the PLACE *on* DALHOUSIE

Melina Marchetta is the bestselling author of nine novels, which have been published in more than twenty countries. Her novels, screenplays and television scripts have won multiple awards. She lives in Sydney.

PRAISE FOR MELINA MARCHETTA'S NOVELS

'Each new Melina Marchetta novel is a revelation; she's always changing, always evolving, and each one performs the miracle of somehow bettering the last.'

MARKUS ZUSAK, BESTSELLING AUTHOR OF *THE BOOK THIEF*

'A master storyteller . . . I've been reading on trains for 16 years and never missed my stop – until now.'

WHO WEEKLY

'Outstanding fiction.'

THE AGE

'On occasion, even cynical reviewers stay up long past bedtime, nodding and turning pages.'

THE SATURDAY PAPER

'This story with its cast of rounded, beautifully crafted characters and dialogue shining with humour, pathos, and a vital spark, makes for a fiercely emotional and entertaining read.'

BOOKSELLER AND PUBLISHER

'A story so full of heart – sorrowful, but warm and funny – it won't be easy to forget.'

THE SYDNEY MORNING HERALD

'Brilliant.'
CANBERRA TIMES

'A novel to rejoice in. A story from the heart.'
BOOKSELLER AND PUBLISHER

'Jam-packed with family drama and heartbreak. Highly recommended.'
LIBRARY JOURNAL

'Often heartbreaking, sometimes heart-stopping, and definitely unforgettable.'
IVY POCHODA, AUTHOR OF *VISITATION STREET*

'Heart-pounding (and heartbreaking) ... [it] grabbed me by the throat and didn't let go until I'd read the last word – and shed the last tear.'
GAYLE FORMAN, BESTSELLING AUTHOR OF *IF I STAY*

'Marchetta is an outstanding writer.'
HERALD SUN

'The vibrant characters leap from the pages as Marchetta builds up the suspense to a superb crescendo.'
THE AUSTRALIAN WOMEN'S WEEKLY

ALSO BY MELINA MARCHETTA

Looking for Alibrandi

Saving Francesca

On the Jellicoe Road

Finnikin of the Rock

The Piper's Son

Froi of the Exiles

The Gorgon in the Gully

Quintana of Charyn

Tell the Truth, Shame the Devil

the
PLACE
on
DALHOUSIE

Melina Marchetta

VIKING
an imprint of
PENGUIN BOOKS

VIKING

UK | USA | Canada | Australia
India | New Zealand | South Africa | China

Penguin Books is part of the Penguin Random House group of companies
whose addresses can be found at global.penguinrandomhouse.com.

Penguin
Random House
Australia

First published by Penguin Random House Australia Pty Ltd 2019

Design by Louisa Maggio © Penguin Random House Australia Pty Ltd
Cover image by Bjanka Kadic / Alamy Stock Photo
Typeset in 11.5/17.5 pt Adobe Caslon Pro by Midland Typesetters, Australia
Printed and bound in Australia by Griffin Press, an accredited ISO AS/NZ 14001
Environmental Management Systems printer.

A catalogue record for this
book is available from the
NATIONAL
LIBRARY National Library of Australia
OF AUSTRALIA

ISBN 978 0 14379 353 3

penguin.com.au

For Brenda
Because I love being a supermodel with you.

p.1 Part One
'When Rosie Met Jim'

p.29 Part Two
The Place tst Sub Butt

p.247 Part Three
'Going Home'

↓
277

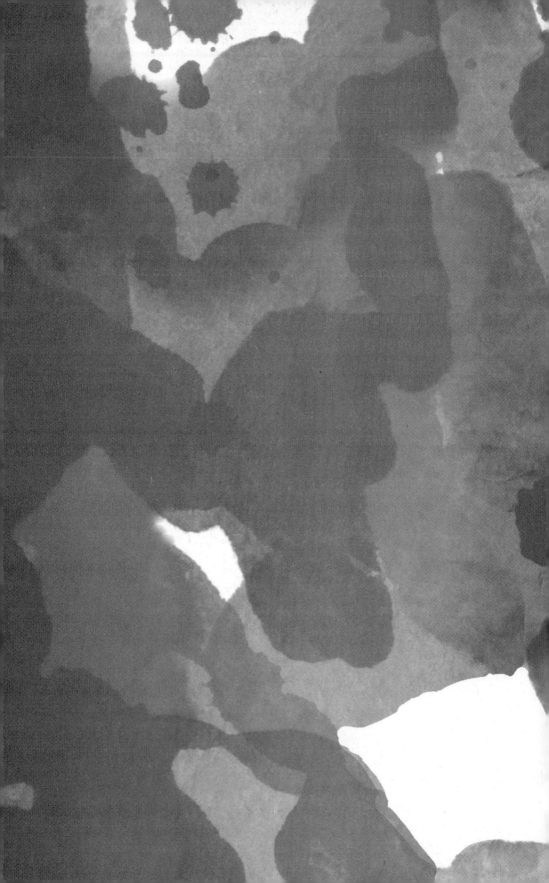

PART ONE

When Rosie met Jim

Chapter One

It's rained for forty days and forty nights, so when a guy who looks like Jesus in orange SES overalls comes to stand next to her, Rosie thinks it's all a bit biblical.

Up on the meat-raffle stage, the pot-bellied chief of emergency services is trying to get a word in. He's just mentioned the words 'forced evacuation' and the whole place is in an uproar. Some old bloke yells out that the Dawson threatens to flood every year and it's nothing to get their knickers in a twist about. The mayor is pushing for evacuation.

'Kev and his people aren't putting their lives at risk for you stubborn mongrels,' he's shouting over everyone. 'Move out of the low-lying areas now or you'll be cut off for at least a week.'

Rosie feels SES Jesus's stare and she makes eye contact. He's a bit older than her, but not that much. Mid-twenties, maybe. Or younger, but he seems like he's been around.

'Jim,' he says.

Crazy eyes. A lunatic. Always the lunatics.

'Rosie.'

'For Rosemary?'

'Rosanna.'

There's a whole lot of shoving around them. On any given night The Royal gets half a dozen patrons, mostly old-timers. But tonight it's packed, and no one wants to leave because Maeve from the news-agency's brought along sandwiches and sausage rolls.

SES Jesus's stare is intense. 'You're pretty.'

Rosie wants to hear something more original than that, but she lets him buy her a beer. What else is there to do but hear stories about the last big flood, of '74, from some of the old blokes who haven't spoken about anything interesting since?

And that's all it takes. A couple of drinks and she's back in some strange guy's room, upstairs at the pub. His calloused fingers find their way between her legs and she realises that she's going to spend another night of her life screwing a guy she doesn't know. Makes her feel as if she can't climb out of the bat cave, and the bleakness is smothering.

'You're going to have to stop doing that,' she hears him say, and Rosie realises that she's crying. He mutters something, but she doesn't catch what it is.

Prickteaser? Bitch? Luke had an arsenal when it came to name-calling.

The guy on top of her – Jim, she remembers – falls back beside her. She can hear his ragged breathing. Wonders how much time she'll let pass before she climbs out of his bed. The walls are paper-thin and she can hear the muffled sounds of two people having it off next door. She makes her move.

'Stay,' he says. It's with a sigh. One of empathy, and she hasn't felt anything close to that for a long time. She turns to face him in the dark, feels the tickle of his beard every time he takes a breath.

The lovers next door are at it. Rosie already knows their names because Stace needs to articulate in the third person everything she wants Roger to do to her.

'Go to sleep,' Jim murmurs.

'While that's going on?'

'It'll be over in less than a minute. Tops. I've listened to this four nights in a row. Roger takes about ten seconds to come.'

A moment later there's silence from next door.

'Told ya.'

Rosie chuckles and he laughs. A warm sound.

He's gone when she wakes in the morning and she's relieved they don't have to do the polite stuff. Outside, it's drizzling and steamy and her tee-shirt's pasted onto her with the grime that comes from humidity and sweat. A couple of utes and four-wheel drives pass by, packed with possessions being taken to higher ground. Rosie wonders if she's left it too late to get out of this town. Wishes Luke was here. Realises she hasn't missed him at all, but he would have been someone to make a decision with. She's been in this town for five weeks now. According to the Tidy Towns sign out on the highway, there are 970 people living here: all whingers, in her eyes.

Those she's met, anyway. Rosie hasn't made a friend the whole time so she has no idea what to do when a flood is on the forecast except for what she heard last night from SES Jesus.

At the cenotaph one of the RSL guys is removing the wreaths, probably as a precaution. She's never been into the whole Anzac thing so it surprises her that she's memorised the twenty-six men who have died in wars since 1914. The names that stick out the most arc the O'Hallorans. They make up eighteen of the dead and she wonders how many of them are left. She's the last Gennaro of her family and the second last on her mother's side. When Rosie and her Nonna Eugenia die, there'll be none of them left. So much for big Italian families.

She crosses the low-lying bridge that takes her over the river and out to the old Simpson Road that backs onto the gully. There are half a dozen properties out here. It's where she's been living since Luke did a runner last week. When they first arrived in town, she found a job looking after someone who'd just had a hip replacement. Rosie hasn't got any qualifications, but she does the housework, feeds the chooks, cooks and buys the old woman beer. There's no love lost between her and Joy Fricker, but Luke's departing gift was also nicking off with the money she had saved, so if Rosie wants to get out of this town sometime soon she doesn't have much choice.

On the Fricker property she can feel the dampness on the grass. It's too much water to have come from the morning drizzle, so she wonders if it's already an overflow from the river. The house is an old two-storey Queenslander on stumps about seventy centimetres above the ground, so Rosie's hoping it'll keep them dry.

'Still in the same clothes from yesterday.'

The ironically named Joy is sitting on the verandah. She wears eighty years of bitterness in a lower lip that hangs down in a constant bag of sourness.

Rosie ignores her and walks into the kitchen to fix breakfast. She whistles for Bruno, but there's no bark of acknowledgement.

'Where's my dog?' she calls out.

Miss Fricker's followed her inside.

'Made a nuisance of himself so I had to tie him up, didn't I?'

Rosie bristles, but holds her tongue. Wants to tell the old woman that if she's strong enough to tie up a kelpie border-collie cross then she can clean up after herself.

They eat in silence before she goes to run Miss Fricker's bath, but nothing comes out. Last night, the head of emergency services was worried the lines would go underwater so she figures they've cut the power. Most properties have a generator that kicks in, but no one's looked in on Miss Fricker since Rosie arrived, so she can't imagine a flood plan's in place.

She spends the morning with SES Jesus's instructions in her head, because he was a talker and didn't shut up the whole night. Removes anything she can off the floor in the living room and kitchen. The cane armchairs, the rug, baskets and vases. The furniture she's able to lift, she piles onto the table. In the kitchen, she grabs some of the china that looks sentimental and packs it away in a box with the photos on the mantelpiece before taking it all upstairs into the spare bedroom. Miss Fricker watches the whole time, her eyes suspicious. Once or twice Rosie hears Bruno barking and peers outside, but it's not until early afternoon that she's alarmed to see water almost up to the chicken coop, about ten metres from the back steps of the house.

'We need to get to the evacuation centre in town,' she tells Miss Fricker.

'I'm not going anywhere.'

'We can't stay here, Joy. We could be cut off for days.'

'This is just a way of getting me out of my house and sticking me in that nursing home!'

It's all Rosie's heard for weeks, because Joy Fricker's nephews are pricks, dying to get their hands on the property to sell. The problem for the Fricker boys is that their aunt still has her wits and isn't going to sign anything over to them. But Rosie doesn't give a shit about the Fricker family problems and she's not staying if the banks of the Dawson have broken. Once she's retrieved Bruno, she's out of here.

Outside, in knee-deep water, she heads to the yard where Miss Fricker's gone and tied Bruno a couple of metres away from the goat. She's thrown by how fast the water's risen. SES Jesus had warned her that when it came, it was full-on. He had seen it down south when he was living in Lismore. He was a city boy, amazed by how everything could change in less than five minutes. It takes Rosie more than one attempt to undo the goat and the moment he's free, he nicks off. Rosie wades over to where Bruno is barking. The water suddenly hurls her forward, slamming her into the fence, winding her. It's only Bruno's whine that has her struggling to her feet to clutch the post and edge towards him, the splinters digging deep into her palm until she feels the wet fur of his coat against her arm. She's frightened to untie him for fear of him being swept away, but can't bear the idea of keeping him tethered in case he goes under and drowns in front of her. Because if he does, Rosie knows she'll let go. Fears she's been wanting to let go for so long now.

Studying the flow around her, she takes a chance. Carefully unties Bruno and wraps the leash around her wrist, but goes under twice and feels herself being swept away. It's only the Hills hoist that she latches herself onto that stops them. She's colder than she's ever been in her life but she doesn't move because the water has a rage beyond anything she's seen, and it wants to snatch them both, wants to fling them against a tree trunk or the side of the house. There's a vengeance to its force and she can't fight it because she's bone-tired. Wants to close her eyes, except Bruno is growling beside her and she knows they have to find their way back up those steps. But as cold and frightened as she is, Rosie feels safe staying put. Because in the backyard of the house in Dalhousie Street, her best memories were of the Hills hoist. Of her mother singing Rosie songs in dialect. Rosie knew them all and she sings them quietly in Bruno's ear until it's her mother's voice she can hear. Clearer than she has for years.

She doesn't know how long they stay. Doesn't know how she finds the strength to let go again, but somehow they make it inside. The entire downstairs is flooded and for an awful moment she thinks Joy Fricker has been swept away. Until she sees the old woman sitting waist-deep in water on the stairs, her teeth chattering.

'Upstairs,' Rosie manages to say. Miss Fricker shakes her head and Rosie figures that she's tried to get up those stairs and failed. For once, she feels sorry for her. There's a vulnerability that Rosie hasn't seen before, even after the hip replacement when she couldn't wipe her bum without help.

'We can't stay down here, Joy. Let's go.'

Rosie's no bigger than Miss Fricker and she buckles under her weight as she helps her step by step, Bruno at their heels shoving them forward. She's worried that she'll snap Miss Fricker's arm, but better a broken arm than being found facedown in rancid water.

In the musty-smelling room that Joy Fricker hasn't used since her operation, Rosie removes the old woman's wet clothing and dresses her. In her own room, she strips off and finds a pair of shorts and a tee-shirt, anything that won't drag her down if she ends up back in the water. The deluge becomes a phantom in her head, and she imagines it creeping its way up, engulfing them, so she drags a chair onto the landing and keeps watch at the top of the stairs. Has no idea what she'll do if that water slinks towards them, but needs to know what she's up against.

Later, in the dark, she feels a shudder of the house, picks up the torch and goes to the window, trying to get a glimpse of whatever's coming downstream to hammer them.

'My father built this house for me.'

Rosie jumps at the sound of her voice, shines the light towards Miss Fricker, who's standing at her bedroom door.

'It's got good foundations.'

Rosie helps the old woman back into bed and then curls up in the tacky velvet armchair close by. On the wall, the Sacred Heart of Mary clock taunts her, moving at the excruciating speed that punishes those who are praying for time to pass.

'If my father knew what his grandsons were trying to do, it would have broken his heart,' Miss Fricker says. For her, there still seems to be a greater malevolence than a flood.

Despite the darkness, Rosie can feel the old woman's bitter scrutiny.

'You look the type to break your father's heart.'

'Yeah, but he broke mine first.'

A voice wakes them. Bruno is barking at the bedroom door and Rosie untangles herself from the chair, blinded by daylight that snuck up on her while she wasn't looking. She wipes saliva from her mouth and heads to the landing.

'Looters,' Miss Fricker whispers from her bed, because everyone is the enemy in her eyes. Rosie puts a finger to her lips and creeps down a step for a look. SES Jesus is standing thigh-deep in water, wearing only his budgie smugglers and orange SES jacket. Not quite an apparition, but Rosie feels a hysterical laugh bubble up inside her at the sight of him.

'Told you to get to higher ground,' he says.

'Have you got a boat?'

He shakes his head. 'The CFA have lent us their truck. Outboard motors are too dangerous. Who knows what's under this water.'

Rosie helps Miss Fricker out of bed and can feel the old woman trembling. On the mantelpiece, she sees a Mary MacKillop brooch and pins it onto Miss Fricker's dress before walking her to the door. The old woman refuses to take another step at the sight of him coming up the stairs.

'Now they're hiring perverts,' she mutters.

'You're going to have to put your arms around my neck,' Jim tells Miss Fricker, 'and I'm going to have one arm around your back and the other under your knees.'

And there's something about the way skinny SES Jesus hitches Miss Fricker up in his arms and wades through the deluge that makes Rosie think that she'd follow him anywhere.

It's the town butcher who drives the CFA truck through the flood-water. He loses control of the wheel more than once, yelling *Christ* at the top of his lungs. Rosie feels the perspiration running down her brow, undoes her seatbelt, readying herself for the inevitable. They'll go under, for sure, trapped in a tomb of water. As if sensing her fear, Jim turns in the front seat, catches her eye.

'Almost there, mate.'

They pass the cenotaph and Rosie sees shops half sub-merged, garbage bins bobbing in filthy brown water and an elderly couple sitting on the roof of their car being towed by a ute. The butcher, Mick, she thinks, swears at a couple of kids watching it all, sitting on the awning above the fish and chips shop, laughing their heads off, oblivious to the fear. And it's only SES Jesus's calm instructions to Mick, suggesting another route down less dangerous roads, that brings Rosie any comfort.

The evacuation centre is in the cottage owned by the Country Women's Association, perched high on a hill. Standing at the entrance Rosie sees a familiar face, one she's locked horns with before. A couple of weeks back she had to pick up medication for Miss Fricker at the hospital pharmacy and was put through the third degree by this woman, a local midwife who had come in to deliver a baby. This morning she looks at Rosie with just as much hostility.

'No dogs allowed, love,' she says.

Rosie can't believe what she's hearing. 'I'm not leaving him outside.'

'I'll take him someplace safe,' Jim says.

But Rosie's shaking her head. 'I'll keep him in a corner and he won't move.'

The midwife holds up a finger of warning at Rosie. 'No dogs allowed,' she repeats before leading Miss Fricker away. Rosie feels tears threatening, but she refuses to cry in front of Jim for a second time. The butcher's honking the horn and Jim holds out a hand to her. She lets him take the leash and he walks away.

Inside the cottage there are three large living spaces, all packed with people, most sleeping on solid-looking mattresses. Rosie notices a couple of the older evacuees are lying on comfy armchairs. She checks on Miss Fricker before searching out the midwife who she finds in the CWA kitchen, boiling water on a portable stove.

'We need one of those armchairs,' Rosie says.

'Be patient,' the other woman says without looking up. 'Everyone's gone through a lot, okay. You're not the only one.'

'Miss Fricker's had a hip replacement,' Rosie insists. 'She needs to be comfortable.'

'Sorry, love, none left for the time being.'

'Don't fucking "sorry love" me again,' Rosie says.

The midwife looks up. Rosie flinches because the woman reminds her too much of her mum. They would have been the same age, both with long black wavy hair and fierce dark eyes, except the midwife's an Islander. And the owner of the mothership of dirty looks.

'You need to change your attitude.'

'I'll change it when you get Miss Fricker onto something comfortable.'

Soon after, two teenagers carry an armchair to where Miss Fricker is sitting on a fold-up seat beside Maeve from the news-agency, who hasn't stopped speaking since they arrived. Rosie's heard Miss Fricker say, 'Shut up, Maeve,' more than once.

'Aunty Min says it's from the office so you better take care of it,' the older of the boys says.

Later, Rosie finds Min the midwife watching them from the door. Regrets not looking away before she's beckoned over by an aggressive hand.

'What?' Rosie says.

Another scathing look.

'Don't you "what" me, you little bitch. Come and help me with morning tea.'

Handing out tea and biscuits means that people want to talk. Most are worried about their homes. Their pets. Their photos. Their insur-ance documents. Maeve is in tears.

'Everything in the shop's gone,' she tells Rosie. 'Everything. What if they won't cover me?'

Rosie's grateful that she has nothing to lose.

'It could be worse, Maeve,' a woman with a couple of kids hanging off her says from across the room. One of her girls has been crying for their dog all morning because they had to leave him behind.

Later that day, it does get worse. SES Kev and a couple of young guys come in, looking gutted. After that, it's like the power company's come in and turned off everyone's voices. Because down by one of the properties backing onto the river, a baby's been swept from his father's arms, and out by the old mill road, two people are missing. Their car went over the embankment.

Min hands Rosie a folder. Tells her to tick off the names from the electoral roll. They need to start working out where everyone is. Most have gone to family and friends on higher ground. Some stayed in their homes and have ended up here. Rosie can't help thinking that she's not on the town electoral roll. If she'd got swept away from the Hills hoist yesterday, she wouldn't have even been considered missing.

Jim comes looking for her later and they just stand around for a while until he says, 'You want to go somewhere?'

And in his room upstairs at the pub, her legs are wrapped around his hips and there isn't really that much time for pleasantries or catch-up, but she doesn't care; for most of it, she's in her world and he's in his and it's fast and she likes the fact that she doesn't have to pretend with this guy.

Later, she asks where he's from.

'Sydney. You?'

She can't believe it. 'Same.'

No more questions, she tells herself.

But can't resist.

'Where?'

'Grew up in Waterloo but mainly hang out in the inner west when I'm home. Close to you?'

Closer than she'd care to admit. She doesn't answer. Rosie doesn't want to think of Dalhousie Street and who lives there now.

'What are the chances?' he says. 'You and me from the same place.'

Rosie's dad believed in chances and fate. He believed in signs. Rosie doesn't believe in anything hopeful.

'What's your story?' he asks.

She shrugs. 'No story.' Because exchanging misery isn't her style, and at the moment even her misery can't top a baby being swept away.

They talk about Bruno.

'He's out on a property off the highway,' Jim tells her. 'You know, near the goods-train track. The family's looking after a few other animals. I don't think he likes goats.'

He glances at her.

'History of goat trouble in his past?'

She laughs for the second time in days.

It's under a dirty hungover sky that the rest of the world arrives a couple of days later. The insurance companies are there first, pitching their tents on the property beside the CWA, along with the Red Cross, RACQ, recovery hubs and state police. The premier visits because she's been up north and the roads there are open. The CWA and St Vinnies people are sorting through the donations that have arrived from the surrounding towns and Min is in charge of feeding whoever turns up. Rosie gets delegated to chopping onions for the sausage sizzle. It all seems productive and warm-hearted, but beneath the surface it's anything but. Some have it in for the cops and the mayor because the evacuation plans came too late. Others complain they were stranded for more than two days without food drops and blame the SES. One woman comes up and gets in Min's face.

'Your husband's useless!'

'You were told to evacuate,' Min says, calmly. 'And you were told to have a flood plan.' Rosie's discovered that Min's husband is the pot-bellied chief of the SES, so Min's pretty particular about how much criticism he gets.

Rosie keeps to herself. She doesn't belong to these people, so the anger and grief isn't hers to own. It stops people talking to her. Confiding. Crying. She sees Jim once that day. Maybe because it's hard to avoid someone you're looking for. He knows how to charm the old CWA women; one hands him a plate of food that he wolfs down. And then he's gone again.

The Red Cross start working out temporary accommodation and Rosie has to tell Miss Fricker that she'll be staying at the nursing home wing of the hospital from tomorrow onwards.

'That's what you think,' Miss Fricker mutters.

'Well, you can't stay here and you can't go back to your place until the clean-up's over.'

'My nephews are behind this, aren't they? Them and those wives of theirs.'

'They have nothing to do with this, Joy.'

Miss Fricker mutters something under her breath.

'Do you want me to set your hair?' Rosie asks. 'They've switched the water back on.'

'What would you know about setting hair?'

'I'm only offering once, so it's a yes or a no.'

Rosie had spied a set of curlers and styling stuff in the St Vinnies donations and ends up setting the hair of at least half a dozen pensioners in the CWA laundry.

Even Min wants a wash and blow-dry. Rosie combs the woman's hair over and over again, because it's what she used to do for her mum before the chemo got to it.

'Are you staying?' Min asks, eyeing her through the mirror.

'No. So if you know anyone heading south . . .'

'Have you got family down there?'

'I've got a house,' Rosie says, briskly.

Min is still studying her. 'What are you going to do with your life, Rosie? Start thinking of that now or you'll waste good opportunities.'

'Do you like your job?' Rosie asks.

Min nods. 'It means I know every baby and kid in this town.'

Rosie's eyes meet hers in the mirror. Thinks of that lost baby.

'Did you deliver –'

'Yes, I did.'

Rosie sees a glimpse of tears, but before she can say anything else Min stands up, already composed.

'There's something about getting your hair done that makes you feel half decent, doll.'

She's lying on top of Jim and he pushes her hair off her face. They're all sweaty skin on skin. She can feel the trickle of sweat between her breasts. Feels his tongue there. She sits up, straddling him, studying his strange face. Not good-looking but behind the beard there's a kind face. Sad crazy eyes.

'Where are you off to next?' he asks.

She shrugs. Hopes he won't ask to tag along, because right now she'd say yes and there's something about this guy that would break her if he ends up being a disappointment.

'You?'

He shrugs. 'Can't go home yet.'

'Why?'

'I'm on a good behaviour bond so I can't leave the state for another eighteen months.'

'What did you do?'

'Drugs.'

'Dealing?'

He shakes his head. 'Possession.'

She feels his stare.

'Min says you keep to yourself.'

Rosie lies back down beside him, unimpressed. 'I don't like people and I don't appreciate being spoken about.'

His tongue is at work again. Apart from his annoying habit of talking while she's having an orgasm, he's pretty generous in the sex department. Makes it last, unlike Roger next door.

'What's your favourite thing to do, Rosie?' he asks when they're still awake in the early hours of the morning watching the shadows playing on the wall.

'Going on road trips. With the right person, that is. Can't stand getting stuck with someone who talks about nothing. Or who doesn't talk at all. The best is when you're with someone who's comfortable with silence, but doesn't make you feel lonely.'

'You feel lonely sometimes?'

Always, she wants to say. Worse is when she feels lonely in the company of others. The ache of it makes her feel weary. Like she isn't nineteen. More like a hundred. SES Jesus must see something in her eyes, because he leans over her, a hand on her cheek.

'The trick is don't give into it, mate.'

'It's a trick, is it?' she asks.

There's nothing held back about him. No cruel games. The yearning in his eyes makes her want to look away but, regardless of the fact that he never shuts up, she feels less alone when she hears his voice so she asks him more.

'My mum . . . she was always a bit crazy,' he says. 'The type to turn up to my primary school off her nut, you know. I was a bit like that. The Ritalin kid. And then one day when I'm ten she goes to Woolies to buy bread and milk and doesn't come back.'

'Ever?'

He shakes his head.

'It got to me a couple of years ago when my grandpop died and I had to get out of our flat because it was housing commission and someone else was waiting in line for it. And I realised I didn't have a home, so I disappeared for about a year. My friends aren't the type to let go, which is a good thing, so I ended up back in Sydney, couch surfing. A couple of months ago, I'm living with my best mate's family and she convinces me to track down my mum.'

'Your best mate's a girl?'

'Italian, like you.'

Rosie feels herself bristling. 'Did you pick me up because you've got a thing for your best friend?'

'No, I picked you up because you were the hottest girl in the pub and I wanted to have sex with you.'

'Using a very unoriginal line.'

'Can I get back to my story?' he says.

'Go on.'

'Anyway, her boyfriend and I are looking online for a car and we come across some guy who's fixed up a Monaro. You know what a Monaro is?'

'Course I do.'

'Course you do.'

'So where's your Monaro?'

'Mate, let me finish the story. We get to this guy's garage and he takes one look at me and that's it. He has a feeling in his bones. I was meant to own this car. And the more he says it, the more I believe it because he doesn't seem like a fake. But my mate, Will, is cautious. Needs to check it out. Rings his brothers who are car experts. That sort of thing. All the while, this guy is staring at me. "Why do you want this car?" he asks, which I thought was a strange question, but I tell him the truth. "Because I'm looking for family." And he just smiles at me. "Buy the car and you'll find your family."'

'That's pretty freaky.'

'He had an accent. Even freakier.'

'Did you find your mum?'

He nods. 'In Lismore.' His voice softens. Rosie likes a guy whose voice softens at the mention of his mother. 'You know how they say people can't turn their lives around? Well, my mother did. Hasn't touched drugs or alcohol in eleven years. Married a born-again Christian. Bawled her eyes out when she saw me. Said she loved me, but made me promise to stay away. She's got a ten-year-old boy and eight-year-old twin girls and she hadn't told them about me.'

He turns to her, a flash of vulnerability in his eyes. 'But she did give me the name of my father. Thinks he lives in Bundaberg. So I took off and ended up in this vicinity. Problem is that last week my car got stolen just outside town at a servo while I was in the dunny.'

'You lost a Monaro?'

'No, it was stolen,' he laughed. 'It's how I met Kev. He was filling up his tank and I hitched a ride into town with him. By that stage it was raining hard up north and I knew I was stuck here for a while, and that's how I ended up volunteering for emergency services.'

'When are you leaving?' she asks.

'When I get myself a cheap car.'

Rosie is worried for him. Doesn't know him from a bar of soap, but knows this guy's heading for disappointment.

'Just say . . . just say your father doesn't want to be found?' she asks.

Jim thinks about it for a moment. 'The man's got a right to know his son. Anyway, I'm one of those crossing-that-bridge-when-I-come-to-it people.'

He leans on his elbow looking down at her, a ghost of a smile on his face.

'You listen too much for someone who doesn't like people.'

'You talk too much for someone who's just interested in sex.'

By the end of the week, the old Simpson Road is reopened. Rosie takes Bruno back to Miss Fricker's place by the gully to check out the damage. The chooks and ducks, and a couple of kittens that had taken refuge in the shed, are all dead, and Rosie finds herself gagging. But the goat comes back. Peeks its head through the door to irritate Bruno.

The backbreaking part of the clean-up is the downstairs area of the house, covered in silt. She works the next couple of days hosing down and scrubbing every wall. The mud has crept into every crevice, but she keeps at it. She knows the drill because she's heard it over and over again this week. Anything made of plastic or wood gets chucked. Disinfect everything. Watch out for snakes. In the kitchen and dining room she pulls up the lino and carpet and drags it out back where the roses are gone and the spotted gum tree has cracked in two and smashed the fence and the henhouse. Working this hard reminds Rosie of being with her parents when she was a kid. Of stripping paint and trawling junkyards with her dad for anything of worth. She remembers the derelict building on Lilyfield Road where they found the old floorboards that ended up on the lounge room floor in the place on Dalhousie Street. Suddenly she's crying. Even after five years without her mother and a year without her dad, the thought of never seeing them again robs her of breath. She's relieved to be on her own because here she can scream with rage, with grief, until her throat feels shredded.

And the only thing that gets her through the depression of her days is the thought of lying next to SES Jesus, listening to the rumble of his voice as she tries to sleep. One night he cries and she doesn't know whether it's because of the bodies they found in a paddock two k's out of town, or because his car got him as far as a town that's soaked with despair. She holds him in her arms and feels the shudders.

'Shh, it's okay. It's okay.'

He clings to her and being this needed feels better than sex. It's when Rosie knows she has to leave this place. Because she could easily love this guy. It's what Rosie does best. She loves broken people who damage her in return.

'I just want to warn you that I'm leaving any day now. Min's helping me find someone who's heading south.'

It's the right thing to say to someone whose mum went to Woolies and didn't come back.

It's only a couple of days later when Min lets Rosie know about one of the SES volunteers from Newcastle who's heading home. Two hours from Sydney.

'Come by the CWA and I'll pack you a lunch, doll,' Min says.

Rosie and Bruno track Jim down to the property he's been helping out on, by the creek. A couple of the younger kids have taken it upon themselves to look after the domestic animals that haven't been claimed. Jim's helping them with an inventory, labelling cages and jotting things down. He lets a galah nip at his finger, right opposite a Persian cat that eyes the bird with disdain and a promise of violence.

'What are you writing?' she asks.

'Just where we found them and if they have a name on a collar. I'll put the details up on the noticeboard in the pub.'

He catches her eye. 'You're leaving.' Not a question.

She nods. 'Can you make sure Miss Fricker gets home sooner rather than later?'

'Am I breaking her out of the nursing home?' he asks, mischief in his eyes.

'She'd like that.'

He takes her hand, linking it with his. 'I'll give you my number,' he says.

She shrugs. 'I don't have a mobile.'

'Take it anyway.' He writes on her palm with the marker. She loves the feel of his knuckles against her palm as he writes, like the sinew of his body against her when they have sex. Rosie feels as if every part of her is stamped by this guy's bony strangeness.

'First chance you get, copy this down on a piece of paper,' he says.

She knows there'll never be a reason to ring this number. She's not a *hello, let's catch-up* type of girl. And then his mouth is on hers and a part of Rosie feels desolate. Because maybe deep down she thought SES Jesus was one of her father's signs after all. Except they're both travelling in opposite directions and she can't think of anything powerful enough to place them on the same path.

She goes back to the nursing home to tell Miss Fricker she's leaving. Wordlessly takes the old woman to the toilet, cleans her up, helps her back to where she was sulking by the window. When she pins the Mary MacKillop brooch on Joy's collar, she feels something press against the palm of her hand. A whole lot of hundred-dollar bills rolled up. Rosie tries to return it but the old woman's hand is a fist.

'Take it. You've wiped my arse and bought me beer. You deserve it.'

Rosie thinks that 'You've wiped my arse and bought me beer' would make a great title to a country and western song.

'Have you seen the house?' Joy asks.

'Been there all week. You'll be ready to go home soon.'

'How are my roses?'

'Dead. Everything outside was wiped out except for the goat.'

'Is the house still standing? Because that's all that counts.'

Rosie nods, goes to walk away but stops herself.

'My father spent eighteen years of his life building a house,' she tells Miss Fricker. 'He wasn't a builder – just one of those guys who knew what he was doing. Anyone who walked past it would say, "That's the house Seb Gennaro's building for his family." But my mum got sick and never got to see it finished and within a year he remarried. Then he died. And now *she* thinks it's hers. Won't move out. The house my dad built for me and my mum.'

She walks away because oversharing isn't her thing.

'Rosie.' It's the first time Miss Fricker has ever used her name.

Rosie turns back one more time.

'Keep away from good-for-nothings. It's what's kept me alive all these years.'

She walks past the cenotaph and up to the main street where everyone's hard at work. Maeve is dumping stuff into a skip bin. Next door, Rockmans is all but ruined. If it's not water, it's mud, but it doesn't stop them working. She envies these people. Some have lost everything and, for the life of her, she can't get that baby being swept away out of her head. Or those who are uninsured because living so close to a river means the insurance companies won't touch them for less than a fortune. They belong to something bigger than Rosie's had for a while and, as depressed as they all seem, the words 'Do you want a cuppa?' seem to change everything for a moment. Rosie hasn't belonged to anything for longer than she can remember. Her fault. Their fault. Whoever's fault it is, the bleakness consumes her. She hears the deluge spoken about over again, but a deluge can't be that bad. It has substance. Rosie wants deluge. She wants to watch her whole life float down the river so she can do what these people are doing now. Go retrieve it. Put their lives back together again.

She sees her ride pull up outside the pub just as it begins to rain. Opens her hand, studies the name. James Hailler. The phone number's already beginning to smudge like she knew it would. She puts her hands into her pockets. Gets into the truck.

'What about this raaaaain?' a nasal ZZ Top–type from Newcastle says as if he's the first to notice the weather in weeks. Rosie knows she's going to be a passenger to someone who doesn't know when to keep his mouth shut.

'You got everything?' he asks.

She thinks for a moment.

And asks for a pen and paper.

PART TWO

The house that Seb built

Chapter Two

To: justmartha@me.com

From: sophiekolotos@gmail.com

Date: 1 March 2011

Subject: Sister Mo is dead

Dear Martha,

Where have you been and why aren't you answering my phone calls? I told George this is the longest you and I haven't spoken since that time in Year Twelve when you misunderstood Elizabeth King's words and imagined that everyone was blaming you after we lost the netball grand finals. Anyway, Sister Mo died on Saturday. I know you've spent the past thirty years avoiding any school reunion, but apparently Alana Charbel went to see her at the nursing home and Mo spoke about you, so I think she'd want you to be at her funeral on Thursday. Martha, please respond! Elizabeth King is after everyone's emails.

Love, Sophie

P.S. Although you would have received the invitation to Scarlett's birthday party, I've attached a photo from the day. You can see how upset she looks because her godmother chose not to turn up.

To: sophiekolotos@gmail.com
From: justmartha@me.com
Date: 1 March 2011
Sophie, you better not have given anyone my email address after I've spent three decades making sure they can't contact me. Just what I need. Another shitload of vacuous emails sent by people who have nothing better to do with their lives. And for the record, what part of 'You lost us the grand finals' spoken by Elizabeth King would I have misunderstood in Year Twelve?
Martha
P.S. We haven't seen each other for two weeks, Sophie. Don't be so dramatic.

To: justmartha@me.com
From: sophiekolotos@gmail.com
Date: 1 March 2011
Subject: The class of '80
Dear Martha,
I had no choice giving Elizabeth your email. She probably won't contact you, anyway. I'm sure she got the hint years ago that you don't want to be part of a reunion.
Love, Sophie

To: acharbel@nsw.edu.au; justmartha@me.com; sophiekolotos@gmail
.com; juleshealy@yahoo.com
From: queenelizabeth3@gmail.com
Date: 1 March 2011
Subject: Sister Maureen Louise Cassidy's funeral
Hi girls,
Now that I've got all your contact details, let's get down to business.
Sister Mo would have loved nothing better than her golden girls doing
the offertory procession on Thursday. I'm not ruling out a liturgical
dance just yet. You know how Mo felt about those she choreographed.
Any preferences on what you want to carry in the procession? Bread,
wine, the napkin?
Regards,
Elizabeth King

To: sophiekolotos@gmail.com
From: justmartha@me.com
Date: 1 March 2011
Obviously she didn't get the hint, Sophie. I'm not spending Thursday
dancing up a church aisle, pretending to hold the body and blood
of Christ, grieving an evil nun who delegated me to wing defence for
six years while the rest of you basked in the glory of being centres
or shooters.

Anyway, I've already reached my funeral quota for the month.
Please decline on my behalf.
Martha

To: justmartha@me.com
From: sophiekolotos@gmail.com
Date: 1 March 2011
Subject: WMD
Dear Martha,

Why aren't I surprised that you brought up the netball team? Remember the 'F' Sister Mo gave us for our assignment on the minority groups persecuted through the ages, and you sketched all the victims wearing WD bibs? You know what you should have had on your bib back then? WMD, not WD. Because you're a weapon of mass destruction when it comes to bringing up anything related to school. It's made you paranoid, Martha!

To: sophiekolotos@gmail.com
From: justmartha@me.com
Date: 1 March 2011
I'm not paranoid, Sophie.

To: justmartha@me.com
From: sophiekolotos@gmail.com
Date: 1 March 2011
At school you were convinced that Julia Healy's brother only went out with centres and shooters. Move on, for crying out loud. George says you're better than that.
Sophie!
P.S. Did you hear Ewan Healy got sacked from his NRL coaching position?

To: sophiekolotos@gmail.com
From: justmartha@me.com
Date: 1 March 2011
I can't believe you discuss me, and the netball days, with George. Is it dinnertime news? Is that why Scarlett looked so depressed in her birthday photo? And here I thought it was because you threw her a fairy party when it's obvious my goddaughter was never meant to be in tulle. And no need to bring up Ewan Healy, thank you. I bumped into him at Charlie P's funeral in the Hunter last week. He didn't even know who I was, so I'm not exactly crying over the fact that he went out with most of you at some time in his life.
Martha

To: justmartha@me.com
From: juleshealy@yahoo.com
Date: 2 March 2011
Subject: It's been a long time
Dear Martha,
Sophie mentioned you might not be at Mo's funeral on Thursday. Alana and I want to have you over for a catch-up.
Best,
Julia
P.S. Did you know my brother was divorced? Are you going out with anyone?

To: sophiekolotos@gmail.com
From: justmartha@me.com
Date: 2 March 2011
Sophie, did you write to Julia Healy and suggest matching me up with her brother?

To: justmartha@me.com
From: sophiekolotos@gmail.com
Date: 2 March 2011
Subject: Olive branch
In a brief IM conversation we had today, Julia mentioned that she's extending an olive branch, Martha. Regardless of how toxic your relationship was in high school, it seems as if she's moved on. You should too.
Love, Sophie

To: sophiekolotos@gmail.com
From: justmartha@me.com
Date: 2 March 2011
Quit the subject lines, Sophie. They're supposed to be a hint of what you're going to say, not a repetition. And you wonder why I don't respond to you sometimes. Subject: Mammogram scare. Subject: Head lice alert. Subject: I'm the prophet of doom. One day, I want you to send me an email that doesn't spell despair before you even say hello.

To: justmartha@me.com

From: sophiekolotos@gmail.com

Date: 2 March 2011

Subject: How can you say that?

Martha, how can you say that? I send you the most beautiful emails and your subject line last month was 'Fuck these angels off'.

To: sophiekolotos@gmail.com

From: justmartha@me.com

Date: 2 March 2011

Because I've told you so many times not to send those chain emails about passing it on to another twenty people so an angel will bless me. I lost my mother and husband within a four-year period, Sophie. Do you honestly believe I'm on an angel's mailing list?

Martha

P.S. Don't you think it's just like Julia to try and match me up with her brother when he no longer resembles JFK Jr? All of a sudden I'm good enough for Ewan Healy because he's jobless at fifty and has love handles.

To: justmartha@me.com

From: sophiekolotos@gmail.com

Date: 2 March 2011

Subject: How do you know Ewan Healy has love handles?

I thought you didn't talk to him at that funeral. Please explain.

To: justmartha@me.com; sophiekolotos@gmail.com; juleshealy
@yahoo.com; queenelizabeth3@gmail.com
From: acharbel@nsw.edu.au
Date: 2 March 2011
Subject: Burwood United
Hear me out, girls, because I think there's a purpose to Sister Mo's
death. Last Saturday Jules and I were up at Cintra Park watching the
kids play netball and we saw those Ashbury trolls who demoralised us
back in '80. They've re-formed a team and they look smug. We have to
get the Burwood United team back together.
Love Alana

To: acharbel@nsw.edu.au; justmartha@me.com; sophiekolotos@gmail
.com; juleshealy@yahoo.com
From: queenelizabeth3@gmail.com
Date: 2 March 2011
Subject: Re: Burwood United
We'll need to find another couple of players to replace Karen and
Mary. They've completely let themselves go and have got Buckley's of
getting into the uniform. Any suggestions?
Elizabeth xx
P.S. Is it true you're putting Dalhousie Street on the market, Martha?

To: queenelizabeth3@gmail.com; acharbel@nsw.edu.au; sophie
kolotos@gmail.com; juleshealy@yahoo.com
From: justmartha@me.com
Date: 2 March 2011
I am not rejoining the team. Please take me off this thread.
M

To: justmartha@me.com

From: sophiekolotos@gmail.com

Date: 2 March 2011

Subject: house on the market???

Martha, what's going on??? You would never put Dalhousie Street on the market unless it was bad news. Don't do anything rash. Please. I've put away money for Scarlett's private school fund (don't tell George that we're going to send her to a private school). If you need money, it's yours. I can't bear the idea of you giving up that house.

Love, Sophie

To: sophiekolotos@gmail.com

From: justmartha@me.com

Date: 2 March 2011

Dear Sophie,

I can't talk about this now. Too depressing. But thank you.

Love Martha

P.S. Nothing will convince me to join The Real Housewives of Burwood United.

To: justmartha@me.com

From: acharbel@nsw.edu.au

Date: 2 March 2011

Subject: You can play centre, Martha.

Are you in?

*

The house that Seb once started building for his other family is almost complete. What's left for Martha is the backyard and the grouting on the kitchen floor and wall tiles. It's all about deciding the colour of the mortar to complement the ceramics. It's been this way for months now but she can't find it in her to finish. Each night she stares at the murky space between the cobalt ceramics, frightened of what the finality of it all means. So it stays undone.

Upstairs she can hear the baby. It's constant, but she's become accustomed to its cry these past weeks. Sooner or later she has to venture up those steps, and perhaps she'll do it tonight. But there's still a tyre to contend with, courtesy of some delinquent who decided to slash hers outside the house. She wants to go out there to change it, but knows Seb's voice will be in her ear, telling her to finish the grouting, and to start on the backyard. Or go upstairs and ask about the baby. So she calls a cab and heads down to Nield Park where Sophie and the others said they'd be training, because putting off the inevitable has been Martha's go-to option for some time now.

She arrives just as the street lights flicker on around the park. Can see Julia Healy running a lap with the same intensity she had in their school days. Close by, Alana Charbel and Elizabeth King are warming up. Martha hasn't seen them in years, but here she is in their company again. First Sister Mo's funeral, now training.

'We thought you'd pike,' Alana says, giving her a quick hug.

'I'm never one to pike.'

Elizabeth King gives Martha a quick appraisal. No love lost between them. They had cohabited the same social group all those years ago because Sophie was the common denominator.

'You look good as a brunette, Martha.'

Martha likes the compliment. It's what she misses about her work environment. A lack of discussion about the important things in life such as semipermanents and shellac.

Julia Healy jogs past and the others join her. 'Alana and I made a bet you'd pike!' she calls out.

Martha catches up with them, already cramping at the twenty-metre mark. 'What's with the taxi?' Julia asks.

'Some dickhead at work put a *cops are tops* sticker on my back window, which inspired another dickhead to slash my tyres.'

'I heard you were working for the police.'

'The minister,' Martha corrects.

Sophie arrives, late as usual, chewing gum as delicately as she can and rubbing her hands with lavender oil, because she's been smoking. She jogs across the oval and falls in next to Martha, shoulder bumps her.

'I told them you'd come.'

It's the reason why Martha has never let go of Sophie. Unconditional love since they were twelve years old, even back at school when the others had become a troika.

'What's your brother doing here, Jules?' Sophie asks.

Martha falters for the slightest of moments. Hopes none of the others have noticed.

'He's training us,' Julia says.

Ewan Healy is heading towards them, a large sports duffel bag slung over his shoulder.

'I've just realised that I've never seen him in anything but shorts and joggers,' Sophie says.

'Martha has,' Julia says.

Martha ignores the scrutiny.

'In his suit at Charlie P's funeral,' Julia says. She's jogging beside Martha now and watching her closely. 'My brother said your speech made grown men cry.'

'I make grown men cry every day. It's too easy.'

When they reach Ewan, he doesn't do eye contact, but he's contemplative, as if he can't find the words to describe what he's just seen. Twice divorced and sacked from a lucrative coaching job, he has truly hit rock bottom training his sister's netball team.

'Too much talking out there, girls.'

'Fuck off, Ewan,' Elizabeth says. He dumped her on the night of their school formal and Elizabeth clearly hasn't forgiven him after all these years. As a punishment, he has them doing wind sprints, followed by a circuit of torture.

Martha's relieved when her phone rings.

'Don't answer that, please,' he politely requests, making eye contact this time.

Finally, Healy.

'Let me tell the Minister for Police that I'm doing squats and can't talk,' she says.

When it's over he goes out to collect the equipment and takes a phone call.

'What a cranky bastard he's turned out to be, Julia,' Sophie says.

'A lot on his plate.' Julia is focused on her brother while fishing in her bag for keys. 'We'll drop you off, Martha.'

Not quite an offer. More like an order. It's one of the reasons Martha and Julia clashed so much in high school. Both refused to be a subordinate of the other.

Ewan returns and he doesn't look happy.

'We're taking Martha home,' Julia tells him.

A look passes between the Healys. 'We've got to get Dad,' he says. 'Maybe someone else can take Martha home.'

'I already offered,' Julia says.

As they walk to the car, there's an uncomfortable silence. Martha doesn't do uncomfortable. Or inadequate. Or not good enough.

'I'll take a cab.'

'Don't take a cab,' Ewan says and she can hear weariness in his voice.

They reach Julia's jeep and the others insist that Martha sits in the front. Without asking for instruction, Julia drives around the Bay Run on Henley Marine Drive where Martha can see a few time-starved joggers hitting the track in the dark. In the back seat, Ewan and Alana sit in silence. Martha doesn't know what it all means. The Healys and Charbels have lived next door to each other all their lives. Julia and Alana have been partners for half that time. It's not exactly strained, but Martha can sense that things aren't right.

'How are the kids?' she asks. Sophie has persisted in keeping Martha up-to-date on all their lives, whether Martha wanted the information or not. Julia and Alana's kids have lived with them for four years now. Like most people caught up in the foster care system, the adoption is taking forever.

'Marley's full of attitude and Samuel's the sensitive one,' Alana says.

'But he's tough and she's a softy,' Julia says. She slows down to an almost stop as they're about to pass the rowing shed and Martha can see the orange glow of the street lights illuminating a lone walker. After a moment Julia picks up a little speed again.

'How old are they now?' Martha asks.

'Eight and six.'

'Jules!' Ewan says.

Martha hears a seatbelt come off in the back seat and feels him brush up against her as he leans in between her and Julia, pointing to a hunched figure walking under the Iron Cove Bridge.

'Is that your father?' Martha asks. 'He's keen.'

Julia stops the car and Ewan gets out, crossing the road, jogging towards him. After a moment, Julia follows. Because of her work, Martha spends too much time reading crime reports and can't help being the alarmist.

'It's dangerous walking out on his own at this time of the night.'

Alana doesn't speak for a moment.

'They're both finding it tough,' she finally says.

Before Martha can ask what she means, Ewan and Julia are heading back towards the car with their father.

The stench of urine is overwhelming. It reminds Martha of the old guys who live out on the streets close to the police headquarters in Surry Hills. She turns in her seat to say hello, surprised by the emotion that comes over her. She hasn't seen Julia's father in more than thirty years, but it feels like yesterday.

'Do you remember me, Mr Healy? Martha Newman. You and Mr Charbel used to do the St Vinnies run with my father.'

He smiles at her, but doesn't respond.

'Martha went to school with Julia, Dad,' Ewan tells his father.

'Who's Julia?'

There's silence and Martha suddenly gets it. Feels for them all. The only relief that came from the death of her mother and father

44

was that they still knew who she was until the very end. There's a tap on her shoulder and she turns back to John Healy.

'I'm off to see my son play footy down at Leichhardt Oval,' he tells Martha. 'Do you know he was chosen for the Balmain Juniors?'

And because the mood in the car is heavy with sadness and she doesn't know what else to say, Martha takes his hand and squeezes it.

'Well, let's hope it doesn't go to his head,' she says.

After a moment she hears a laugh from the back seat.

They pull up in front of her house a little while later.

'A neighbour of ours used to deliver mail here on this street,' Alana says, 'and he'd go on about how the man who bought the hoarder's place on Dalhousie Street wasted his money.'

Martha had heard it all before. Most people would say that after eighteen years Seb'd never finish it. He used to be a joke, until he was a tragedy. But he didn't care what people thought. Anyone who sees the house now understands why.

'No such thing as wasting money on a house in this area,' Julia says.

Martha's phone rings. 'Thanks for the lift,' she says, getting out and answering it.

After thirty minutes of trying to avoid a media shitstorm concerning the part-time hours of a local police station, Martha stays outside in the dark changing the tyre. Teresa from next door comes out and offers her husband's help, but Martha waves it off. Teresa leaves the light on and it's not until Martha's inside that it's turned off. She doesn't want to contemplate moving away from their kindness. Their inclusion. The quick night-time visits offering a leg of lamb they had just won up at the club, or a couple of tomatoes from their garden. Teresa and Marco have been Haberfield people all their lives, their families living within backyard shouting distance, their three children brought up between at least four households in as many streets surrounding them.

Once inside, she heads to the kitchen, because that's always her first port of call when she gets home. It's where she places her keys, hangs up her bag and sits down at the breakfast nook for a cup of tea. Seb was adamant that the stairs leading to the attic would originate from here because the kitchen is the most communal place in any home. He wasn't as interested in the front room, which accommodated a three-seater sofa and TV. He thought that people were more comfortable around a kitchen table. It was a place to be together. To break bread. And in Seb's heart he always believed Rosie would return to live with them. After a trip out to Camden to tow a client's car he returned with a second-hand timber butcher's trolley that served as a main table and a sideboard made of a recycled barn door that accommodated her mother's Hummel porcelain figurines and wireless. The space is the greatest reminder Martha has of Lotte and especially of Seb. Of how, back then, the house smelt of coffee beans and what she called peasant food. Soaked breadcrumbs, sardines, anchovies, fennel. Despite Seb refusing to romanticise the Sicily he left behind in the late eighties, he couldn't let go of it either.

From above she hears the screaming baby again. If the truth were told, Martha's worried. The cry has been a constant since it arrived and she doesn't think that's normal. Sooner or later she has to climb those stairs, but when she fails again she takes a shower and watches TV because, to avoid the grouting and the backyard, and climbing up those stairs, Martha's just got cable. She's catching up on every movie she's missed since marrying Seb and losing him. That covers six years and anything made since 2005. Last week she was engrossed in the *Sex and the City* movie, which did inspire her to go from blonde to brunette because the change of hair colour seemed to work a treat in the film. And she found herself watching it over and over again, just to get to the part where Carrie Bradshaw compares the loss of the unreliable Big, who stands her up at the altar, with the death of a loved one. Not even close, Carrie. Because men who stand you up at the altar still get to walk back into your life a year later holding a pair of Manolo Blahnik shoes. Dead ones stay dead. This week she's moved on to the foreign films. She's given up on the French masterpiece *Hidden*, because the meaning of it was too hidden, so now she's onto a Romanian one.

When the doorbell rings, she's hesitant at first. Perhaps her tyre slasher is getting bolder, but she can see the shadow behind the glass and knows who it is. And all Martha wants to do is go back to that day a month ago. Because it changed everything she had started to work out about going forward. Hadn't she finished with a certain part of her life? Men? Sex? The bullshit that comes with it. But Charlie P's funeral changed everything for more reasons than one. He hadn't just been a work colleague; they'd been friends forever. Over the years Martha had lost a lot of male friends to their relationships. Catching up one-on-one had either stopped, or changed to group drinks. But Charlie's wife Astrid had never felt threatened, had never felt the need to crash the friendship or even be part of it. Martha and Charlie had the same taste in music so she was his gig date. At his wake, Astrid had asked her to speak because the family didn't want it to be all cop talk. Martha hadn't been able to speak at either of her parents' funerals, or Seb's. At her mother

Lotte's funeral, she couldn't even open her mouth to mutter thanks to anyone. Sophie had taken care of that. Had organised the eulogies, made sure they played '*Befiehl du deine Wege*' for the procession, had enlisted the Kolotos tribe to prepare the food for the wake and had written the thank-you cards. Seb's funeral was even more of a blur. But Martha had to be present for Charlie's funeral. So at the wake she told a story of being at a David Gray concert with him and how they spoke about what they wanted sung at their funerals and his choice was 'Babylon'. Later, Ewan Healy approached. Martha had seen him once or twice on sport segments in the news, mumbling in that testy tone most football coaches seemed to have post-game.

'Nice,' was all he said to her. A simple word, but loaded. In the past couple of years, Martha had slipped into that invisibility that belonged to a woman of a certain age. She hadn't let herself go, but it was as if the world had let go of her. It wasn't just men. In pubs and bars and the non-virtual world of socialising, a reminder from the age-police that strappy shoes belonged to the younger generation. Skinny jeans did too. The words 'age appropriate' were reintroduced into her life. It was different with her work team because Martha had been there long enough to count. But outside her job and home, she couldn't quite grasp what her place was. Ewan Healy's 'nice' changed that. In high school, he was crush material for the simple fact that he was someone's older brother. And that he was male. Which meant everything to the daughter of strict German migrants who had never been allowed out.

'Do you remember me?' she had asked. 'Martha Newman.'

A blank look.

'Julia's friend from school.' Martha grabbed another glass of wine off a tray that was doing the rounds. 'You asked me to dance at the Year Ten St Pat's school dance.'

'Yeah, course,' he said, but she could tell he was lying. Not that she was heartbroken, but there was no harm in letting him suffer slightly.

'What was the song?' she asked.

'What song?'

'The one you asked me to dance to?'

'You've got to be joking.' And she saw the hint of a grin. 'Am I supposed to remember that?'

She shrugged. 'I remember.'

'Are you going to hold that against me?'

He had eyes that were kind and a smile that still had clout and, after all these years, she realised that it hid shyness. That's what his good looks and sporting ability had done back when they were teenagers. What his post-game mumbling meant. It hid a sort of awkwardness with the world. And in the corner of that function room, beside the floral wreaths and amongst drunken cops, they covered everything. Grief. Humiliation. Family. She even found herself telling him about the step-demon who was twenty-one and had gone AWOL. And then they ended up on the balcony. She was drunk. He wasn't. But he let her talk, because that's what Martha was good at. Talking. About singing 'Babylon' with Charlie P at the top of their voices at a David Gray concert in 2009. Ewan had known Charlie since his days in the juniors. When he got sacked from his club, Charlie was the first to reach out to him. Martha could see Ewan's eyes water as he told the story. And that happened more than once. She liked that about him. She liked his mannerisms.

The scratching of his bottom lip with his thumb when he was about to laugh. The habit of touching her hands as they spoke. It was intimate, not accidental. It's how they had first kissed that night. Talking, and hand lingering. And then they were in his car making out like bloody stupid kids. Martha couldn't compare it to what she had felt with Seb, because that relationship was about grief and companionship before it was romantic. Working on the house had brought them solace. But with Ewan Healy, it was about the giddy buzz of attraction and suddenly in that car she felt inhibited.

'I wasn't prepared for this,' she had said after they came up for air. 'I've got a Bavarian forest down there and I don't want to be doing a Brazilian or whatever's needed to keep a man interested.'

Too much information, Martha.

And here he is, weeks later, on her doorstep.

'I thought I'd look at your car,' he says. 'Jules said you had a flat tyre.'

'I was married to a mechanic for three years,' she says. 'First thing he taught me was how to change a tyre.'

He goes to speak, but she stops him.

'The whole sleeping-with-a-guy-and-waiting-for-him-to-call got old when I was in my thirties. So I'm going to say a *no thanks* to you coming inside, and see you next week at training.'

But then her traitorous dog comes outside, acting as if she's never received affection from her owner. Suki ignores Martha and cries, pressing against Ewan's leg. He crouches for a play before looking up, a sad smile on his face.

'Lost mine last year,' he says.

She nods, knows the old girl is ready to die, but Martha's not ready to let go.

'You didn't tell me your dad was that far gone,' she says, because maybe she doesn't want him to leave just yet.

He nods. Doesn't speak.

There's a cry from upstairs, then another round of barking. Ewan looks up at the window, surprised, before sending her a questioning look.

'The step-demon is back,' she says. 'With child and dog.'

'I thought you said she was a kid.'

'She's twenty-one.'

'How old's the baby?'

'Who knows. We don't engage in conversation. All I know is that she disappeared two years ago with Seb's dog and a dropkick, and came back last month with a baby and the dog.'

Martha knows the baby is about to walk because her stunning banister has been fitted with an un-stunning child gate.

When there seems nothing left to say, Ewan turns to walk away, but stops.

'Actually I lied,' he says. 'I didn't come about the tyre. I just want to say something and you've got to let me say it.'

Martha stays silent. So does he. She points to her watch.

'I've got a Romanian film about genocide I'm dying to get back to.'

Still more silence. He's a pause man. Martha isn't.

'I'm having a bit of a fucked year,' he finally says, 'and to top it off, I'm contemplating putting my father into a nursing home, and that makes me feel like a prick because John Healy's been a hero all my life, and the last thing he remembers about the son he gave everything to is that I'm a failure who got sacked from a dream job because I wasn't good enough.'

Martha gets a sense that it's the most he's said in a lifetime.

'But last month, I went to an old mate's funeral, and that day was something better than it should have been. Because of you, and that speech, and the fact that you didn't stop talking, after I've spent years with two different women who had nothing to say. And I know I'm wanting this at a time that I don't have much to give in return, Martha, but if you're interested I'd really like us to go out sometime and, who knows, I might get to see Bavaria again –'

'Let's lay that analogy to rest.'

'Agreed.'

Martha nudges Suki towards the door, but this time she stops.

'The way I see it, the last thing John Healy remembers is that his son was good enough to get chosen for the Balmain Juniors,' she says.

And his smile has more than just clout so she nudges the dog inside before they both invite him in.

'I'm going to remember that song, you know,' he says. 'The one I asked you to dance to. I've been going through all my LPs so I've narrowed it down to something from Elvis Costello or The Cure.'

'Dream on that you were that cool back then,' she says, shutting the door.

But she can't help smiling herself.

Frankie Spinelli ^{girl}
'girls'
Tom Mackee
+ Tara

Chapter Three

He's home, and he knows he's home because they're here and that's the way it is, just the certainty that one of them will always be around, and it feels like everything's going to be okay in a way that it hasn't since that phone call, and he's hugging the three of them because he's become the sort of person who goes straight for the clinch, because once that hug came from Frankie Spinelli years ago he knew his days of holding back were over. And everything looks the same and different, and he has one of those epiphanies in front of the clocks outside Central on Elizabeth Street next to a guy selling *The Big Issue*. That regardless of where his car took him and what he didn't end up finding, he's part of this city too and he realises that they're all laughing and that he's said it all out loud.

'Shut up, Jimmy!'

And the girls link their arms with his and Mackee takes Jimmy's duffel, and he's so overwhelmed by them, and the city, and being home, that he forgets why he's really here, and just lets it all settle in. That he's home.

And they take him to a café and fill him in on what he hasn't heard in phone calls. That Justine's still in 'fucking Melbourne'.

'It's what we call it now,' Frankie tells him.

'Because we're sick of hearing how cool it is down there and how fantastic the music scene is, and how it's less expensive than Sydney, and Melbourne Melbourne fucking Melbourne,' Tara says.

'The whole of Queensland got the treatment while you were there,' Mackee explains. 'Jimmy's in fucking Queensland, we'd tell people. And because Siobhan's still in London, it's fucked as well, and so is wherever the fuck in Europe Will is.'

'Stuttgart,' Frankie tells him. 'Fucking Stuttgart.'

And Jimmy can't help laughing because they do idiotic conversations better than anyone he knows.

'So you're staying with us?' Tara says.

'One of our housemates is in Pakistan so you get his room,' Mackee adds. He's wearing a tie, which isn't really a Tom Mackee thing to do.

'What's with the noose?' Jimmy asks.

'Brace yourself,' Frankie says.

'Because Tom goes by the title *Sir* these days,' Tara tells him.

'Teaching?' Jimmy's more than surprised. 'Mate, no.'

'He got his Dip. Ed. last year,' Tara says. 'He's back to wearing the sexy Design and Technology apron and goggles.'

'Ah come on, Tara, do you have to tell people what we get up to in the bedroom?'

Tara's laughing and it's good to see. Because two years ago when Jimmy was last in Sydney, Mackee and Tara were feeling their way around being together and it all seemed raw.

And they don't stop talking for hours, and later he can't even remember what it was they spoke about. All they want to hear is what he's been up to in better detail than they get over the phone. So Jimmy tells them how he's driving dump trucks for the mines and he tries to pretend that Tara isn't about to have a major brain freeze at the mention of mines, and that he's working one week on, one week off, and how the company flies him to Brisbane but anywhere else is at his expense. And he's talking a mile a minute about town-hopping and how he got his big vehicle licence, and how he really wants to save up enough so he can get into the paramedics one day. And when Jimmy's covered everything, he figures it's time to tell them why he's really in Sydney, apart from wanting to see them after a two-year good behaviour bond kept him in Queensland.

'Promise you won't freak out.'

Wrong way to start things because Frankie's about to have a meltdown.

'I'm not dying and I'm not going to jail.'

'Probably should have started with that,' Mackee says.

For a moment he's silent. He's only had five days to process this himself.

'I got a girl pregnant,' he says.

For the first time since he got off the train, there's silence.

'Is she going through with it?' Mackee finally asks.

'She's already had it,' he says.

The silence this time is a beat longer.

'Why didn't you tell us?' Frankie asks, and Jimmy can hear the hurt.

'Because I didn't know, mate.'

He has to start somewhere, but even in his own head he hasn't worked out where.

'I met her about two years ago up north during the floods. We went our separate ways. Apparently she got pregnant. Remember when I changed phone numbers about a year ago because I couldn't find my phone? Well, I found it in my duffel bag when I returned to Rockhampton a year after she contacted me. He's fifteen months old.'

'How do you know it's yours?' Tara asks.

'Because she says it is.'

There's more silence after that.

'I don't know how to pronounce his name,' he says because everything feels so intense. 'You're going to have to help me here, Frankie. It's Toto.'

Jimmy tries to say it the way he heard it over the phone when he spoke to Rosie, but seems to fail.

'You got an Italian girl pregnant?' Frankie asks.

'Yes, and you're not going to believe where she lives,' he says. 'Haberfield. So I better go see her sooner rather than later.'

Mackee's nodding in agreement. 'Nothing worse than bumping into the girl you knocked up while stuffing your face with the Italian cheesecake at Papa's.'

And it all seems wrong but they're pissing themselves laughing.

Mackee and Tara take him home to the two-storey Victorian terrace they rent across from the railway line in Petersham. They share it with two friends, one who's overseas and the other who's out bush for six months. Mackee leads him up the stairs and hands him a towel from the linen cupboard.

'You know you can stay as long as you want, mate,' he says.

It's heartfelt, no matter how it's delivered, and it's the thing that Jimmy's worked out about his relationship with Mackee. That their connection is strong, despite the lack of dialogue between them. Before the girls came along in Year Eleven, they had never exchanged a word. Nor had the girls, and they'd come over from the same school. Frankie said the six of them were the loneliest people in the world until they became a group. But even then, Jimmy and Mackee only got to know each other in fragments. Until a couple of years back when Jimmy disappeared from their lives and Mackee tracked him down and asked for help working on a community building project in Walgett with Tom's father and grandpop. Working with them was tough at first, because the Mackees were dealing with their own shit, and most times it was Jimmy who did the talking. Mackee's dad later wrote to say that Jimmy had filled in the silence for them, and it made all the difference.

In the shower he can hear the rumble of their voices and he's comforted by the sound. He hasn't lived in a house since Frankie's place more than two years ago. It's been a whole lot of motel rooms and boarding houses and makeshift accommodation out at the mines.

In the kitchen, Mackee is cooking and Tara has work spread out on the dining table. Her computer sounds the Skype ringtone just as Jimmy sits down.

'That was quick,' Tara says. 'Siobhan.'

Jimmy owes Siobhan a couple of phone calls, so he goes straight into an apology when her face appears on the screen. She's been working in London for the past five years on a British passport because her mum was born there. She was the screw-up when they were at school. Now she has her life worked out better than any of them and dishes out advice and threats from the other side of the world.

'Can we just skip the pleasantries while I find the one key word that's gone through my head since Frankie texted?' she says.

'Brace yourself,' Mackee says from the sink.

'*Condom!*'

'They didn't hear you in Sheffield, Siobhan,' Mackee calls out.

'And he's working for the mines as well,' Tara says, leaning over Jimmy's shoulder.

'Go ahead, ruin the environment and knock up girls you meet in floods,' Siobhan says. 'She is the flood chick, isn't she?'

Tom sings a couple of lines about floods and fools as he chops up the vegies.

'And have you spoken to Frankie?' Siobhan asks.

'About what?'

'About Will.'

'None of our business, Siobhan,' Tara says, but Mackee is sitting next to Jimmy now, so it seems serious.

'Well, he's in Germany and she's here,' Mackee says. 'And the deal was that they'd both be living overseas together for a year.'

'Talk to her, Jimmy,' Siobhan says.

Later, the three of them sit on the front verandah eating Mackee's tacos and drinking beer, accompanied by the rattle of the trains.

Tara's telling them about her work at Barangaroo and how it's part of the C40 Cities climate program. Her passion for urban renewal comes through in every word she speaks. 'The pay's shit, but it's an amazing opportunity.'

'How can you afford to keep this place?'

'We sort of can't,' Tara says. 'But I'm working full-time and Tom is still getting shifts at the Union, as well as casual teaching, so we manage to make the rent.'

'We share a mobile phone and go without pay TV,' Mackee informs him.

'Which means we watched the first episode of *Game of Thrones* at my parents' place last week,' Tara says.

'Where Jaime and Cersei declared their familial love for each other,' Mackee added. 'Never again.'

A train rattles by and it lulls them into silence. A comfortable one. And Jimmy wonders if this is what Mackee and Tara do when they're alone. Sit side by side on an ancient vinyl couch without the need to fill the silence with banal talk.

Much later they head back inside.

'I thought she was just some girl you met and forgot,' Mackee says, as if he's been thinking about it all this time.

Jimmy shrugs.

'Were you in love with her?' Tara asks.

'Didn't know her long enough. She was a train wreck. I was one. A good fit.'

He takes one of the buses that travels along Parramatta Road and walks down to the Haberfield shops. He's been here once or twice with Frankie, mostly to pick up Italian sweets or groceries for her grandmother, who won't get her homemade pasta or deli food from anywhere else. It's a couple of blocks of the essentials. A newsagency, drycleaners, cafés, restaurants and pasticcerias. They're mostly grassroots businesses, like the hole-in-the-wall bakery or the IGA. It hasn't had a makeover like plenty of the other main streets in the inner west, and he figures that's the way the locals want things.

Rosie's place is on Dalhousie Street and he needs to check his phone for the number. Finds the house soon enough. A small cottage surrounded by pretty impressive Federation homes. In the front yard is a tiny box garden of wild grass and flowers that gives it an unkempt feel, contradicted by the homeliness of the verandah, where a couple of cane armchairs, same as those outside the Queenslander houses up in the Burdekin, sit, a small ceramic table between them. Like Mackee and Tara's train-watching vinyl couch, they speak of home. He rings the doorbell and regrets it a moment later, because he figures he's woken up the baby. When no one answers, he peers through one of the windows and between the curtains. Jimmy can see a fireplace with a cuckoo clock above it. He walks across to the other window and realises he's looking into someone's bedroom.

'What are you doing?'

Behind him a woman is standing at the gate, unimpressed. She's dressed in a suit; obviously home from work, judging from the oversized bag she's holding. She's sort of beautiful in an older woman way, but Jimmy's too intimidated by her hostility to ponder the beauty. Rosie never mentioned parents so he doesn't know how the two are related.

'I'm looking for Rosie,' he says.

She continues to stare at him without responding.

'Can you let her know I'm here?'

'I'm not her receptionist.'

He's about to turn and head home, but knows he has to work out the truth sooner or later.

'I think it's important that I see her . . . them.'

Jimmy notices the flash of realisation. She's just made the connection and couldn't look more unimpressed, shouldering him out of the way to unlock the door.

Although there's no invitation to follow, Jimmy steps inside after her.

She disappears into the bedroom so he walks into the room with the fireplace, wondering if he's meant to wait. It's small, so the TV's mounted on a cream-coloured wall to save space, and there's a three-seater sitting the right distance away. He likes the cuckoo clock. Maybe a bit kitsch, but he figures the 'Made in Germany' label means it's the real thing. When he figures that no one is returning for him, Jimmy explores the house. Apart from the bathroom, the rest of the place is an open-plan kitchen and living area with impressive jarrah floorboards. Jimmy's worked with Bob Spinelli on properties around the city and Mackee's a carpentry freak, so he's been dragged to enough timber-recycling sheds to appreciate how the red tinge of the wood works well with the colours surrounding it. Although he sees the wood's imperfections, the polish makes him want to take off his shoes. His favourite thing about the place is the natural light coming through a couple of French doors at the back, enviable after some of the places Jimmy's lived in.

He's just about to look outside when he hears a sound above him. Walks to the foot of a narrow staircase where he sees Rosie standing at the top. He makes his way to her and they stand before each other for the first time in two years. When Jimmy met Rosie that time up north, her hair was cropped and he couldn't keep his eyes off her face. Stared at her for at least half an hour before he had the guts to approach. He remembers the singlet and shorts she was wearing and the colour of her skin, and the way she folded her arms while she was listening to the information being handed out. Jimmy honestly thought that a pasty-skinned, bushy-bearded weirdo in orange work gear didn't stand a chance.

Her hair's longer now, shoved back in a ponytail and looking like it hasn't been washed in weeks. Her dark eyes are accentuated by darker circles. Even so, if he walked into a pub today and saw her standing there, he'd still wait thirty minutes to take a chance. The thump of his heart gives that away. She's studying him now and Jimmy wonders what she's looking for. Resemblance to her child? A disbelief that she ever saw anything in him? Behind her, he sees another living area, different from downstairs. Toys and cushions scattered over the floor, a sofa covered by an old sheet and a bag with nappies spilling out. The back end of the room is the best thing about it. Wall-to-wall glass with a view of the backyard. From where he's standing, Jimmy can see a mess of a garden.

'How have you been?' he asks.

She doesn't respond.

'Like I said on the phone,' he says, 'I'm sorry it took so long. I lost my mobile . . .'

'You lose a lot of things.'

He remembers once how they were lying in bed and talking about the stolen Monaro. Jimmy's suddenly overcome by the memory. The sex. The chemistry. The sorrow of that town.

A cry interrupts the silence between them and Rosie disappears into the next room. Jimmy's pulse is going for it, because he's not ready for this. He hears murmuring and the crying stops and she reappears, holding the kid who looks heavy in her arms. A good-looking baby, caramel hair and same coloured eyes. He starts crying again when he sees Jimmy, and Rosie balances him on her hip and grabs a baby bottle that's lying on a milk crate.

'Have you ever held one of these?' she wants to know.

Jimmy doesn't respond. And that's how they spend the hour. No one speaking and a baby wailing.

One that looks absolutely nothing like Jimmy.

'I'll come back tomorrow if you like,' he says.

'Up to you.'

The next day he gets there earlier so he doesn't have to deal with the hostile woman in the suit. This time it's Rosie who answers the door.

'Are you okay?' he asks.

'Why wouldn't I be?'

Because she's in her pyjamas at eleven o'clock in the morning, and yesterday she was in the same pyjamas at five-thirty in the afternoon. Jimmy follows her upstairs where the baby is crying again. She disappears inside the bedroom to get him.

'Who lives here with you?' he calls out. 'Is it your mum?'

She comes out holding the baby. The now ear-piercing screeching is taking swipes at Jimmy's temples.

'As if I look anything like her.'

True. The woman is fair-skinned and blue-eyed, but she doesn't seem the type to be renting out her attic space, so Jimmy figures she's somehow related.

'She was my father's other wife.'

'Was' could mean two things about Rosie's father. Divorced or dead. He goes for the latter.

'It's a great space,' he says. 'It doesn't look this big outside.'

'My father did it himself.'

'He was a builder?'

'No.'

She holds out the crying kid for Jimmy to take, but he doesn't.

'When he gets used to me, maybe,' he says.

Rosie cradles the sobbing baby, but it doesn't seem to help. And that's it for the day. No more talking, just a lot of standing around and soaking in the mess.

He takes a bus out to Waterloo, back to the housing commission block of flats he lived in most of his life. Thirteen floors of misery, his mum used to say. Jimmy doesn't know whether that's true now, but it was a place of fear for him then. Not for his life, but for hers. He remembers the older kids who used to sell ciggies in the toilet block. They'd tell him that the newspaper called this place Suicide Towers. From that moment on, until his mum left him behind, Jimmy was convinced she'd walk up to the roof and throw herself off. The area had changed now. More hipsters moving in and a lot more families with better lives than theirs. Maybe that's not a bad thing but it depresses Jimmy. Makes his life feel even more forgotten.

His phone rings and it's Frankie.

'Are you okay?' she asks.

'Are you?'

'Come over tonight. My mum's asking about you.'

Jimmy enjoys the idea of being asked after. There'd been moments in the past two years where he'd felt himself disappearing off the grid.

*

Later that afternoon, when Mia Spinelli opens the door, she hugs Jimmy with that intensity and promise that he's always found in his embraces with this family. When he first met them in Year Eleven, Mia was suffering depression and Frankie was dealing with her only spiral into something close to it. For some reason, he connected with Mia during her illness. She calls him her second son, and he wishes it were true. Wishes these people weren't his on loan. Even Nonna Anna, who's staying with them because she's had a hip replacement, welcomes Jimmy as if he belongs to them.

'Too skinny,' she says, her accent heavy with warmth.

He does the rounds with Frankie. Dropping off her brother Luca who's doing a health science degree and working part-time at one of the local primary schools at their after-hours day care. Then taking Will's grandmother to the physio before heading in to work to pick up her pay.

'Are you and Will okay?' he asks, because he figures that if she's hanging out with Will's family everything should be fine. The two have been a thing for eight years. Have been in love for even longer. Jimmy isn't one to live through other people's relationships, but he can't fathom the idea of them not making it. Their public displays of affection may be too much, but they're the sort of people who rarely fall out with friends or relatives. Despite Will being an introvert and Frankie being the exact opposite, they have a great friendship. An enviable one. Three years ago when Jimmy was in Sydney, he felt as if he really got to know Will and he still receives a text at least once a month asking, *Have you found the Monaro?*

'Who's saying we're not?' Frankie asks.

'No one,' he sort of lies. 'But he's in Germany and you aren't.'

'We've been apart before,' she says.

'I thought the plan was that you'd live overseas together.'

'We will,' she says. 'But I'm in the middle of sorting things out and I can't just pick up and take off.'

Jimmy leaves it at that because he can tell she's getting irritated.

She parks in a no-standing zone at King Street Wharf where clubs and restaurants line the road, and tells him to keep an eye out for parking police while she runs in to grab her pay. He can't keep count of how many jobs she has these days.

'You must be knackered, mate,' he says when she returns.

'I'm still paying off my HECS loan, my credit card, my phone, plus I need to save.'

Jimmy's noticed that everyone's talking about saving money, or paying off loans, and stuff they didn't seem to worry about a couple of years ago. He doesn't know how to be part of that yet. He may understand what he wants to do for a living, but he doesn't have a plan that takes him into a financial future. It just hasn't been a priority. These past eighteen months he's made good money, and he's learnt to spend good money. On flying up to the Cape to fish. On watching the V8 Supercars in Townsville. On grog.

'We're not twenty-four anymore, Jimmy.'

'I can't see the big difference between being twenty-four and twenty-five.'

'Quarter of a century!' she says.

Back at Frankie's place, he has dinner with the family. Here, it's always chatty. As if they haven't been together for weeks and need to fill each other in on fragments of their day that are neither trivial or profound, but provide him with a comfort beyond words. There's constant talk over each other, but no one gets irate. Tonight it's a switch from English to Italian and back again, but Jimmy doesn't know whether they're translating for him or Mia's mother. They are known to each other in a way Jimmy's family wasn't. When his grandpop died, the old guy was still a mystery to him. An angry man who raised a broken daughter who walked away from Jimmy because she woke up one morning and couldn't find a way out of that life except to leave. It's what she told him that time he tracked her down in Lismore. Jimmy is certain of two things: that he was no better off with the old guy, and that his mother's decision to leave led him to this table. For that, he's grateful. After dinner, Frankie heads off to the UTS library and promises to be back in a couple of hours. Jimmy helps Bob wash up and then sits with Mia, who's marking a batch of uni essays.

'Have you seen him?' she asks, and he doesn't question to whom she's referring.

Jimmy nods.

'And Rosie? Is that her name?'

'Yeah. Rosanna.'

'What's the surname? We may know the family.'

'I have no idea,' he says. 'And I don't know how to bring it up without sounding like a dick.'

'Then ask her the baby's full name.'

Simple solution. Why didn't he think of that?

'I don't think she's coping,' he says. 'I recognise the signs and I want to do the right thing, you know, I don't want to let her down.'

'But?'

He looks up, meets her eyes, because he can pretty much bullshit anyone including himself, but not Mia Spinelli.

'I don't know if he's mine.'

And Jimmy feels like a bastard saying that. Has no idea what he owes Rosie, but it's not calling her a liar.

'Then find out. Regardless of where you want to go with this, you can't have that question lingering every time you're with them.'

She googles something on her laptop and scribbles it down on a post-it note.

'Tell her to ring one of these numbers. They know how to deal with babies and mums.'

He takes the post-it note, but can't imagine Rosie appreciating him talking about her with other people.

Frankie comes home and they head down to meet Tara and Mackee at the Union. Jimmy is meant to fly out tomorrow and his head is no clearer than it was a couple of days ago when he arrived.

'Are you coming back?' Mackee asks.

'The room's there for you,' Tara says.

Jimmy's relieved by the offer because it makes going away a lot easier. But it's the fear of returning to Sydney and Rosie's house that keeps him awake. And he's frightened of the weak reckless side of him that wants to return up north to stuff things up, good and proper. So that it'll be more than a good behaviour bond keeping him from ever coming home again.

Chapter Four

The crying is endless. It's a sound that has embedded itself into the part of her head that can't block noise out anymore. She wakes to it, showers to it, walks the streets to it, breathes in rhythm to it, and Rosie takes the blame for it all. Ten weeks of not giving a shit what she drank or smoked or what pills she took while he was in her belly. When he was born, she thought Toto had escaped any of the damage she did because the nurses said he was perfect, but Rosie was kidding herself because that's what she does.

Today she leaves the house because Tuesday has incentives. It's the day that gives her a reason to get out of her pyjamas and have a shower because the mornings are the worst and most days she talks herself out of walking down the stairs. Most days there are too many people to avoid. Martha downstairs. Or Teresa next door. She seems to have a radar that detects the moment Rosie and Toto hit the pavement.

'Rosie, why don't you come in and –'

Rosie keeps pushing the pram up Dalhousie, but really she wants to turn back and tell Teresa exactly what she thinks of her. For forgetting Rosie's mum the moment she died all those years ago, even though they were best friends. For welcoming the second wife with open arms too soon after. Rosie hears them outside the window. Teresa and Marco and Martha chatting away about the house mostly. As if the house, like their neighbours, belonged to Martha from the beginning, when it was Rosie's mum who came first. She passes St Joan of Arc's Church and old Signora Bitch Face from across the road is gossiping to one of her cronies, giving Rosie the evil eye. Fuck you all, she wants to say. Toto is crying again and she wants to yell the same thing to him, and it makes her feel like a monster, and she's crying as she pushes the pram, praying she won't do something to hurt Toto, like those women who drive their kids into lakes or leave them behind in hot cars for hours. She keeps on hearing Min's voice in her head. *What are you going to do with your life, Rosie?*

So she's been trying to move forward. She went to Leichhardt Library a couple of weeks ago and found an advertisement on the community noticeboard for those who didn't get to join a mothers' group when their baby was born. That's where she ends up on Tuesdays. Meeting at an old church hall in Lilyfield with at least nine other mothers, three who are vying for leadership. Passive-aggressive Caterina, Yolanda the foghorn, and cardio mum, who's determined that everyone is going to lose post-baby fat. A few of the others seem friendly, but they don't want to commit to the first person who smiles at them in case someone better comes along. One or two don't contribute at all, like the mum sitting beside Rosie who checks her phone every time it beeps as if missing a tweet is going to ruin her life. Or the Chinese girl who hasn't spoken a word. Rosie finds them all irritating. She's either ignored or paid too much attention.

'Oh, you're so young,' passive-aggressive Caterina says, as if it's something to be sympathetic about. She reminds Rosie of the girls in the neighbourhood who used to bitch about what she was getting up to with their brothers and cousins, rather than what their brothers and cousins were getting up to with her.

'He's so big for his age.' Definitely a reprimand from cardio mum who Rosie is convinced has already put her baby on a diet. The woman's first question every week has been, 'Is he walking yet?'

And then in that first week, the topic she most dreads comes up. The exchange of 'When did you stop breastfeeding?' stories. By the time they get to Rosie, some of the others are in tears from the trauma of moving onto formula.

'I didn't breastfeed,' she says. 'It was too painful.'

'Oh, you poor thing.'

Rosie's grateful for even a bit of patronising sympathy from passive-aggressive Caterina until she realises the woman is talking to Toto. Had Rosie given up too soon? Her mother would have endured the bleeding and scabby nipples. Her mother endured years of cancer.

'Where's the next meeting?' Rosie asks.

'We'll put things up on the Facebook page,' Caterina says. It seems as though it's only on a need-to-know basis. As if they're a group of operatives who have something to hide.

'I'm not on Facebook,' Rosie says. 'Could someone text me?'

No one commits to doing that.

Cardio mum tells them about a 'Mums with Gloves' program she's starting up at one of the parks just off the Bay Run and then goes into nutrition news again to help anyone who wants to lose the baby fat. Yolanda bristles through the whole spiel.

And then there's Toto's incessant crying. It stops conversation most times. Produces strained smiles from the others that don't quite reach their eyes. Yolanda pulls Rosie aside when she goes to makes herself an instant coffee. She's an Indigenous girl who's just moved to Sydney from Moree with her partner and, apart from bristling whenever cardio mum speaks, Yolanda's brought up how crap Sydney is about three times now.

'It's his teeth,' Yolanda tells her.

'What?'

'Your bub. He's crying because of his teeth.'

'He's never had trouble with his teeth,' Rosie says.

'But the molars are painful and you should –'

'It's none of your business, Yolanda.'

'I don't like your tone.'

Obviously a teacher. Rosie's history with teachers is worse than her history with girls from the neighbourhood. Before they leave, Caterina wants a photo of all the babies together because she thinks they're the most culturally diverse mothers' group in the area and is patting herself on the back for bringing them together.

But Rosie goes back each Tuesday regardless, because it's company. Because some days she just needs to speak to someone other than Toto. A few of the mums are close to going back to work soon and there's a lot of talk about professions. Banking. Pharmaceuticals. IT. It's yet another question Rosie dreads.

They bypass some of the others but Caterina insists that someone Rosie's age must have a story.

'I've enrolled in a nursing degree,' she lies. She's enquired about it, anyway. Researched it online at the library. Next time they ask, she'll fill in the details. About how she's thinking of midwifery because of Min during the floods.

But today, after four weeks of mothers' group, they aren't there. Nine women with prams, the United Nations of the inner west, on the run from Rosie.

So she takes the bus to the city for the first time with Toto, worried that she won't be able to get the pram on and off in time, but a couple of people help her when she gets off at UTS. She heads to the Student Association and browses the pamphlets outside the door. Takes one about free legal advice for UTS students. Once inside, a guy her age helps her download an application form and she wants to weep with gratitude because kindness disarms her these days. Lachlan, or Lachie as he likes to be called, is doing a Bachelor of Mathematics and Computing. Beautiful straight teeth and a great smile. Tells her to come back on Thursday and he'll help with the application. Rosie contemplates the offer in his eyes, because he doesn't seem to be fazed by a sleeping baby. And as far as she's concerned, she doesn't owe SES Jesus anything.

But that afternoon he turns up on her doorstep. He says something about working in the mines up north, one week on, one week off, but Rosie figures that's just some bullshit lie. She can tell he's not interested in Toto. Hasn't touched him once, and the moment he walks up those stairs he's itching to leave. He doesn't have the beard anymore. It softened him. During the floods it made him look kind.

She hears a ringtone. Not hers, because Rosie doesn't get phone calls. 'Jimmy here,' he says, and then he mumbles to whomever he's speaking to. The fragments she knows about him begin to disappear.

'You're Jimmy, not Jim,' she says, when he hangs up.

'My friends call me Jimmy.'

Toto doesn't want to be contained because he's tasted the freedom that feet bring him, and he wants more. In Rosie's arms he headbutts her and for a moment she's stunned by the force of it, but she doesn't let on.

'Do you want me to call you Jim or Jimmy?' she asks.

'You can call me whatever you want.'

She remembers the nights during the floods lying beside him when he didn't shut up. Now she gets short abrupt statements and little else. Rosie hates small talk. Hates people who force her to indulge in it. But that's who she's become now. Someone satisfied by the mundane. The girl who pushes prams through shopping centres just to enjoy the pace of a flat surface because it calms her down.

'I won a raffle at Marketplace,' she tells him. 'I've got a portrait of Toto and they're giving me three copies, so you can have one. He's pretty photogenic.'

Rosie holds the baby out to him, but Jim's hands stay at his side. So she puts Toto on the floor and lets him try to walk. He falls, hits his head, and starts to cry.

'I'm sorry,' she whispers, holding him tight. 'I'm sorry.' Because it's all she says to him these days.

'Are you sure he's mine?'

Jim's words clench something in her gut.

'Why would you ask that?'

'Because he looks nothing like me.'

'Toto's yours,' she says.

Apart from the coldness in Jim's voice, there's also pity in his eyes.

'How can you be sure, Rosie?'

'Trust me, he looks like you! When he smiles, he looks just like you.'

'He doesn't!'

Toto jumps in her arms, his little heart beating fast. And that's it for Rosie. Gennaros don't beg. It was her father's golden rule. She takes Toto into the bedroom, puts him down in the cot and then returns.

'I want you to leave,' she says. 'You don't respect me and I don't need that in Toto's life. I told you he was yours because I know how you felt about your mother not letting your father be part of your life. You said any man should have the right to know.'

He doesn't respond, and she shoves him.

'If you don't want to be part of this, then go away, *Jimmy*, or whatever the fuck your name is. I don't want your darkness in his life.'

'I'm worried about you, Rosie,' he says. He takes something out of his pocket. A post-it note with a couple of phone numbers on it. 'These people might be able to help.'

'Why would you care?'

'Because I just do.'

'You don't even know me. I'm just some girl you picked up who you think is a liar!'

*

After she manages to put Toto down for a sleep, she heads to the kitchen to organise food. It's the Heinz stuff from the supermarket for the time being because she doesn't have it in her to prepare any-thing else. She hears the front door open and starts to head upstairs. There's an unspoken rule between them not to be in the same room. But Rosie stops herself, because this is her house. Her kitchen. Bruno comes down the stairs and walks towards Martha, but Rosie calls him back and sends him up again. Martha puts the groceries down on the butcher's trolley, her icy blue stare on Rosie for the first time since Rosie's returned. She's darkened her blonde hair lately. When Rosie first saw her in that cancer ward all those years ago, she thought Martha was the good witch Glinda from *The Wizard of Oz*. Some things changed over the years. Same land, different witch.

Rosie wants to be the first to speak because she needs that control.

'Where's my father's wedding ring?'

Martha seems surprised by the question. 'In my jewellery box.'

'I mean his real wedding ring.'

Martha's eyes meet hers. When it comes to staring, Rosie can win this. Almost.

'No disrespect to your mother, Rosie, but I do consider my marriage to your father the real thing.'

'I don't give a shit, Martha. Where have you put my parents' stuff?'

'You took most of your mum's things when you left.'

'And what right did you have taking down photos of my mother in the living room?'

'Once again, no disrespect to Loredana, but why would I have photos of her in a house that I've been the sole occupant of for almost three years?'

'Because it's my house.'

'Yes, but also mine. I've lived here for six years, Rosie. Your father and I worked on it together. Both of us. He didn't just work on it alone.'

Together. Us. When those words come out of Martha's mouth, Rosie wants to slap her hard.

'My father never worked on this house alone before my mother died. It was the three of us.'

And all Rosie can see in the kitchen now is a photo of Martha and her father stuck on the fridge. Must have been taken just before he died. The only photo she has with her parents is from around the year 2000, before her mother was diagnosed, when Rosie was ten. The house was still a shell back then. But it didn't matter, because they were happy. As if nothing could break them.

'I've already seen a solicitor and they said I have the right to this house over you,' Rosie says. 'You need to move out.'

'That's not true and you know it.'

'Then I'll take you to court.'

'With what, Rosie?'

'My nonna in Italy's given me money.'

'Eugenia doesn't have money!'

'You know nothing about my family,' Rosie says. 'Eugenia would do anything for me to have this house, because it was built for my mother and me.'

Rosie watches Martha fill up the kettle with water and switch it on. As if she's calm, but her hands are shaking.

'You want me out of here, Rosie? Then how are you going to manage a mortgage?'

'The house doesn't have a mortgage.'

Martha shakes her head with disbelief.

'Of course it has a mortgage.'

'My father worked on this house for years without getting into debt.'

'Rosie, they didn't have health insurance. Any money he made went to paying your mum's hospital bills.'

'Don't blame my mother.'

Upstairs, Toto wakes up and is wailing. Rosie sees Martha's eyes flicker towards the sound.

'How about we have this discussion when you've had a bit more sleep?' Martha says.

'I don't want you living here with us!'

'Then we sell the house, Rosie!'

Rosie is stunned to hear the words.

'Is that what you want? Because we both can't afford to buy each other out.'

'I'm not moving! This is Toto's home.'

Toto's cry turns into a bloodcurdling sound.

'Seb said –'

Rosie doesn't want to hear another word about what her father and Martha said or did together. She grabs the photo off the fridge and tears it in pieces. She sees Martha's teeth clench.

'Go and calm him down –'

'Fuck you, Martha. What would you know about calming down babies?'

And then groundhog day begins again. With wailing. With Teresa next door calling out to her. With Signora outside St Joan of Arc's, reprimand in her eyes, watching Rosie push that pram. With the realisation that SES Jesus is another disappointment in a line of useless guys in her life. And, to top it all off, she picks up the portraits of Toto at Marketplace and sees the mothers' group, laughing in a café on Marion Street. Without her.

And back in the only place that makes sense to Rosie, she closes her eyes to the sound of crying, and in the end she doesn't know if it's Toto's or hers.

Chapter Five

If it's Seb who instructs Martha during the day, it's her mother Lotte who wakes her up most mornings. It's usually with a gentle order. Sometimes a reminder to ring Oberammergau because it's Tante Kristiana's birthday, or that it'd be rude not to take up Voula Kolotos's offer to join the family this Greek Easter. For the past two days Lotte has raised concerns about the silence upstairs. 'Come on, *honigbiene*,' she whispers in her ear, so Martha finally gives in and follows her mother's voice up those steps. But there's no one there and it makes her stomach churn. Rosie disappearing two years ago was one thing, but this time she's taken a baby with her and left Bruno behind. He's sitting at the bottom of the stairs, brooding, while Suki's in Martha's bedroom, dying.

*

At work, a brief lands on her desk. She stares at it a moment, before heading to the chief of staff's office.

'Can you get someone else to do this?' she asks Matthew Solloway. He wants Martha to report back to the minister later in the week about her findings, as if there's supposed to be a profound one. People drink and drive. Loved ones die. Everyone's devastated. End of story. Martha can't understand the need to spin it into something more than that.

'How about I work on the firearms policy and Leon takes over with this?' she asks.

Martha should let him know that Leon is in over his head with the firearms policy, but it's not her style to report one of her team.

'How about you continue working on what I gave you, Martha?'

Out at training that night, she's relieved to be pumping blood into her brain. She likes the laps the most. Sometimes it's the only peace and quiet she's had all day, but then one of the others will catch up and they get to talk and she'll enjoy that as well. Tonight, it's Alana giving her a rundown on being principal at a new school out west, and how hard it's been balancing Julia and the kids with all the students at school, but sometimes she sees a glimmer of results. Martha loves people's passion for their work. She doesn't feel a passion for hers, but a commitment. Hers is a job of great emotion controlled by useless bureaucracy. This week it's a backlash against the revenue cash cow of speed cameras. Road carnage is the hardest topic for Martha to deal with, so spending today reading emails from grieving parents and partners and siblings and neighbours and friends of those who've been killed or damaged beyond repair has her dancing at the edge of something dangerous. She doesn't want to be so committed anymore.

Ewan catches up while she runs her third lap.

'Two's enough,' he says. And there it is. The resonance of his voice that brings a pleasure beyond words.

'I need to say something and I don't want you to react,' he says.

And she knows that it's a 'yes please' to whether she'll go out with him. No beating around the bush this time.

'You know you don't have to preface everything with "I need to say something" although I find it very endearing,' she says.

She can't help smiling because that's what she does in his presence.

'So you're going to be okay about not playing centre,' he asks, 'because honestly –'

Martha puts up a hand to stop him speaking because if she doesn't give it a purpose at the moment, it might just slap his face.

'I've mapped it all out and you need to be in a defence position because of your height and your intimidating demeanour.'

Martha points to the others who are doing push-ups on the freshly cut grass, like a squadron out of a *G.I. Jane* movie. 'I think I come in a close fourth when it comes to intimidating demeanour.'

'You're tall and I need you as a goal defender,' he says. Now he's speaking to her as though she's one of his ex-footy players.

'I was invited into this team to play centre or shooter, Ewan, and if I don't get to play those positions, I'm walking away.'

'For crying out loud, Martha.'

'Don't you "For crying out loud, Martha" me.'

She breaks into a sprint that she regrets about ten metres in, forced to slow down. It leaves him with two options: pass her or jog alongside her.

'So what are my chances of taking you out to dinner now?' he says, going for the latter.

And that's the humiliating part. His chances haven't diminished at all.

'Saturday night,' he says. 'Food, film, footy or –'

'Stop with the Fs or I'm going home.'

He laughs into a cough, because the others are watching them approach.

'What happened out there?' his sister asks.

Martha checks a stitch. 'He told me I can't play centre.'

The others are outraged. Martha's sort of flattered. Surprised.

'Honestly, you're a C-bomb, Ewan!' Elizabeth says.

'Are we playing for the Sydney Swifts or the Commonwealth Games?' Alana asks.

'As if it matters who plays what,' Sophie argues.

Ewan's unimpressed by their wrath. 'I don't train a team to lose, or to catch-up and chat,' he says. 'And don't be fooled into thinking people in this comp are ready to be put out to pasture.'

'We could do without the cow references, Ewan,' Elizabeth says.

'Martha's playing goal keeper,' he tells them, 'because if she was standing in front of me with a hand to my face while I was trying to score, I'd crumble.'

His face reddens under everyone's scrutiny. After a moment, Martha gets the same treatment from the others, but there's no blushing from her because she thinks it's all pretty funny.

*

They go for a drink at the Rowers, still berating him. Not as much as one of the patrons ordering at the bar, who recognises Ewan and decides to approach.

'You ruined that club, you arsehole,' the woman says, two small kids at her side.

'Greed ruined that club, fool,' Julia says. Martha would pay good money to take a Julia masterclass on how to use that word so calmly and with that much edge. Especially when the trio of Ewan-haters walk away with a bit less puff in their steam.

'And shame on you for using that language in front of your kids!' Alana shouts after the woman. She turns back to Ewan. 'It's been six months. How much fucking longer do you have to put up with this?'

Martha's seen enough coverage on the news to know that Ewan's been called worse.

'George reckons you should have challenged the board instead of walking away,' Sophie says.

'George is an accountant, Sophie,' Julia says. 'I'd like to see him go and challenge his board.'

Ewan clearly doesn't want to discuss it and they head to a table out back. He sits opposite Martha and she likes the eye contact they make once in a while.

'You're coming to work for me,' Alana says to him.

'Christ,' he mutters.

'My staff are taking a group of our best players on a four-day sports camp and I want you running it.'

'Larns –'

'I've got funding, Ewan.'

'She's asking because you're good, not because you're desperate,' his sister says.

It's obvious that Alana and Julia have rehearsed this.

'What else are you going to do? Sit at home and wallow when disadvantaged kids would appreciate your expertise?' Alana asks.

'You are the first to say that you can't stand the "disadvantaged kids" label,' he accuses her.

'I said I can't stand the western-suburbs-disadvantaged-kids label,' she says.

'But you use it every single time you want something for that school.'

'Do you know how I get results? By hand-picking my staff, and my number one criteria is passion. You've still got it.'

Elizabeth returns with a tray of drinks, handing them out. 'He doesn't want to be known as the has-been NRL coach saving the kids of the western suburbs.'

'Yeah, thanks Elizabeth,' he says, drily.

'They don't need saving,' Alana says. 'They need funding and opportunity.'

Martha can see Ewan is caving in.

'So when is it?' he asks.

'This weekend.'

Ewan's and Martha's eyes meet again.

'Well, there goes your effing Saturday night, Ewan,' she says. He laughs. And Martha realises that she looks forward to these training nights not only because of Ewan Healy, but because she misses talking to people about important things like education and foster care and big messy families and vegie patches and food, over unapologetic glasses of wine that don't lead to fatalities.

*

At home she calls out, hoping for a response but there's none. Bruno looks depressed, but not as bad as Suki. While Martha's trying to coax her to eat, the doorbell rings and she's desperately hoping it's Rosie, despite the fact that she has her own key.

'Who is it?'

'Jimmy.'

'Who?'

She realises it's the dropkick boyfriend. Martha would bet her life on the fact that he's a drug dealer.

'She's not here,' Martha tells him, opening the door but keeping the security screen door locked.

'Do you know when she'll be back?'

'She hasn't been home in two days.'

'Where is she?'

'I don't know where she is.'

Martha goes to close the door, but he stops her.

'What do you mean you don't know?' he asks. 'You live with them.'

'She lives upstairs. I live downstairs. Rosie's a big girl. She can look after herself.'

He slams a hand against the screen door. 'Are you kidding me?'

'Cut the aggression or I'm calling the police.'

He walks away at the first mention of the cops. Martha's sure he's the one who slashed her tyres.

She spends the day with the minister, taking meetings with friends and family of a nineteen-year-old killed in a car accident on the Pacific Highway. At lunchtime, she attempts another discussion with Matthew Solloway.

'Just give me the report, Martha, and it will be done and dusted.'

Martha inherited an ironclad work ethic from Otto and Lotte and has never walked away from a task. She stays late that night until she finishes writing the report, returning it to Solloway, who is still in his office.

'I'm taking long service leave,' she says.

At least that piece of information has him looking up from his work.

'When?'

'Now.'

He throws his pen onto the desk and studies her.

'Is this about Charlie P dying? I know you two were tight, so how about you take a week's stress leave?'

'I'm not taking stress leave. I'm taking the long service leave owed to me. That I've been asking for since October 2009. If I take stress leave, it'll go on my record and then I'll never get another position, because women my age don't get an adviser-to-the-minister job back if they take stress leave!'

'Calm down, Martha.'

'Don't tell me to calm down.'

'You're shouting and you sound shrill.'

She grabs a post-it note and writes, *LSL NOW*.

In silence.

The minister pays her a visit just as Martha is logging off.

'Matthew says you're having meltdowns all over the office.'

She counts to ten because she respects the team too much and doesn't want the story to go around that she told the minister where to go. There are much bigger battles to wage on this job and she doesn't want to take it out on the overworked.

'I'm owed twelve months,' she says.

He shakes his head, irritated. 'I'll give you six weeks' family leave, just because I'm feeling generous, but next time plan this in advance.'

He's not a bad person. Neither is Solloway. But if Martha doesn't see them both for a long time, she'll be happy.

She stands up. Doesn't do it often, but towering over the minister brings her great satisfaction.

'Can I give you a few "next times" of my own?' she asks. 'Next time a grieving family comes in with photos of their dead son lying by the side of the road after some coked-up arsehole crashes into him, don't send in the widow of a man who died in similar circumstances.'

She sees his grimace.

'Shit, Martha. Solloway wasn't thinking.'

'And nor were you. So you better work out a way to replace me temporarily.'

The messages go off in her bag all the way home but she ignores her phone. Ignores the look from the guy next to her who has to deal with a vibration against his leg. Her stomach is churning. Not from the confrontation at work but from the fear of silence in the attic space. Once she's home, Martha's desperate to get inside, needs to know that Rosie's brought that baby home safe.

'Rosie!'

But nothing.

'Fuck you, Rosie!'

She searches through Seb's paperwork for any trace of his mother-in-law's phone number in Sicily and finds nothing. On her way back upstairs to go through Rosie's things, she notices Suki's untouched food. Martha knows that this is it. Because seventeen years with a dog who's never said no to food means it's time. So she collects Suki's bed and one of her toys and drives her up to the vet hospital on Ramsay Street. The nurse recommends that Martha makes a decision sooner rather than later.

Bruno's at the door waiting when she returns home.

'Go away,' she says. Years ago he belonged to Seb and lapped up any attention Martha gave him, but Rosie was always Bruno's favourite and now Martha refuses to be the substitute.

She picks up her phone and reads the messages. Lots of worry from the team. Mostly because they don't know how to move forward on a brief without her. When the phone rings this time she notices it's Solloway.

'Five months' long service leave,' he says.

All of a sudden, the idea of finding something to do for half a year is frightening.

'I'll see you in October,' she says before hanging up.

Rosie's boyfriend is outside the house the next morning.

'Are they back?' he asks, his tone a bit more on the polite side.

'No.'

Martha keeps walking and he catches up with her.

'Then can you give me –'

'Listen,' she says, before he can say another word, 'the vet's putting down my dog and I don't want to be late.'

Martha says it very matter of fact. The vet's putting down the dog. I'm going shopping for some shoes. It's recycling pick-up on Tuesday.

She walks past her favourite house in the neighbourhood and reaches out and squeezes a stem of lavender, enjoying the scent of it on her fingers. Even at the worst of times, the street is a comfort to her. Brush box trees and decorative parapets and timber fences and striped bull-nose roofs and wide verandahs. Back in the early 1900s, when the suburb was created, they were aiming for harmony with the landscape. The Italians who arrived in the 60s weren't interested in harmony with landscape. Just family harmony, so they built accordingly, much to the chagrin of the local historical society. Seb may have arrived in a different decade to the others, but he was at war with the council over his plans to build an attic space. Martha learnt to swear in Italian because of them.

At the vet, she sits in a sterile little room with Suki. Holds her for a while, whispers into her ear that she was the greatest consolation in her life on too many occasions to count. The vet's lovely, reassuring Martha that Suki won't feel any pain. Out in the foyer the receptionist speaks in a hushed tone as she tells Martha that it'll cost her three hundred and fifty dollars. Martha takes out her Visa card and hands it over. She's doing a good job of not crying. She lets Otto Neumann take over. There's Otto emotion and there's Lotte emotion. All her life, Martha's chosen which of her parents' personalities to use. Today, it has to be Otto.

Except Rosie's idiot boyfriend is there. Standing at the lights on Ramsay Street waiting for her. She's about to let fly, but this time he gets in first.

'Mate, I'll walk you home,' he says. 'Thought you might want the company.'

Martha bursts into tears because her dog is dead and this skinny guy with no sense of boundaries is here to take her home. He puts an arm around her, lets her cry some more. And once back at Dalhousie Street he makes a pot of English breakfast and finds a KitKat in the pantry and gives her half.

'Do you think they mightn't come back, Martha?' he asks later, his voice low. 'Because I keep going through it in my head and I know she wouldn't leave Bruno. That time in the floods she almost refused to stay in the evac centre because they weren't letting him in, so it's freaking me out, mate. Honest. Because she wasn't coping last time I was here and I didn't make it easy for her and I should have.'

Since Rosie's return, Martha's tried to work out her movements of the past two years. It's come to her in crumbs of information. Now she knows that Rosie was up in Queensland during one of the 2009 floods.

'How long were you together?' she asks.

'Two weeks.'

'What's wrong with you kids? It never occurred to you to use a condom?'

'It was a strange time,' he says. There's a wistfulness in his voice. He feels something for Rosie. Martha can see it.

'She has a grandmother in Sicily. Eugenia. That's all I know of her. A first name. I don't know whether the baby has a passport. Rosie's phone and her clothes and all the baby stuff is upstairs.'

'What about her parents?' he asks. 'What happened to them?'

'Her mum died when she was fourteen. Cancer. And then Seb was killed when Rosie was just about to turn eighteen.'

There's a whole lot of information Martha's left out. Fifteen-year-old Rosie nicking off to live with Seb's mother-in-law in Sicily, refusing to return for more than a year because he got married to Martha. Rosie living with a boyfriend's family when she was sixteen because she couldn't stand the sight of Martha in her home. Rosie getting expelled from two schools. Rosie lying under her father's coffin-stand at the funeral home the night before they buried him. Jimmy, in the floods, must have met a mess of a Rosie. Martha had lived on and off with all that adolescent grief and fury for three years. She's lived without it for just as long, but Rosie's absence now is frightening.

'How did he die?' Jimmy asks.

'He stopped on the M4 to help a young guy change a tyre and some woman off her face on drugs swerved into the car and it crushed him.'

He reaches out and takes her hand and Martha wants to cry again because that's what he's turned her into. A sobbing mess. It's people's empathy that always gets her in the end. It's how she bonded with Seb outside the cancer ward.

'Do you know if Rosie's got any friends around?' he asks.

She shakes her head.

'Then why haven't you called the cops?' he asks, and she hears the frustration in his voice. 'Doesn't this all make her a missing person? With a baby.'

'Jimmy, I work with the cops. I know how they operate. If they go looking for Rosie and they figure she's not coping with that baby, they'll involve DOCS.'

He stands up abruptly. 'Can I look around up there?'

Martha lets him because maybe he'll see something she missed. But when the silence upstairs stretches out for too long, she can't help thinking that he's stealing something of Rosie's. It makes

Martha feel guilty to think of him as a thief, but she knows nothing about this guy, regardless of him sticking around today. She gives him a few minutes more and then goes to check out what's keeping him.

He's in Rosie's room staring at the photo of the kid on the mantelpiece. It's one of those studio shots and, despite having lived in the same house for more than a couple of weeks now, Martha gets her first good look at the baby.

'He's all Seb Gennaro,' she says, a catch in her throat. 'Except that twisted smile. Seb's was a grin. He always seemed as if he was having a joke on the world.'

Jimmy hasn't spoken yet and when she finally looks at him, she notices how pale he is.

'He was crying every time I saw him,' he says. 'I didn't get to see the smile . . . but it's all Gary Hailler.'

It takes a while to understand his mood. 'You didn't believe her, did you?'

Jimmy shakes his head.

'She doesn't lie. The exact opposite, really. She's very blunt.' Martha studies him. 'Was Gary Hailler a nice man?'

'No, not really. He was okay with me, but he was a shit husband and father, apparently. I don't think he dared try anything with me. He knew I could beat him up.'

'You don't look the beating-up type.'

He laughs, and she can't help looking back at the photo.

'You're wrong,' she says. 'His smile isn't all Gary Hailler. It's yours, Jimmy. You get to claim it.'

*

Sophie texts her that night with a *Let's catch-up, Martha*, and because she runs a household, holds down a part-time job, checks in on her sick father every day and helps out at Scarlett's school, Martha allows herself to be squeezed in to Sophie's schedule. It means Saturday morning at Scarlett's gymnastics class, viewed from the mezzanine level and being interrupted by every second person that knows Sophie. She's collected people ever since she could crawl.

'But I love you best, darling,' she says often enough. It'd break Martha's heart if she found out Sophie was saying that to anyone else. They chat about George and his long hours and his mother who's just flown over to Greece for six months. 'Thank God for the Peloponnesus,' Sophie says every April. And then after she's lulled Martha into the comfort of other people's messy lives, she cuts to the chase.

'What's really going on, Martha?'

Martha's furious with herself for walking into this trap. She concentrates on Scarlett, who's just done a cartwheel on the beam, and it reminds her of when she and Sophie went through their Nadia Comăneci obsession during the 1976 Olympics, begging their mums to let them be gymnasts. When Sophie asks again, Martha figures it's no use beating around the bush.

'Rosie came back with a baby. I quit work for five months. Suki's dead. Rosie's disappeared with her baby.'

Sophie looks taken aback.

'Don't worry about me,' Martha says. 'I'm going to Bunnings to buy a tool belt.' She stands up and gives Sophie a quick hug. 'Tell your mum I'll be at Greek Easter.'

That, at least, will placate Sophie for the time being.

'Greek Easter was a week ago, Martha.'

Martha sits back down, stunned. No quick getaway for her today.

'Is Voula angry?' she asks.

'Furious.'

'How furious?'

'My mother refused to freeze any leftovers for you except for the *pastitsio*, *keftethes*, *yemista*, *spanakopita* and *tsoureki*.'

Martha can't help laughing, and when Sophie goes off to order banana bread to share, she doesn't argue.

On her first day off in years, she goes to Bunnings and gets some grout for the tiles. Ends up buying at least two hundred dollars worth of other goods because that's the effect Bunnings has on her. She dumps it all in the laundry and makes herself a cup of tea. And then she hears the sound upstairs. A baby's laugh. The relief she feels is beyond words.

Bruno comes to greet her, his moping gone. And then he plants himself on the fourth step.

'Clever dog,' Martha mutters.

But he gets a treat for being that smart.

Chapter Six

Jimmy receives a text from an unknown number. It says, *They're home.* He knows it's from Martha, and in the housing on the site that he shares with three other guys he's trying not to react, but his hands are shaking and there's this part of him that wants to get on a plane and try to make things right. But he doesn't know how. He's brought a DVD with him. About an Italian kid who's in love with films. Jimmy watches it because Mia told him that there's a kid called Toto in it, so he figures it's a good way of learning how to say his son's name without making it sound like Dorothy's dog. By the end of the film, he's bawling. Jimmy shows a scene to Norm who drives the dump trucks with him. Asks if he's got the pronunciation of Toto right.

'Fucked if I know, mate.'

Norm follows it with advice Jimmy doesn't necessarily ask for. 'You owe her nothing.'

There's a suppressed rage in Norm's voice when he says the word 'her'.

'She probably did it on purpose to get money from you, so remember that you're just as much a victim of this as she is.'

Not really, Jimmy wants to tell him. But the question of what he owes her is forever on his mind, even when he doesn't return to Sydney on his week off. They fly down to Brisbane and Norm convinces him to stay and Jimmy's on a blinder, listening to advice from a man who's got six kids by four different women and refers to them as bitches and slags. In the middle of one of Norm's rants, Siobhan rings him, like she always does when she's pissed on a night out in London.

'What are you doing, Jimmy?' she asks. He can hear the slur in her voice. At school she was the crying drunk, sleeping around with the wrong guys. Nowadays, everything seems to be on her terms, including sex and relationships.

'Same as you, mate,' he says.

'Not the same as me, Jimmy. Go home.'

And because Norm starts up again, and Jimmy can't handle the mess of someone else's hate mixed with grog, he finds himself at the airport spending too much money on a last-minute ticket to Sydney.

In the early hours of the morning, he wakes to a fight upstairs. Mackee and Tara aren't the arguing type, so it surprises him. They're not much into public displays of affection, nor do they talk each other up, or live in their own world of relationship bliss. But Jimmy thinks they're solid most days. A couple of weeks back, he arrived late from hanging out at Frankie's and they were lying on the couch with their feet in each other's faces killing themselves laughing at something on TV. Jimmy sat with them and watched it and couldn't for the life of him follow the humour. Frankie calls their house the Petersham Embassy. If they're not entertaining friends from East Timor, they're accommodating a couple of teachers from Kiribati who are trying to raise awareness about what's going on in some of the low-lying islands battling climate change in the Pacific. It's strangely believable that Mackee can switch from politics to sport to music in seconds while talking about the importance of letting wine breathe between courses.

Later that morning, he watches from the front window just to make sure they're okay. Most days, Tara takes the train and Mackee the bus. Their usual practice is to stop at the front gate and exchange some sort of dialogue with their lips almost touching. Whatever takes place at the front gate seems sincere and Jimmy's curious to find out what it is. Today's no different but they seem tentative and he figures the tension is coming from Mackee. He's not the same as he was at school. Moodier. Easily frustrated. Back in 2005 his uncle Joe died in the London bombings and after six years Mackee still carries it. Joe was a teacher and Jimmy knows that Mackee's searching for the perfect teaching position because it has to mean something to him.

He showers and heads off to Rosie's, rehearsing what he's going to say. Jimmy doesn't have much encouragement to go by, because she hasn't responded to any of the texts he's sent. At the house on Dalhousie Street he rings the doorbell and waits. After a couple of minutes he hears the sound of footsteps coming towards the door. Rosie doesn't seem surprised, or impressed that he's there, but she lets him in wordlessly. He's relieved to see that she's not in her pyjamas. Doesn't realise until he's following her up the stairs, that he's angry.

'Where were you?' he asks. 'Because I was worried and you can't just nick off without telling people.'

'Yes, I can.'

She's lost the vulnerability of a couple of weeks ago. And the heat between them during the floods is packed away someplace, because it would be reckless to let it out. Jimmy has to play differently with this version of Rosie.

'Where were you?' he asks again.

'I went to Tresillian.'

'Who?'

'You gave me the number,' she says, irritated. 'You said, "These people might be able to help".'

Upstairs he notices that the sunroom is tidy. Cosy. She doesn't invite him to sit down. Instead she picks up a few of the toys lying around and throws them into a big bright Elmo tub. When she bends, he can see down her top and he feels like a perve because she's not wearing a bra and he can't look away.

'Is Toto okay?'

She rolls her eyes. Probably at Jimmy's pronunciation. 'He's fine.'

'Can I see him?'

'Why? So you can pull out a piece of his hair and check his DNA?'

'I know he's mine so let's not revisit that conversation.'

He follows her into the bedroom where Toto is standing up in a cot beside a leadlight window, clutching onto the rails and looking pleased with himself. He's different to the crying miserable baby of a few weeks ago, and the moment Toto sees Rosie he bucks like crazy and his eyes light up. She picks him up and murmurs something to him and then puts him on the floor.

'Keep an eye on him,' she says, disappearing into the ensuite.

Toto manages to get himself onto his feet and Jimmy realises that he's learnt to walk these past couple of weeks. It's a tiptoeing sort of walk and the kid's pleased with himself again, chuckling as he heads straight for Jimmy, who's used to people walking away. So he's hesitant when Toto gets too close. Holds out a hand to steady him, but he doesn't let their fingers connect and the kid falls, surprised for a moment, before he picks himself up. There's the flush of the toilet and Rosie's out again, and Jimmy spends the next hour watching her with Toto, trying to steer his eyes away from her tee-shirt every time she bends. He wants to ask her questions, but it's stilted between them and he doesn't know how to break the ice. He doesn't know how to go back to that place where they connected during the flood.

'Do you want to go for a walk?' he asks. She doesn't answer, but disappears into her room and comes back in a different tee-shirt.

They venture out just as Martha's walking into the house. There's a guy with her, about Martha's age. Fit-looking, in long shorts and joggers.

'Hey, Martha,' Jimmy says.

'Ewan, this is Rosie and Jimmy,' she says.

Jimmy holds up a hand in acknowledgement, but Rosie ignores them and keeps walking, pushing the pram past. She reaches the front door. 'Bruno!'

Bruno hurries after her, just in case Rosie's going to change her mind.

The Ewan guy looks taken aback.

'Wow, she's a charmer,' he says to Martha.

Outside Jimmy catches up with Rosie.

'You're on first-name terms with her, are you?' It's an accusation.

'Martha was worried about you and –'

'Don't involve yourself in stuff you know nothing about.'

'I know about being worried.'

Toto is shrieking out to anyone who passes them by and an elderly lady with tight curls and drawn-on eyebrows tries to engage with him, but Rosie doesn't stop for anyone.

'I think she wanted to see the baby. Do you know her?'

'None of your business.'

She struggles at the lights with the pram and he helps her steer it back in place as they cross the road.

'Can I do that?' he asked, indicating to the pram.

'No.'

At Algie Park she takes Toto out of his pram and puts him on the grass, which he seems to enjoy. Bruno's all over him and he loves that even more. Close by, a group of little girls are being trained in ball games and Toto is fascinated by the sound of their laughter. The kid is already a speedster, and he goes tottering past Jimmy and falls. It's Rosie who picks him up and Jimmy can feel the accusation in her eyes.

'Why are you here?' she asks, and he doesn't know how to respond, so the question goes unanswered.

*

He visits Frankie and her family later because being with them is effortless. Not that Mackee and Tara's place isn't welcoming, but the shouting he heard during the night has unnerved him. Frankie's interviewing her grandmother in the same way that she seems to be interviewing every Italian person over seventy that comes through the front door. She's talking PhDs and going down to Canberra to do some research at the National Museum, and they plan to go together on one of Jimmy's weeks off.

He does the taxidriver rounds with her. Dropping off both her nonnas and also Will's at the Leagues Club in Ashfield that puts on a seniors buffet every Tuesday night. Then they drive over to Darlinghurst and hang out at one of the cafés on Victoria Street until it's time for senior pick-up. They're interrupted frequently. Frankie's worked in a couple of the bars up and down this strip and seems to know everyone. She's one of those people that the rest of the world genuinely want to be around. It could be because she's beautiful, but Jimmy puts it down to her energy and warmth. Most of those who stop at their table ask about Will and she uses the standard line. 'He's thriving over there. Doesn't want to come back.' And then she laughs and asks them a plethora of questions. Jimmy's known her long enough to work out that Frankie's fascination for other people is also a way to fob off talking about herself. Since they left school she's got herself a history degree and a masters, formed a band with Mackee and Justine, worked in pubs, made wedding dresses with her grandmother. Hard work has camouflaged her lack of direction. And her anxiety. Jimmy was like that in high school, minus the hard work. Back then he was perceived as a weirdo. Other kids were put off by the attention he paid them, but at least it stopped them asking questions about his life.

'What do you and Will talk about every day?' he asks after some-one puts a macchiato in front of her before she's even asked for it.

'He'll have a short black,' she says to the waitress. 'Why do you ask?'

'Because I can't understand how people fill their day with talk without it becoming empty.'

'Are you having trouble talking to her?'

At least they don't have to beat around the bush. He nods.

'While Will's there, he wants to know about everyone here. People mostly. He keeps up with news and stuff online, but he misses family and our friends. He misses us.'

She gives him a look and there's laughter in her eyes. 'He'll never get over the Monaro.'

'Yeah, neither will I,' he says. And then, 'Is he thriving? Doesn't want to come back?'

She doesn't respond for a moment, but he gets that look.

'He is thriving. He's making a shitload of money. He's mak-ing amazing connections, so he doesn't necessarily want to come back now.'

'But?'

She's annoyed again. Like the last time they had a discussion about Will.

'Do you know the worst thing about being in a relationship this long?' she asks.

Jimmy shakes his head. Hasn't been in one long enough to know.

'It's that everyone wants to talk about your relationship. They want to dissect it. Speculate on whether it's run its course.'

'Why would they think that?'

'Because according to the experts, relationships that begin at the end of high school last about seven years. Most split up when they're about twenty-three, twenty-four.'

His coffee comes and she passes him the sugar.

'I don't like being a stat,' she says. 'So let's get back to the lack of discussion between you and the baby mama.'

Jimmy would rather be speaking about her than himself.

'She sort of shuts down conversation before it starts,' he says.

Nothing changes at Dalhousie Street for the rest of his time in Sydney. Sometimes Toto totters or crawls towards him and hands over a plastic block that's dripping with saliva. Every day they go for a walk down to Algie Park and Jimmy asks Rosie if he can push the pram and she barely acknowledges the request. It pisses him off. Jimmy doesn't want to spend the rest of his life on the back foot with Toto just because he was one year late.

'Is it a control thing?' he asks her, the day before he's due to fly out.

They're on Ramsay Street, and he doesn't want an argument outside the busiest bakery on the block but he can't hold back.

'I can push a pram, you know. It's pretty obvious you don't need a brain to do it,' he says.

Rosie puts the brake on the pram and hands Toto a rusk to slobber over. At first Jimmy thinks she's ignoring him, but then he gets the full impact of her stare.

'What are you, five?' she says. 'Ask me if you can hold him and I might say yes. Because he's not going to remember who pushed him in a pram!'

He doesn't respond and that seems to irritate her even more.

'All he wants is to be fed and held, and you can't even do that, and I don't get it because you were the most touchy-feely guy I ever came across. And I'm not. So he got that from you.'

Toto drops the rusk and Jimmy picks it up, but she snatches it from him and throws it in the bin. As if she doesn't even trust Jimmy to do that himself.

At her place, he watches her struggle up the steps holding Toto and once they're in the sunroom Jimmy figures there's no use staying because the silence between them is too toxic.

'I've got to go,' he says. 'See you in a week.'

He heads down the stairs to where Martha's sitting at the table, drinking tea and reading the paper. She glances up and he must look like shit because she points to her mug and, instead of walking out, he nods.

'That guy – is he your boyfriend?' he asks when he's sitting before her.

'Ewan.' Martha looks up from what she's reading to think about it. 'We're flirting.'

'He looks familiar.'

'Sacked NRL coach.'

'Who isn't these days? It's such a pathetic game.'

She laughs again. 'Isn't it just? You're obviously not a fan?'

'Naw. I like cars. It's the adrenaline.'

She gives him a look. 'Well, you've bred into the right family.'

The kettle sings and he gets up to make his own cup of tea. Can't help noticing the splashback. 'You know, I can do the grouting for you guys. It'll look amazing once you finish.'

'I'm now officially on leave so I'll get around to doing it myself.'

After a moment Martha puts down what she's reading.

'Where did Rosie go?' she asks, her voice low and as if she's been waiting a while to ask.

'Tresillian? Does that make sense?'

She nods. 'It's a clinic to help mums with babies. At least she knows how to ask for help.'

He tops up her mug and they sit for a while talking about how FIFO works. He used to think it was a good perk, but flying in and out only gets him as far as Brisbane.

'Are you thinking of moving back here?' she asks.

He shakes his head. 'The money's too good. I'd never get that sort of pay here.'

'You need to make this work, Jimmy,' she says.

He volunteers to go grocery shopping with Tara the next morning because Mackee trains his little cousin's soccer team on Saturdays. Jimmy hasn't spent much time with Tara without Frankie or Mackee around. Sort of knows her the least. At school she called him a dickhead a lot. Not out of affection either. She was a bit militant back then – perhaps as lonely as the rest of them.

Jimmy's surrounded by women who won't let him take control of the wheels, because at Coles Tara won't let him push the shopping cart. She has a system and is very particular about sticking to the grocery list she's holding.

'I don't do lists,' he says. 'I just grab what I need.'

'If I don't stick to a list I go over our budget.' Her tone is cold, abrupt.

'You're pissed off at me.'

'I'm pissed off at you,' she says.

'I'm sorry?'

'We were expecting you on Saturday. Now whenever you don't turn up, we think you'll disappear again.'

'Frankie's fine about –'

'Frankie's good cop at the moment. We take turns.'

'When is she bad cop?'

'When Tom's being a dick.'

'Was Tom being a dick the other night?'

The question surprises her. He doesn't know whether her reaction is because he overheard them, or just that he's bringing it up. But throughout the whole toiletry aisle, she doesn't speak.

'The other night was Tom having an anxiety attack,' she finally says, 'and then he doesn't cope and he gets even more agitated and goes for walks at two in the morning and that freaks me out because I think a group of drunks are going to king-hit him on Stanmore Road and, as much as my heart is telling me not to shout at him, my mouth is saying, "Where the hell have you been?"'

'Understandable.'

He glances at her, hoping he's not overstepping the mark. 'I miss the way Mackee was when we were at school.'

'I do too, but I'm sort of more in love with this version of him.'

And that's the thing with Tara Finke. She can deliver sincerity in such a practical way.

'Dating is the fun part,' she tells him. 'Living together is complicated. It means that when he doesn't speak for the whole morning, you're wondering if everything's okay. When you're dating, by the time he drives over in the morning, he's worked everything out.'

'You're good with him.'

He feels the intense study again. 'And that surprises you?'

He laughs. 'Yeah, actually it does. The same way it surprises me that Siobhan can dish out good advice when she used to be the worst at taking it.'

Tara focuses on handing over the groceries in the order of how she wants them packed.

'I jumped the dating part,' he finds himself saying. 'I just got her pregnant and you can't go backwards from that. The chance is gone, you know.'

'Would you have liked to have dated her?'

He hands over cash as she's taking out her Visa card to stop her from paying.

'I thought I had it all worked out,' he tells her. 'I've been saving for ages and I figured I had another year then I could come back here and apply to the paramedics. It's a three-year course and I wouldn't be making much on a base wage. But I'd have a profession, you know. For once in the history of my family. Both sides. They're not bad people. They're just so fucking useless, that's all.'

'Jimmy –'

'I don't know how to be a father,' he interrupts, and he can't understand why he's admitting it to Tara. 'So that means I'm just like the rest of the people I come from. I don't know how to be anything but a big disappointment in someone's life.'

He takes the shopping trolley and they start walking.

'She's given you a way in,' Tara says after a while. 'What's her name?'

'Rosie.'

'And she didn't have to. Take it. I don't think that kid is going to have a better life because he has a father, Jimmy. I think he's going to have a better life because he has you.'

Jimmy thinks Tara's just crossed into good-cop territory.

'Don't ask me to explain a compliment,' she says, briskly.

And her words take him back to Dalhousie Street. Martha lets him in and he says he's sorry for disturbing her again, and goes upstairs to where Rosie is bathing Toto. The bathroom light is crap and she looks even more beat. He doesn't know whether she's a good mum or not, but what he does know is that she loves the baby. Toto's at least happy to see Jimmy because he smiles in that twisted crazy Hailler way.

'I have held one of those,' Jimmy tells her. 'I was with Kev the day after the water went down. We got access to that area beyond the mill and we found him . . . that baby . . . and Kev had a meltdown . . . and I just picked him up, this little thing, and he was so cold and I can't forget how it felt and I don't want to touch yours . . . ours . . . because he deserves better than hands that held a dead baby.'

Jimmy sees Rosie's eyes water and he knows she hasn't forgotten anything about that town. She reaches out and grabs a towel that's sitting on the sink.

'My father believed in signs,' she says. 'Not that they change events or predict what's going to happen. It's more about what we do when we come across one.'

She removes Toto from the bath and wraps him in the towel.

'I was going to have an abortion, you know. And the night before I was booked to have one, I had a dream. Not of my mother or my father or of anyone telling me anything profound.' Her eyes meet his and she's trying not to cry. 'I dreamt of the flood and of the town and I dreamt that someone found that baby alive. I don't know who it was, except that Min was holding him.'

She looks at Toto, who loves the attention. Post-clinic Toto seems to love everything.

'Honestly, I know what everyone thinks. That I'm like any other dropkick who has a baby because at least then there'll be someone out there who loves them. But the dream was a sign. I felt it here,' she says, pointing to her heart. 'So you're wrong if you think your hands only held death.'

And she holds Toto out to him and Jimmy takes his son.

Chapter Seven

Rosie has nowhere she needs to be. Five minutes into a job interview at the nursing home she walks out. It makes her regret the money she spent keeping Toto in the council-run occasional day care for two hours, although she's relieved to have found a place that only charges ten dollars an hour. Her plan is to find a job that can offer her a couple of shifts a week and then she'll add on from there. But five minutes into the interview she picks up her bag, and says, 'I'm out of here.'

She's walking out of the grounds when she spots the guy Martha's been hanging out with on the front verandah of the house for the past couple of weeks. Rosie can hear everything from her window. It's nauseating to listen to, but she knows everything about him. The latest is that his father has had a fall and it's become obvious to everyone that he can't stay home. It's turned Irwin, or whatever his name is, into even more of a misery guts. She'll never understand why people whinge about their parents getting old and all the things that come with it. Rosie would give anything to push her mother and father around in a chair. She wouldn't care if they were dribbling and didn't know who she was, or if they pissed their pants every morning and every night. The woman in the interview asked her why she was interested in working with old people. Someone as young as her. She didn't say her real reason. Because no one in her family except for Nonna Eugenia got to grow old.

Today, he's pushing a guy in a wheelchair who is obviously his father, and they're coming towards her and she's about to look down and ignore them, but then she doesn't. Because of the way he brushes the old man's cheek with the back of his hand with an affection that makes Rosie's eyes water.

'Can I give you some advice?' she says.

It takes him a moment to recognise her.

'Rosie, is it?' he asks.

She nods and goes to speak, but he stops her. 'Look, I don't want to get involved in whatever this is between you and Martha, because you need to sort it –'

She holds up a hand to shut him up.

'I don't like it here,' she tells him. 'Regardless of whether your father remembers you, it doesn't mean he's given up on feeling any-thing. If he stays at this place, he'll die sooner. I've seen it happen. There are better homes.'

He looks taken aback. 'Like where?'

Rosie likes the fact that he's asked and she names a few, but then gets pissed off.

'Just do your research and don't be so fricken lazy.'

His phone rings and he answers it. Rosie moves his father's chair before heading off, because the sun is directly in the old guy's eyes.

She gets a haircut next, seeing as she's paid for two hours of day care. Stares at herself in the mirror and contemplates her instructions for the girl at JustCuts. Rosie doesn't have one of those elfin faces that look fantastic with cropped hair because she took after her father and everything about her face is too pronounced, but she's got good skin courtesy of her mum. So she goes for a buzz cut.

Later, when she picks up Toto, his hands go straight to it, chuckling, and the day-care girls laugh at the sound. They love Toto, and that's going to be Rosie's yardstick in life. She'll love anyone who loves her son.

On the way home, her phone beeps a message and her heart leaps for an instant and it's how she knows. It's a Pavlov's dog thing. The only person who texts her is SES Jesus so the instant euphoria at the sound of the buzz spells trouble. He's texted her once or twice during the week. Wants to know how Toto's doing, so she sends a photo. Wants to know how she's doing. *You okay?* Rosie's trying to have a guy-free year just to prove to herself that she can. She's surprised that she misses talking most of all because she didn't date many guys who were chatty. But he was. Not as much anymore. She decides not to respond to texts asking how she is, because then Rosie'll end up sleeping with this guy and him being Toto's father is tricky. She can't go around screwing up that situation. He needs to be Toto's father above everything else.

When he flew in last week it was a bit less awkward than the last time. He couldn't keep his eyes off Toto. Laughed when he saw him totter around on tiptoes. Rosie tells herself that she loves his laugh because it reminds her of Toto, but then she remembers the Pavlov's dog thing and realises it's because she's got a thing for this guy.

'It'll be sort of sad when he works out that the rest of the world can walk by the time they're one,' she had said.

'Naw, let him go on thinking he's special.'

And Rosie could tell that no one had ever told Jimmy he was special.

She tries to stay upbeat despite unsuccessful interviews. Because there are moments with Toto that make Rosie feel euphoric. The unconditional love from him, and the way his face lights up when he sees her. But there's always something to crush the joy. At a café in Rozelle where she's getting a latte, Rosie notices two of the women from the mothers' group. Yolanda the megamouth and the Chinese girl who never said a word. Rosie's not interested in being seen, so she turns the pram, accidentally blocks the entrance and gets the huffing and puffing sound annoying people make when they don't have the guts to say, 'Get out of the bloody way'. Rosie refuses to move, which sort of causes a scene. It means Yolanda and the other one spot her. Suddenly the two are on their feet, shoving their prams between patrons to reach her.

'For your information, what you did was rude,' Yolanda says.

Rosie has no idea what she's done to them but she's trying to get out of pramageddon to avoid scaring the babies. And then someone comes up behind them and gets all hot and bothered because now three prams are in the way.

'Oh, shut up!' the Chinese girl says.

*

They sit in the park with their takeaway coffees because the owner of the café bans them from coming back in.

The other one's name is Tess and what the three of them have in common, apart from babies and prams, is that they were all shunned by the mothers' group.

'Secret Service Caterina stopped posting on the Facebook page, so I figured we were all meeting at the community centre,' Yolanda says. 'But Tess was the only one there.'

'Let's not talk about them again.' Tess gives her daughter very sensible snacks out of colour-coded containers. Toto's hoeing into a not-so-sensible chocolate-chip muffin. 'They weren't the type of people I'd ever want to hang out with anyway so I'm angry at myself for caring.'

'Yeah, just because we pushed babies out of our vag doesn't mean we have anything in common,' Yolanda says, going after her daughter, who's a future sprinter for sure. Both baby girls have been walking for months and Toto tries to follow them every time but falls on his face. Rosie notices that they say words as well while Toto is all sounds and gibberish. She worries he's going to be the last baby to do everything. Knows it's her fault for doing it all wrong. She wrests the muffin from between his fingers because he's heading for the sandpit.

'That pram's going to kill you,' Yolanda tells her as they move their stuff over to the pit. 'There's an inner west mums' page on Facebook where you can get a better one for a good price.'

'Rosie's not on Facebook,' Tess says. She seems to have picked up a lot of information during mothers' group despite her silence. She's from Wagga and worked in HR for the council there, but her husband was offered a town planner job for Leichhardt Council and they decided to move.

'Are there many Chinese people in Wagga?' Rosie asks, politely.

'I have no idea,' Tess says. 'My family's Vietnamese.'

Rosie avoids Yolanda's stare. She can imagine how loaded it is with disapproval. Yolanda's also from the country and Rosie makes a point to remember how to say Kamilaroi, because Yolanda speaks about being part of that nation. She talks about being homesick for family and how lonely it is in the city and Tess agrees. Rosie wants to tell them that she's from the city, but just as homesick for family. And lonely.

'Where's your mob from?' Yolanda asks.

'I have a grandmother in Italy,' Rosie says. There's no response after that, as if it's her fault for not having enough family to fill the silence.

The wind has picked up and both Tess and Yolanda remove baby puffer jackets out of the bottomless pits of their bags.

'Your bub needs to be in layers now that it's getting cold,' Yolanda says.

Toto's sucking on his muffin-mixed-with-sand-covered fingers.

'At least he's not crying anymore,' Tess says, handing Rosie a wipe.

'I took him to Tresillian.'

'What was the problem?'

'Back molars,' Rosie says. 'So I guess it's an I-told-you-so, Yolanda.'

Yolanda is instantly pissed off. 'You don't know anything about me, so don't presume I'm going to say that.'

'I know enough.'

'No, you don't!'

'Bet you're a teacher.'

Yolanda stares at Rosie. She's only a couple of years older, but has a look in her eye that belongs to someone who's fifty.

'You do sound like one, Yolanda,' Tess says. 'And in saying that, I loved all of mine.'

Yolanda teaches PE, which is why she wanted to slap cardio mum across the face every time she gave out dangerous training advice. She's also the oldest of twenty-three cousins so she's used to dishing out the threats and advice.

'Are you on your own?' she asks Rosie.

'No. Sort of.'

Yolanda takes out her phone. 'Give me your number.'

Rosie gives it to her and a moment later, the phone rings in her bag.

'Just in case.'

She starts cooking again. Tonight, Martha's out at her middle-aged netballers' training night, so it feels good to have the kitchen to herself and Rosie makes some of the dishes her mum taught her. *Caponata, sugo, parmigiana.* She figures if she freezes it all, they can live on it for the next month or so. Jimmy's back in Sydney and he fixes the highchair Rosie found outside someone's house for council pick-up. When he's done with the chair, he gives it a good clean and fits Toto into it. In the past couple of weeks, he's fixed the cot railing that never worked because Rosie bought it second-hand on Gumtree, as well as the mini mover with a wonky wheel. He's functional and Rosie hasn't come across a functional guy since her father.

When Jimmy doesn't have furniture to fix he stands around in that fidgety way, as if he doesn't know how to take it easy around her. Rosie puts a plate of *caponata* close to where he's standing at the breakfast bar. He points to himself and she just ignores him, goes back to soaking the breadcrumbs for the meatballs. He sits down and starts eating, reaches out for the bread so he can wipe the plate clean like some sort of peasant. He knows the food and she figures it's the Italian best-friend connection.

'Can we talk about money . . . without it being awkward?' he says, picking up Toto's water bottle for the fourth time. Toto thinks it's a game and Jimmy lets him play.

'I'm on a pension,' she tells him and he shakes his head.

'No. No pension.'

She puts down the mince that she's rolling and washes her hands because she needs to be focused. 'It's not really your decision,' she tells him.

'I can give you money every week,' he says. 'You don't have to be on a pension.'

'Let's keep it uncomplicated.'

His stare is unrelenting. She can tell he's trying to rein something in.

'I come from four generations of handouts,' he finally says. 'I don't want him being part of that cycle.'

'And I come from hard workers so he'll be taken care of. Don't worry.'

'You're making this about you.'

'And you're not?'

The mood is broken only by the water bottle on the ground again. Rosie picks it up before Jimmy does and puts it in the sink. Toto's unimpressed and starts howling.

'I don't want to sit around every week waiting for you to give me money,' she says. 'It'll mean I owe you something.'

He stands up abruptly and she thinks he's going to leave.

'If you're suggesting what I think you are, I don't work that way. You owe me nothing.' He unbuckles Toto from the highchair and puts him into the mini mover and Rosie can't believe he's giving in to Toto so easily.

'I don't like borrowing money,' she says. 'I don't like owing money. The moment I start working, I won't need the pension.'

'No one's judging you, Rosie.'

'What would you know?' she says. 'I grew up in this area. Everyone's judging me.'

'If it's Martha –'

'Don't bring up Martha as if she's your best mate!'

Toto's ramming the mini mover into every piece of furniture he can find and laughing with the delight that comes with noise and destruction.

'He's going to be a revhead,' Jimmy says, and he laughs and there's that part of Toto again. The part that makes Rosie a little sad because it means her son doesn't completely belong to her anymore. Jimmy looks up and she sees a flash of something in his eyes and it makes her wonder if his heart leaps when she texts him.

When he says goodbye to Toto he presses a kiss to his brow. It's the first time Rosie's seen intimacy between the two.

'I like your hair, by the way,' he says at the door.

She shrugs. 'It's easier this way.'

But she's lying because the haircut makes her feel cool in a way that she hasn't felt for a long time.

She's run out of containers to store the last of the pasta, so she puts it on a plate and covers it with foil. Martha comes home and Rosie can hear murmuring at the front door. Coach Whinger must be out there with her. He's nothing like her dad, who never complained a day in his life. Rosie stays in the kitchen and waits, because she needs to get the business side of things sorted out. Finding out that money was owing on the house was a game changer. (P.78)

'How much are the mortgage payments?' she asks, when Martha finally walks into the kitchen.

Martha makes a sound of disbelief and shakes her head, before putting her head in the fridge.

'Where's my couscous salad?'

'I chucked it. It was stinking out the fridge.'

Rosie shoves the foiled plate towards her because Martha can't cook to save her life, and Rosie doesn't want to see food go to waste.

'Once I'm working, I'm paying my share,' she says, before heading upstairs.

Despite buzz cuts and cooking, the pit of loneliness becomes bigger. She thinks of Jimmy living with friends, or soaking his bread around a noisy kitchen table. She watches people in their workplaces, laughing as they make lattes and dish out panini. Everyone seems to know each other except for Rosie. She thinks it'll change soon, but can't see the signs. She goes for another interview and knows it's the sort of place she could like. So when they ring to tell her that they were impressed but gave the job to a uni student who was studying occupational therapy, she stops believing that she'll get out of this rut. Stops telling herself that she's luckier than most because she's got this house. Sees herself as one of those girls who'll always be dependent on someone.

At the UTS student centre, she highlights the questions on the application form that she needs to go back to. Lachlan is there to help with a few of them, but most of the others mean she has to search for her school records and official documentation and that's easier said than done. He asks if she wants to have a coffee and they head over to the Marketplace food court. She organises some fruit for Toto and lets Lachlan buy the coffee and sushi.

'I think it's impressive what you're doing,' he says, glancing down at Toto.

Rosie's never been described as impressive. Maybe beautiful and pretty, but however he's dressed it Rosie's been paid a compliment and she likes it. Being turned on by one can't be a bad thing. Better than being turned on by an insult.

'Can I have your number?' he asks.

'No,' she says. 'It's nothing personal but I don't want to be tiptoeing into the student centre just because you didn't ring me. As if I did something wrong.'

'Okay,' he says, and then he laughs as if he's processing it. 'How about if you say your number out loud and it won't feel as if you've given it to me?'

'Same thing,' she says. 'And you won't remember it anyway, and then you'll use that as an excuse.'

'I have a 98.9 per cent success rate when it comes to keeping promises and honouring conditions,' Lachlan says. 'The 1.1 per cent failure mostly revolves around returning library books.'

She can't help smiling.

'And I've got a great memory for numbers, so try me.'

*

The next morning, Rosie pushes the pram out onto the street and sees Teresa watering the plants. She's a hairdresser who now runs her business at home so she and her fifteen-year-old daughter, Bianca, always look like they've literally stepped out of a salon. Rosie is about to ignore the greeting that she knows is coming, but the words come out of her mouth before she can stop them.

'I don't want to sit in your kitchen because it'll make me too sad.'

Because it will haunt Rosie with the smell of coffee and the memory of dialect and emphatic gestures. Teresa and Rosie's mum weren't just neighbours. They had been best friends from the moment Rosie's parents moved into the dump next door. As a kid, Rosie remembered often walking to Ramsay Street with them, both women perved on by men driving by.

Teresa folds the hose to stop the water.

'Can I at least hold him, *bella*?'

While Teresa has a cuddle, Rosie's phone beeps and she fumbles for it. She reads the message and it gives her hope because today she has a place she needs to be.

> *Do you guys want to get kicked out of another café?*

Chapter Eight

'We do the garden last, Marta.'

At the house on Dalhousie Street there's the lawn and then there's the beyond.

The beyond is what lies at the bottom of the backyard. It's a vegetable patch gone feral, now sprouting capsicums off the side of the house, tangled with every shrub, creeper and weed known to existence, roots entwined deep and tight, a mockery of humans' belief that they have some sort of dominance over nature.

Martha rejects every quote, stunned by the costs involved in taming it. Deep down she knows it's not about the money. Ever since her argument with Rosie about the property, she's imagined Seb's voice. Remembered those nights when they'd lie in bed talking about the house. Always the house. 'It never gets sold, Marta. We finish the garden and that night we sit in the banana chairs and we wait for the solar lights to come on and we say, *basta*. Next time we move is when they put us in the ground.'

Basta. Enough.

The taming of the beyond will be the completion of Seb Gennaro's dream.

He had never told Martha much about his life before coming to this country, but she knew it was a less romanticised version than that of the older Italians in the area who had migrated in the fifties. Seb would say with great bitterness that there was no future tense in the Sicilian language, and little wonder. Back in the eighties, he would have done anything to take Loredana away from the housing projects and the crime they had grown up with in a place called San Filippo Neri, on the outskirts of Palermo. Deep down, Martha figures he did the 'anything', although she never discovered what that was. Seb was a version of Martha's own father, who never looked back. One changed the spelling of his name; the other bought into the dream of owning something in his life despite it being a hovel. When he first showed Martha photos of what the property looked like when he had bought it, they were still strangers outside the cancer ward of the RPA. She couldn't quite believe that houses like that had still existed in Sydney back in the nineties. No inside toilet and one liveable room, he told her, but still better than any place he or Loredana had lived in their entire lives.

And now, she's breaking a promise to him. Martha's made a couple of calls to local real estate agents to get an idea of where they stand. Today's agent is all bright-eyed excitement. Until she looks out at the beyond.

'You're going to have to do something about that before

you put it on the market,' she says. 'Do you want to go inside and talk?'

'I don't have time,' Martha says. 'I've got to be somewhere.'

It's Saturday and Martha and the women have their first netball game. It's a loss, but not dismal and they're pretty impressed with themselves. Ewan isn't.

'You lost,' he says, his tone blunt. 'Do you think a footy player would be cheering about that score?'

'Fuck off, Ewan,' Elizabeth says. 'Can't we just celebrate not getting carried away on stretchers?' She's brought along her twenty-one-year-old doppelganger daughter – one expression fits all. Louise King spends the entire game sitting on the sideline with a hoodie over her head.

'Can I put an end to your celebration of averageness,' Ewan says, 'and ask that you take this seriously?'

He walks away and there's plenty of muttering.

'He's struggling,' Julia tells them.

The team do that thing where they say goodbye next to Julia and Alana's car but spend the next forty minutes talking. Martha finds herself telling the others about the house and its beyond and Rosie and the baby and Jimmy Hailler, who looks like he should be in jail, but who took care of her after she had the dog put down.

'And she forgot Greek Easter,' Sophie says.

'How the hell could you avoid seeing ten thousand Greeks bearing crucifixes in a procession?'

'That's an exaggeration, Elizabeth.'

'Excuse me, St Spyridon. The cops closed down Gardeners Road, Sophie.'

'If you say this Jimmy guy's a local, I'll ask around,' Alana volunteers.

'You won't know him.'

'Trust me. She's a Charbel. Alana'll find a degree of separation,' Julia says, getting into the car.

'Drinks Wednesday night?' Elizabeth suggests, and there's another twenty-minute discussion at the car window about where they should go.

Later, while Martha's looking out at the beyond, wearing her brand-new gardening gloves, Ewan texts to say that he's at the front, and she heads out to see him.

'Are you over your tantrum?' she asks.

'Am I the only person who takes the team seriously?' he wants to know.

'I take it seriously,' she says. 'Just not the competition.'

'You want to go for a drive?' he asks.

'Where's your father?'

'A mate's taken him down to the club to watch the game.'

'You don't want to watch the game?'

'Not this one,' he says.

On Cronulla Beach they watch the diehard surfers sit in wait for the perfect wave. More silence. Up until now the list of Ewan Healy traits had been positive apart from a touch of grumpiness and the fact that he can't remember the song they danced to. But now she has to head the negative list with the word 'moody'. Martha's history with moody people began with Julia Healy in high school. An irritating self-indulgent trait that always had her walking on eggshells until she got to an age where eggshell-walking didn't appeal to her.

'My father used to take me here for training,' he finally says. 'One minute we'd be doing wind sprints up those sand dunes and next he'd tell me to get into the water, no matter how cold, and I'd hit the waves crying, praying that he didn't notice.'

'Did he?'

'Who knows? He'd never say anything. Later, we'd sit on the rocks and discuss John Healy's version of the meaning of life.'

'I'm going to say no thanks to that baptism of male nonsense,' she says. 'If you want my version of the meaning of life, let's do it over a Reschs.'

He laughs. She glances at him, takes in the solidness of his shoulders and the power in his hands. She wants to hold them because they seem to promise something that sort of thrills her. It's what she remembers from their time in the back seat of his Hilux after Charlie's funeral. But there's a part of him that's been diminished by the sacking and she doesn't know if she can take that on board. Because she can feel herself slipping towards something dark within herself that she hasn't felt before. Mocking her for thinking that she could survive the death of her mother and Seb and even Charlie, who had made her work day bearable, without hurting an inch of her soul.

'Is your team playing tonight?' she asks. 'Is that why you're not with your dad?'

'They're not my team,' he says.

She figures he's not ready to talk about it. Perhaps he can't. Last she heard it was tied up in legals. She shivers from a touch of ice in the wind and he shuffles closer and places an arm around her.

'Nothing worse than a public sacking,' he finally says.

'Jules and Alana blame the club.'

'I have to take some of the blame, but it still pisses me off. Five losses in a row and then everyone forgets that you almost got them to the minor premiership twice in four years and next minute you're hearing about the club deciding your future on the morning news.'

'Do you know what Lotte Newman would have said? *Durch Schaden wird man klug*. A bad experience brings wisdom.'

'I don't feel wise at all. Just pissed off most of the time.'

'So what next?'

He sighs. 'Options.'

'How can options be a bad thing, Ewan?'

'Because the best offers come from the UK,' he says. 'The next best are for being part of the coaching team for the Warriors, or a developmental role with the Cowboys.'

He looks at her. 'That's how options can be a bad thing.'

Martha meets a guy she could remotely be interested in dating, and he's either off to England, New Zealand or Townsville.

'What would Lotte Newman say to that?' he asks. 'Because listening to you speak German is strangely exciting me.'

'Really? I actually know all the words to "99 *Luftballons*" if you want me to sing.'

'Even more of a turn on.'

She laughs, but then thinks of Lotte and it makes her sad. '*Ach du lieber Gott*. My mother was an *Oh my God* sort of person.'

'You miss her?'

How can Martha even try to answer that? She's reminded of Lotte every single day. When she goes into the IGA at Haberfield, they play Lotte's radio station and either Petula Clark is belting out 'Downtown' or The Seekers are singing 'I'll never find another you'. Next door she'll see the affection between Teresa and Bianca, and she'll remember walking to school with Lotte, arm in arm. It was the way they'd stroll together for the rest of her mother's life. Lotte was a joy, although damaged by her childhood in the war, with its constant evacuations and bombs and death. She'd hoard groceries in the cupboard just in case, was frightened by authority and had nightmares all her life. Lotte wasn't overly religious, but when she was dying she promised Martha that she'd be her *Schutzengel*. Her guardian angel.

'Okay, I've changed my mind,' she says to Ewan, standing up, stripping down to her undies and singlet and racing for the ocean before she can talk herself out of it. Has regrets the moment she hits the water. Sobs from the shock of icy waves hitting her in the face, and the only way she can stop her teeth chattering from the pain of it all is by screaming, and she doesn't want to stop because the ocean is swallowing up the sound and it gives her a freedom beyond words to do something she hasn't been able to do inside her house or out on the streets or anywhere else in the world.

Ewan at least follows her out into the surf and she feels his arms clasped around her. Much like his father, if he notices her crying he doesn't say. But afterwards he gets her dry and they lie huddled on the sand together in their clothes minus underwear.

'You know we're entering that age bracket where pneumonia can kill us,' he says.

'I never listen to stats about people our age,' she says. 'And you didn't have to follow me in.'

'I figured there was zero chance of me making progress with you if I stayed put.'

She looks at him. 'Progress was made, my friend.' And they lie there glued to each other because the wind's now cruel, but his arm around her feels good.

'What are you thinking?' she asks.

'Frankie Goes to Hollywood's "The Power of Love" or Foreigner's "I Want to Know What Love Is"?' he answers.

'Wrong decade, so not even close.'

Outside the house she doesn't see the point in putting him through any more grief. She doesn't care who's upstairs in her home. Her home. Her room that she shared with Seb. His room that he shared with Loredana in some shape or form before the renovation. If Martha could make love to a man with a photo of his dead wife in his wallet, she can make love to another man with a photo of her dead husband on the mantelpiece. She takes his hand and they're about to head inside when a taxi pulls up in front of Teresa and Marco's place. The driver removes a suitcase from the boot and a woman gets out, in her sixties, but with a walk that most women seem to leave behind in their forties, and it's not until she's dragging the bag towards them that it hits Martha. She feels Ewan flinch, not realising until then that her fingers are digging into his arm.

'Martha?' he asks.

And then she's here on Martha's verandah and under the harsh light she looks older. Grey coarse long hair and kohl-rimmed dark eyes. She begins talking at Martha and it's rapid and blunt. Martha doesn't understand a word, but she gets the nucleus of the conversation. With shaking hands she unlocks the door, steps aside and lets her in.

'*Rosanna!*'

It's a raspy voice. Scraped out of a throat that's smoked thousands of cigarettes in her lifetime. Martha hears the quick footsteps down the stairs, sees Rosie there with the baby in her arms. Stunned at first and then bawling. Rosie's a silent crier, always has been, and she's perfected the art of expressing gut-wrenching emotion without uttering a sound. And shit, she looks young. Martha watches as rough hands grab Rosie's face, kissing her, grabbing the baby, who is staring wide-eyed at all the drama unfolding around him and then he's laughing with glee because, whichever side he takes after, this kid will be attracted to bedlam. Rapid Sicilian bounces off the walls, and Rosie's grabbing the suitcase, dragging it down the corridor, scratching the hell out of Martha's floorboards, *thump, thump, thump*ing all the way up the stairs while the woman wails out a song to the baby, who bucks to the beat of its mayhem.

'What just happened?' Ewan asks.

Martha can't respond for a moment. The woman's emotion at the front door was potent and all she could understand were two names: *Rosanna* and *Loredana*.

'Eugenia.'

'Who?'

'Seb's mother-in-law.'

'Staying in your house? Why?'

Because Martha may be living on less than two hundred square metres, but Seb's mother-in-law is going to make sure that Rosie gets her share.

'I'm sorry, but I don't think you staying is a good idea,' she says.

Ewan is still holding her hand and he gently pulls her closer. 'How can sleeping with me under the same roof as your husband's mother-in-law not be a good idea?' he asks.

She laughs because she's about a microsecond away from crying.

'Come home with me,' he says. 'You don't need this shit.'

She shakes her head.

'But thanks for asking.'

The next morning Seb's mother-in-law is in the kitchen, looking surprised to see Martha up so early as if it's her home already and Martha's the intruder. There's another serving to be had from Eugenia, this time in a hissed, hushed voice.

'I don't understand,' Martha says, although she understands enough. They want her house.

Seb's mother-in-law is pointing upstairs, talking talking talking at Martha until furious tears well up in the older woman's hard wild eyes.

'It's my house as well, Eugenia.'

Eugenia doesn't give a shit who else owns the house, she just keeps on talking until Martha has had enough and walks back into her bedroom, locking the door.

Later, when she hears the front door slam and footsteps and banging against furniture, she ventures out again and sees Rosie and her baby in the kitchen. Martha can't hold back any longer, even though there's a smidgeon of guilt that it's the happiest she has ever seen Rosie.

'I'm not going to be bullied out of this house by your grandmother.'

Rosie stares up at her, annoyed. Dismissive.

'You're a paranoid psycho, Martha. My nonna's come to see Toto and me. It's not always about you!'

That night, Seb's mother-in-law decides that upstairs is too confined for her and takes up residence in the kitchen. Not cooking, because Rosie tends to do that, but it's where the older woman claps loud out-of-tune Sicilian songs to the baby, who crashes his Little Tikes SUV from one piece of furniture to another in time with the music.

When Rosie leaves the next morning, Eugenia goes for another round with Martha, demanding something from her that Martha hasn't quite worked out. To get out of the house? To sell? God forbid, to let them stay indefinitely? And as the days pass, Eugenia and her presence spreads from the kitchen to the living area where Toto, a Damien from *The Omen* child, has found more corners to crash into. Martha's place of solace becomes the exact opposite while Eugenia's power spills out onto Dalhousie Street. If she's not talking to Marco and Teresa over the fence as though they're long-lost friends, she's taking Signora De Lorenzo from the house on the corner for a walk around the neighbourhood with Bruno the dog and Rosie sulking behind her with the pram. There's bad blood between Rosie and Signora, but now that Eugenia's here the procession passing Martha's house looks like a Michelangelo Antonioni film, headed by a dog. Martha's now familiar with his work after moving away from Romanian films to Italian existential cinema.

'Martha,' Teresa calls out. 'Come over for a coffee tomorrow.'

'I've got a lot on my plate, Teresa,' Martha says, her tone brisk. Her neighbour looks a bit taken aback. Martha doesn't care because it should be Teresa who feels guilty. Martha was her friend first, not Eugenia.

Four nights into Eugenia's reign on Dalhousie Street, Martha needs space and finds herself driving to Ewan's townhouse in Drummoyne.

'You okay?' he asks when he opens the door to her, and Martha wonders when kindness became an aphrodisiac. If it's an age thing, she'll embrace it with open arms. She's comforted to know that she does have a place to go, because tonight she doesn't want to be sleeping in her house. She's about to let him know he's going to get lucky, when she sees the wheelchair out on the back verandah.

'Your dad's here,' she says.

He nods. 'We packed up his things and I'm moving him over to the nursing home tomorrow.'

'How's Julia taking it?' she asks.

'The kids are upset.' He nods, and she can see he's trying to contain himself. His eyes well up. 'John played a big part in them coming to live with Jules and Alana and we don't think they understand most of this.'

'They've come out of the system. They probably understand more than you think.'

He steps back, inviting her in.

She shakes her head. 'You need to be with your dad.'

*

Sophie's husband George is kind enough to sleep in the spare room, and lying beside her reminds Martha of being thirteen when they'd have sleepovers and talk about the evil Julia Healy and Elizabeth King.

'Why did we hate them so much in first form?' Sophie asks.

'Because they were racist bitches back then. Remember, Elizabeth called you Sophie Souvlaki and me SS Martha.'

'True.'

'Do you think Elizabeth's punishment is the weirdo daughter?' Martha asks.

'I think bad karma's visited her more than once.'

Back in the nineties, Elizabeth King was the girl most likely to run the country, and married a banker from the UK who worked in futures. Martha was long out of their lives by then, but Sophie had been invited to one of the couple's extravaganzas and, even though Sophie was a party girl back then, she opted out of going to any others. 'Another world,' she had told Martha. 'A bad one.' In 2000, Elizabeth's husband seemed to drop off the radar and Sophie and Martha had speculated about what happened to him over the years. No one seemed to know. Whatever the truth, it forced Elizabeth back into her parents' home in Croydon with two young kids, working as a buyer for DJs.

'I think Elizabeth wants Louise to join the team,' Sophie says.

'That'll bring a burst of joy to our lives.'

Sophie takes the remote from her. '*Gilmore Girls* or *Breaking Bad?*'

'They're our options? No one in between Lorelai and Walter?'

Scarlett gets into bed with them and they watch a collection of one-minute films she's made using an app on her mum's phone. Martha's favourite belongs to the horror genre, starring the family cavalier, and it makes her laugh until she has tears in her eyes. Another reason she loves Sophie. Despite waiting forever, Sophie and George managed to produce one of Martha's favourite people of all time.

'If anyone ever calls this one Scarlett Souvlaki, I'll smash them in the face,' she tells Sophie.

'That's such a lovely thing to say, Martha.'

She gets home the next day at midday and within minutes Teresa is out front.

'Can we talk, Martha?'

Martha bristles. 'I don't know what Eugenia's been telling you, Teresa, but it's no one's business except Rosie's and mine.'

Teresa's usually animated face looks pained. 'This is hard for me, Martha, but it has to be done. So let me translate and I promise I'll go back inside my house and not interfere again.'

Martha's front door opens and Eugenia is there, barking out demands to Teresa for translation. There's contempt in Seb's mother-in-law's eyes that Martha doesn't recognise from any of that generation. Her own mother and Alana's and Sophie's were strict, but devoted and warm. Seb had alluded to his mother-in-law's reputation in their neighbourhood, but he respected her. She lacked hypocrisy and malice, but he warned that he wouldn't want to cross her.

'Eugenia wants Rosie –'

Martha cuts her off. 'I've lived next door to you for six years, Teresa, and you've seen how much work I've done on this house. So for you to come to my house and take their side . . .'

Teresa is close to tears.

'It's not what you think, Martha. And I really didn't want to do this at your front door, but Eugenia's come a long way and I respect that. She's lost a mother, a daughter and two sisters to cancer and she can't seem to convince Rosie to have a check-up because Rosie won't be told anything these days. Eugenia wants you to take her grand-daughter to the breast clinic to make sure everything's okay, because if something happens to Rosie they'll have to put Eugenia in the ground with her.'

Martha feels Eugenia's stare. Meets it.

'She knows it's how you lost your mother and that you'd under-stand,' Teresa adds.

Martha nods, because she can't speak, and then Teresa is embrac-ing her and Martha doesn't want to let go.

'Marco and I are worried about you, *bella*.'

With the arrival of Eugenia, the ghost of her daughter Loredana joins Lotte in waking Martha up in the morning.

Forza, Marta.

Martha has never sensed Loredana in this house before, but she's imagined her languorous walk down Dalhousie chatting to every second person outside their home, as they watered their plants or collected their mail. That husky strong accent attracting the foreigners, the rapid musical dialect comforting the old-timers. Seb and Loredana may have been on their own out here, but the upside was that it freed them from the angst most people in this neighbourhood had at the hands of in-laws and relatives. In the cancer ward Loredana had been indifferent to Martha, but she bewitched Lotte, with her charisma and disregard for hospital rules, even when they were dying. More than once, Martha would find them giggling together. She was jealous of that, maybe more than the fact that Loredana was Seb's first wife. And here they both are in Martha's ear, and together they are a force to be reckoned with.

So she ventures outside to the beyond. Finds Seb's mother-in-law hacking at the triffids. When Eugenia sees Martha, she calls out, explaining what needs to be done. Not that Martha understands a word, but it's all in the tone and gestures. Eugenia holds out the sickle.

Forza, Marta.

And it's how Martha and Seb's mother-in-law spend their days. Hacking at years of failed gardening and talking to each other in a language that the other doesn't understand. Once or twice Rosie watches them suspiciously from her window and Eugenia murmurs something to Martha.

'Yes, what a little shit,' Martha says in return and Eugenia laughs as if she knows exactly what Martha said.

Chapter Nine

He misses driving. Not like he does with the dump trucks at the mines. Back in Sydney he's at the mercy of public transport and other people's timetables, when all he wants to do is get in a car and see Toto. Maybe her as well. To have the freedom of taking them places. But if he thinks of driving, it'll remind him of the car and those never-ending highways up north. The temptations they presented.

Rosie's coming out of the house with the pram as he walks up, and he helps her down the step.

'Just got in,' he says, although she hasn't asked. Toto gives him a tired smile and Jimmy figures he just woke up. 'It's like I can't stop thinking of him, you know, and it's freaking me out because every other week I feel forgotten. As if I have to start all over again. I'm worried that he won't remember me.'

It's blurted, but he has to get it out. The problem with being away is that it means Jimmy spends too much time in his head, and all sorts of things happen in there.

He's suddenly aware of someone else on the verandah.

'My Nonna Eugenia is here from Sicily,' Rosie tells him.

He expected a small woman with hair set immaculately like both of Frankie's nonnas, or even Mackee's Nanna Grace. They could be described as stern or haughty, but warm. Rosie's grandmother has a hardness in her eyes that makes him flinch.

'She doesn't like me,' he says to Rosie when Eugenia relinquishes the pram to stop for a ciggie outside the community centre.

'Does she have to?'

Jimmy was hoping she'd contradict him.

'Her father was a good-for-nothing, she was married to a good-for-nothing, her neighbours are good-for-nothing. So as far as she's concerned, men don't rate.'

'What about her son?' he asks. 'She would have loved your father, right?'

Jimmy doesn't know why he says that because it's not as if he's top priority when it comes to his mother.

'Son-in-law,' she says. 'And my father was in a class of his own.'

A car races around the corner of Ramsay and Dalhousie and almost mounts the kerb where they're walking. Jimmy grabs Rosie's hand and pulls her back. He doesn't even try to wrest Toto from Eugenia. A fortnight ago he convinced Rosie to share the pram and now her grandmother comes along and she's not in on the agreement.

They spend the next half hour walking the two blocks of the main drag. Here, there seems to be a place for every deli item.

The shop to buy cheese, the one to buy fresh pasta, the fruit shop, the delicatessen for pickled vegetables, and then the IGA, where they take a ticket and wait for twenty minutes, just so Rosie can buy one hundred grams of salami. For the life of him, Jimmy can't understand why she doesn't get her groceries all in one place. Finally, they wait in a queue outside the hole-in-the-wall bakery, another one of those family-owned businesses with more charm than sparkle, selling a variety of stone-baked Italian breads, and pizza loaves and cakes. Nothing like the flashier pasticcerias up the road. When Rosie's paid up, the woman behind the counter gives her a free bread roll for Toto to gnaw at. They head back home and Jimmy notices that she gets a couple of text messages.

'Are you going out with someone?' he asks.

She shrugs. 'Maybe. I haven't decided yet.'

'Has he met Toto?'

'Yes.' After a moment she glances at him. 'What about you?'

'Nothing serious.'

'I'd hate to be described that way. Nothing serious.'

The girl he's seeing does the accounts for the mines and he can't imagine her losing sleep because she's 'nothing serious' to him. Jimmy is probably less than nothing serious to her.

Rosie eyes him and then looks at her grandmother.

'Do you want to take him for the afternoon?' she asks.

He'd never pick Rosie for someone who doesn't make her own decisions, but Eugenia's definitely in charge here.

'Are you okay with that?' he asks. 'Because I want it to come from you, Rosie. I want to know that you trust me with him. It's what you and I need between us. I don't want to be tiptoeing twenty-four seven.'

143

'If I wasn't okay with it, you wouldn't be taking him,' Rosie says.

Eugenia says something to her and Rosie nods in agreement.

'What did she say?'

'I'm not a translator,' she says, irritated.

'I don't want to be second-guessing what your grandmother's saying about me.'

'You talk too much. That's what she's saying.'

Outside the house, Rosie crouches down and kisses Toto.

'Two rules. Keep him warm and don't swear in front of him. He's about a second away from saying his first words and I don't want them to be *Fuck you.*'

'Fair enough.'

'And don't get excited if he says *Dada*. It's not exactly a first word; it's more of a tongue placement behind his teeth thing.'

'Won't get excited.'

He doesn't mean for it to come out the way it does. She glances up at him and something softens in her eyes.

'It's just that when he says it for real, you'll want it to mean something more than baby sounds.'

Jimmy sends the gang a message telling them he has Toto for the afternoon. He asks whether they want to catch-up even though he knows they're either working or in lectures. Frankie and Mackee take less than a minute to respond and, according to Mackee, Tara says she's chucking a sickie for the afternoon and orders them not to leave until she gets there. The pram's a shocker, flat in one wheel and lopsided. Jimmy stops at a servo to pump it up, but it's more of a puncture than a flat. It must wipe Rosie out going uphill.

He takes Toto onto a bus down Parramatta Road and gets out at Camperdown where he's to meet Frankie and Mackee outside the Deus Ex Machina motorbike shop. Mackee's already there, waiting. He crouches beside the pram and peers in.

'Hey, Totes,' he says.

'No swearing in front of him, okay?' Jimmy takes Toto out of the pram and places him on the ground while he tries to fix the wheel for the tenth time.

Mackee grips Toto's hand and looks up at Jimmy. 'You never let go, mate. Never.'

Frankie arrives and she gets eye level with Toto. Jimmy sees tears well up in her eyes.

'I can't believe we've started breeding,' she says, picking Toto up.

'He's made us old,' Mackee laughs.

'You're the one wearing a tie and talking shares and the stock market.'

'*Guys!*'

They watch as Tara, weighed down by a satchel and briefcase, waves at them from the middle of Parramatta Road. She's perched on the thin medium strip with cars racing past her both ways.

'Use the lights!' Mackee shouts. She ignores him and races across the road the moment she gets a chance.

'Oh my God, he's gorgeous.' She shoves all her stuff onto Mackee and holds out her hands to Toto.

'I dislocated my shoulder last month and you didn't take time off work,' Tom accuses her.

'I gave you a sponge bath for a week,' she says. 'Be grateful.'

Toto goes to her, solemn at first, and then he laughs.

'Fuuuck, it's Hailler in Year Eleven detention,' Mackee says.

'What did I say about swearing?'

'Justine wants to Skype with us from fucking Melbourne,' Frankie says, taking out her phone.

In true Justine fashion she cries when they hold Toto up to the screen. Jimmy hasn't seen her in years, but it feels like less. She'd have to be one of the most generous people he's ever known. At school, if he wanted moments away from Frankie's dramas, or lectures from Tara, or descriptions of Siobhan's sex life, there'd be Justine in the music room. Today, she's rehearsing for a gig and plays Toto a piece of crazy music on the piano accordion and Toto loves it. Tara has a bit of a sway with him while Frankie sings an Italian song until Mackee tells them to hang up or he'll walk away. Inside the café, Mackee tries to fold up the pram.

'In what century did she buy this thing?' he says, while Tara grabs the first waitress they see. 'We need a highchair!' As if Toto's the first baby to ever enter the joint.

And it's all manic and sort of emotional.

When they're settled, Jimmy looks at the menu, wishing there was something that suggested what to feed a seventeen-month-old.

'Do you think he can have French fries?'

'Course,' Mackee says. 'I took my cousin Billy to Macca's when he was about one.'

Frankie is studying Toto. 'You're pretty adorable,' she tells him. 'Very Italian-looking.'

'So why did she name him after my dad's favourite band?' Mackee asks.

Jimmy shrugs.

'I reckon she named him after Toto Cutugno. He's an Italian icon,' Frankie says. She breaks out into one of his songs.

'I think it's a family name.'

'Toto comes from Salvatore,' Frankie explains to the others.

'Sounds nothing like it,' Mackee says, taking off his tie.

Tara leans into him. 'How was the interview?'

He shrugs. 'Pretty ordinary.'

Despite still getting casual work, Jimmy can tell Mackee is getting frustrated with the finding-a-real-job process.

Frankie brings up her project and Tara's impressed that she's presenting two papers at a symposium. It makes Jimmy feel guilty that he hasn't asked what she's studying.

'Family history,' she explains. 'There's so much information around for people whose families migrated from the UK and Ireland,' Frankie tells them. 'But not that much for everyone else.'

'I didn't know you were interested,' Mackee says.

'Accidentally to begin with,' she says. 'As part of my degree I did a genealogy elective and, this one night, a friend of my parents was over for dinner talking about how his parents died without them having written anything down about their migration or history. So I started doing research for him, wrote to libraries and organisations all over Italy, managed to find records six generations back, and then I put it into a booklet for his family. They were weeping.'

She looks at them, nodding.

'Anyway, they wanted to pay me. I said no. They said yes. I said no. My mother said, "You're not living with us forever so take the money."'

Jimmy can imagine Mia saying that.

'How much did you charge?' Tara asks.

'It was about twenty hours' work and I charged thirty dollars an hour.'

'Not enough,' Mackee says. 'You've got a masters.'

'I'm working on at least half a dozen at the moment. All word of mouth. But the best part is that I decided to write an article for an online magazine about migration since the 1920s. It sort of focuses on reasons and experiences and how they've changed depending on what decade they arrived.'

'I want to read it,' Tara says.

'I really wanted to go into what we can learn when it comes to refugees arriving here today. Drum roll, please.'

'Aren't you loud enough?' Mackee says.

'Last week,' she says, ignoring him, 'I got an offer from ANU to do my PhD on the topic.'

'Jealous,' Tara says. 'Very jealous. You're a bloody superstar.'

'No swearing,' Jimmy pleads.

Tara sends a wistful glance at Tom. 'Should I do a PhD?'

'No. Earn money, woman.'

'When did everything become about earning money?' Jimmy asks.

'She wants a couple of those,' Tom says, pointing to the baby.

'He wants a couple of them as well,' Tara says.

'But we're not fornicating for the purpose of procreation until we can afford to live on a single income,' Mackee explains.

Tara's fingers creep up Toto's hand and he chuckles.

'I never pegged you as clucky,' Jimmy says.

'What a ridiculous word that is,' Frankie says.

'Archaic,' Tara agrees.

'Every time I hug one of my baby cousins or godchildren, the relatives are all, "Oh my God, she's next. She's so clucky" and I'm like, "It's a hug, people."'

'So no babies for now,' Mackee says. He gently pokes Toto on the chest. 'You, number one son, Toto.'

'You have to get the pronunciation right,' Jimmy says.

Mackee takes out his phone. 'I'm googling how to pronounce Toto in Italian.'

Toto's amused by their laughter. Jimmy is moved by it. These guys always came up with the goods. Great families to be part of, beds to sleep on, food on the table every time he was in their homes. But Toto's the first thing Jimmy has had to offer and he's overcome by what it means to him.

Upstairs at Rosie's place, Toto does that bucking thing he always does when he sees his mother. She's got eye make-up on and looks hot and it means she's going out with the guy who's met Toto, and Jimmy figures he doesn't have the right to feel jealous. They don't have memories or history. Jimmy didn't get a girlfriend pregnant. He got a stranger he had known for two weeks pregnant. It's as bloodless as it can possibly be. Rosie looks up and it's only her grandmother being there that makes him head down the stairs.

'I've got an interview this week,' Rosie calls after him. 'At a nursing home in Chiswick. Eugenia can look after him for now if I get it, but I need to work something out for when she leaves.'

'What are the options?'

'Occasional day care.' She shrugs. 'And Signora across the road might agree to do it. She used to babysit me.'

He comes back up the stairs because he thinks any progress with Rosie is important.

'I'll pay for any child care while I'm not in Sydney, but when I'm here I really want to look after him.'

She doesn't look impressed. 'You can't go around promising things and then not delivering.'

'Who says I won't be delivering, Rosie?'

'I rang your number for a year!'

'I couldn't . . .'

'I don't give a shit where you left the phone, Jimmy. You didn't deliver.'

Not that much progress after all.

'Enjoy your date,' he mutters, walking away.

Frankie takes him to drinks at the Old Clare, celebrating an engagement of a couple of her friends. The place is packed and she's waved over by a group of mostly guys. All of them pissed.

'Will's friends from uni,' she says, introducing them. 'Jimmy.'

The taller of the guys feigns a sob. 'Your friends too, Francesca.'

She laughs and Jimmy can tell she likes these people.

'And they've just come back from the big drunken tour of Europe and saw him in Germany.'

'Stuttgart!' the guys holler to each other, as if it's a trigger word for another swig of beer.

'We had so much fun,' the only girl says. Erin is her name, he thinks.

They bring up the pipeline project Will's working on and Frankie nods a lot and Jimmy can't understand a word they're saying. Another guy joins them, holding two beers and sipping from both, so pissed he can hardly string a sentence together. He ogles Frankie until one of the guys introduces her as 'Will's Plus One'.

Jimmy sees a flash of irritation cross her face.

'Will told us you're back at uni,' Erin says to her. 'Doing what? Top-up courses?'

Before Frankie has a chance to respond, she says, 'You're a crazy girl not wanting to spend a year in Europe.' Erin nudges the tall guy. 'The moment this one gets a job overseas I'm following him over.'

'Who says you're invited?' the boyfriend says with a laugh.

'As if I'd trust you on your own, babe.'

She looks at Frankie, waves away what she just said, coming up close.

'Will and I had a D & M about you. He can't understand why you're not with him.'

'Did the dickhead stop asking you to marry him, Francesca?' one of the guys asks. 'Is that why you're not over there?'

'I'll marry you,' the drunk says.

The space invasion is full on and Frankie steps away from the intensity of the group.

'See you guys later.'

Jimmy follows her as they push towards the couple getting engaged. Along the way friends recognise her and there's a whole lot of 'How's Will?', 'Where's Will?', 'Why aren't you with Will?'

They stay a while and Jimmy gets talking to a couple of their friends whom he's met before. It feels good to talk about work. Engineers understand mines and Jimmy doesn't have to apologise about what he does. Outside when they leave, Frankie's quiet. Not unhappy, but he knows something's not right. It's crowded on Broadway tonight and they don't have much luck getting on a bus.

'Let's walk,' she says, although it'll take them about forty minutes, especially in the heels Frankie's wearing.

'And just for the record, I am no one's plus one,' she says, out of the blue.

'Good to hear.'

'Because that's what I am to some people. Will's hot girlfriend. While they're speaking pipelines and formulas, no one truly asks what I do. Just, "Oh, you're in the band" or "You make bridal wear, how lovely". And then it's back to pipelines and infrastructure and aren't I lucky because Will's going to be able to pick and choose who to work for one day, and Will would be a fool not to take up an offer in Europe this year because Will's got a future more important than mine and I'd be a "crazy girl" not to go to Europe because everyone wants to spend a year hanging out in Germany as their boyfriend's plus one.'

'For the record, you're not that hot.'

She grins, because she can't help herself. Jimmy doesn't know how else to respond. Has to admit that he's always had a sort of reverence for the rise and rise of Will, because it's mostly due to pretty intense hard work and intelligence.

Frankie's phone rings and Jimmy figures it's the aforementioned at this time of the night. She looks at the screen. Shows him.

'Stuttgart!' she hollers and Jimmy laughs because she's spot-on with the drunk impersonation. She answers the phone and walks ahead of him.

Rosie lets him take Toto for a couple of hours every day. Same instructions. 'No swearing. Keep him warm.' Jimmy is to ring her the moment Toto says his first words. On Friday, he heads back to Mackee and Tara's place. Mackee hasn't got any casual work today and is in front of a computer screen, browsing Seek.

'The paramedics are advertising for interns,' Mackee tells Jimmy, handing over some information he's downloaded and taking Toto from him. Both he and Tara have collected toys that Mackee retrieves from a basket in the corner. 'First thing you have to do online is prove you're eligible. Send in a résumé and two referees.'

Jimmy reads the info pack. Once they clear his eligibility, he's to do an online aptitude test and then wait to see if he's made the next round. There are plenty of rounds. Too many. He wants this more than anything, but can't help noticing the opening salary for a trainee. At least thirty thousand less than what he's earning in the mines. He wouldn't have cared a couple of months ago, but he's just told Rosie that he wants to pay for day care and everything else. He doesn't know what he'll be able to afford if he settles in Sydney, pays rent and tries to support a kid.

Later, while Jimmy's playing with Toto, Mackee types up his résumé.

'This Kev guy should be your referee,' he tells Jimmy. 'Did you get to know him well?'

'I stayed for a couple of months after the floods. Helped with the clean-up. I haven't been in contact because I'm pretty slack in that way, but I can't imagine him not vouching for me.'

'My dad can be your character reference,' Mackee says.

Jimmy doesn't know when Mackee got so responsible, but the application and supporting stuff is done within the hour.

*

They head over to Mackee's aunt Georgie's place to spend the afternoon at the park across the road with Toto and Georgie's four-year-old, Billy. Mackee's sister Anabel pops over, because she lives around the corner. Today she's sporting a Princess Leia hairdo and has her trumpet. Year Twelve music exam trials are on soon and she's practising twenty-four seven.

While she grabs an orange and cuts it into quarters, she nudges Jimmy.

'So you got a girl pregnant?'

Jimmy can't help laughing. There was never any beating around the bush when it came to Anabel. Her phone buzzes and she grabs it before her brother does.

'It's from her girlfriend.' Mackee is making kissing sounds.

'Grow up,' she says, sticking a quarter of the orange in her mouth and giving Billy and Toto an orange-peel twisted smile. Billy thinks it's funny and Toto is in awe of both of them. Anabel grabs her trumpet and her phone and does a dramatic prance around the park, playing a marching tune, while Billy follows.

'Did Tommy tell you about the pram?' Georgie asks Jimmy.

'We all put in to buy Georgie a pram when Billy was born,' Mackee says, 'because she was this geriatric mother who couldn't even walk to the station without a whinge, and now it's collecting cobwebs in the garden shed.'

'It's yours on loan until someone in the family needs it again,' Georgie says.

Jimmy goes to shake his head. 'Take it,' Mackee says. 'It's worth more than her car.'

Georgie laughs. 'Sadly true.'

Jimmy embraces her. 'Mate, too generous.'

'Auntie Margie Finch still goes on about that lovely friend of Tommy's who came out to Walgett to help build the community centre back in 2007,' she says, referring to Mackee's great-aunt who's a nun.

Jimmy can't hide the grimace. 'I was a bit lost back then.'

'Weren't we all?'

Georgie's pram is a breeze and Jimmy almost breaks into a jog with it. Toto sits up, holding tight to the bar and staring out at the world. He drops a new toy that came with the pram and starts crying. Jimmy picks it up and crouches, looking into his caramel eyes.

'I'm Jimmy,' he whispers, 'and you're the first thing I've ever sort of owned and I don't want to get this wrong.'

Toto has a ghost of a smile on his face. A knowing one. Of course Jimmy's going to get it wrong. It's how he ended up in detention all his school life. And on a good behaviour bond for two years. It's how he lost a Monaro.

Rosie's sitting on the front doorstep waiting when they get home. She isn't impressed with the pram.

'I'm going to have to give them money,' she says, trying to take Toto out, frustrated with the shoulder straps.

'No, it's on loan.'

'But I have to give them something.'

Jimmy takes over with the straps and lifts Toto out, handing him to her.

'They won't accept anything,' he says.

'I don't like owing people.'

'You owe them nothing, Rosie. Maybe a thank-you note and leave it at that.'

'I want you to return it,' she says.

Jimmy doesn't want to insult Georgie and the Mackees, and he can't think of any reason why they need to. He pushes the pram back to the front gate. 'Come on.'

'Where?' she asks.

He takes Toto from her and puts him back into the pram.

'Uphill.'

Ten minutes up Waratah Street and Rosie's changed her mind.

'It's like the V8 of prams,' she says. 'A Holden twin-throttle 5.0 litre.'

'No, it's a Ford Barra 4.0 litre six cylinder.'

She's trying not to smile, but then she does. He hasn't seen much of a happy Rosie. Even Toto seems to respond with a chuckle of his own.

Jimmy does an elaborate show of how he can spin the pram around effortlessly and they head home.

'How come you know your V8s?' he asks.

'I was the son my father never had.'

He glances at her. 'What would he have done about a stolen Monaro?'

'He would have hunted the thief down. My mum was the proud owner of one. "*Da Fiat is shiiiiit.*"' Jimmy figures Rosie's impersonating her mum. There's a bittersweet smile on her face. 'Go figure. She loved an Aussie car.'

'Did they ever watch the V8s?' he asks.

'Too expensive. You?'

He nods. 'The Gold Coast. Ipswich. Townsville.'

'I'd love to watch the race on Phillip Island,' she says.

'I'll take you there, one day.'

The words come out before he can stop himself, but they don't seem to bother her.

'Where's your nan?' he asks.

'Eugenia's not a naaaaan,' she says, but she smiles and he can't stop looking at her.

'You want to get something to eat?' he asks.

She shakes her head. 'I want to take Eugenia to the cemetery.'

'I can stay and look after Toto?' he asks. 'If you don't mind me hanging out at the house.'

She thinks for a moment and shrugs. Nods.

Jimmy's in the kitchen with Toto when Martha arrives home. He helps her with the groceries while Toto's in the mini mover ramming into walls. Martha puts on the jug just as the home phone rings, but she ignores it and the answering machine clicks on.

'*Martha, pick up the phone!*'

Jimmy sits at the butcher's trolley expecting Martha to pick up, but she makes herself comfortable opposite him.

'Whoever it is sounds pissed off,' he says.

He checks himself too late, looks over at Toto and hopes his first words aren't *pissed off*.

'You won't remember this because you're too young,' Martha says, 'but there was a time in life when you could go an entire day without speaking to anyone on the phone. And it was liberating. And very unstressful. And you didn't get phone calls such as

"Hi, it's me, I'm on the bus" or "Hi, it's me, I'm buying the milk".
I mean, who gives a rat's arse?'

Jimmy points to Toto. 'No swearing. He's just about to say his
first words and it's freaking me out because I think it's going to be
something pretty awful on my watch.'

They look down at Toto, who's smashing into the sideboard with
his car. The porcelain figurines on top of it are shaking, as if they
sense life is no longer safe. Martha gets up and approaches him,
crouches at eye level.

'Listen, Seb Gennaro, you've got to stop ruining my furniture.'

'Do you have a photo of him?' Jimmy asks. Because he's keen to
see this resemblance. 'Seb?'

'Course I do. But what about Rosie's photos?'

He shrugs. 'She says they're in storage, but I think there's more
to it.'

The phone rings again and the machine switches on. There's
another *Where are you, Martha?* which she ignores again.

'I'll get you a photo,' she says at the same time as Toto shouts out.
Martha stops, looks at Jimmy.

'Did he just say what I thought he said?' Jimmy asks.

They wait and watch.

'A one-off,' Martha reassures him.

Jimmy isn't so convinced. 'She'll kill me.'

On cue the front door opens and Jimmy hears Rosie and
Eugenia's voices.

Toto sets off on his walker in the direction of his mum's voice,
chuffed with himself.

'Marta. Marta. Marta.'

Chapter Ten

Rosie would have preferred Toto's first words to be 'Fuck you'. Worse still, he's turned Martha into a martyr and what she is, at the end of the day, is a thief. Because of her there's no trace of Rosie's mum in the house. At least she can sneak into Martha's room and stare at the photo of her father on the mantelpiece, marvelling at how much Toto looks like him. But her mother's disappeared and Rosie's frightened that she's forgetting what she looked like. Eugenia being here has made the yearning worse because there's a tease of resemblance. Once or twice while they lie in bed together, she reaches out to touch the parts of Eugenia's face that remind Rosie of her mum, but her nonna isn't much for physical affection and pushes her hand away with irritation.

'*Smettila*, Rosanna.'

But Rosie doesn't want to stop it. So she goes searching for fragments of Loredana. There are reminders in the neighbourhood.

Some people know where to get the best *pane di casa* and *arancini*. Rosie knows where to find women who speak the dialect. She can't go overboard because she's on a budget, so it's one hundred grams of prosciutto from Lamonica IGA, a tub of fresh ricotta at Paesanella, a small container of *giardiniera* from Zanetti's. There are the terms of endearment she waits to hear. *Bella. Gioia. Tesoro.* Words that cocooned Rosie's childhood. Missing ever since her mum died.

When she's not stalking Sicilian-speaking women on Ramsay Street, she goes for more job interviews and is offered a couple of shifts at the nursing home down in Chiswick. But she can't provide one hundred points of identification because her driver's licence has expired and her name's not on a utility bill or council rates. She doesn't have a credit card. Her Medicare card only gets her twenty-five points and she's got an ID card for her pension that's worth forty. But to reach one hundred, she needs her passport. Her birth certificate. Which means that Luke the C-bomb has to come back into her life after dumping her in Queensland two years ago. He doesn't just have her legal documents, but her mother's wedding dress. And all her photos. Packed away in two suitcases sitting in his shed in Maroubra. Rosie left them there before they headed up north because she didn't want anything she loved under Martha's roof. Luke's changed his number and she manages to track down one of the guys they met in Coffs Harbour, who gives her a more current one.

'It's Rosie,' she says.

'How did you get this number?'

'I want my stuff, Luke.'

'Then come and get it.'

'I don't have a car.'

'Not my problem.'

'Then tell me when you're home.'

Lachlan rings and it's good to contrast guys. She's hung out with him since Eugenia's arrival and it makes her feel normal, like other people her age who get to hang out and laugh and not give a shit about anything but exams. It feels good knowing she can attract guys with decent histories. He still lives at home, in the sort of family that has dinner together at six p.m. with a mum who calls out 'Lachlan, set the table' every time Rosie's there. His family ask about the baby without an inch of judgement and Rosie laughs at everyone's attempt to pronounce Toto's name. She tells them that it's not so strange a name in Sicily. Tonight Lachlan wants to veg and watch a movie together in his room, but then changes his mind and suggests they head down to The Rose in case his friends are there. By the time they settle back to watch TV a second time, he's changed his mind again and they head out for a drink. Deep down she thinks he has a fear of missing out.

He introduces her to his friends and they seem decent, all study-ing economics or law or both. They talk about taking Nō-Dōz and speed to keep them awake to study and reassure her that they're not junkies, just stressed out about exams. Lachlan seems to inter-pret her silence as disapproval and he takes her hand under the table, squeezing it. But it's not disapproval. Just indifference. Rosie's been there, done that, with drugs and they don't interest her anymore. They failed to live up to any expectations and one of her few blessings is that she doesn't have an addictive personality. Just a destructive one.

Back at his place they have sex. He's cautious, apologises a couple of times, asks permission. She finds it endearing. Later, when he drives her home he whistles a tune. She can tell he's happy and it's because of her. It gives her the courage to ask a favour.

'My ex-boyfriend has a suitcase of some really important stuff of mine and I was wondering if you could drive me there to pick it up?'

'Is he a psycho?'

'No. Just a dickhead.'

'Is he Toto's dad?'

She shakes her head. She gets a sense he doesn't want to do it and instantly regrets asking.

'Look, don't worry about it,' she says. 'It's cool.'

'You sure?'

'Yeah. It's all good.'

The next day, she leaves Toto with Eugenia and takes a couple of buses to Maroubra, planning to drag the two suitcases back the same way. Out front, Luke's place looks like a hoarder's hovel. A rusty boat trailer, half on its side. A soiled mattress piled high with split garbage bags filled with rubbish that have been put out for collection for what seems like weeks. Filthy bath fittings, mops, rusty hinges. On the front verandah, a collection of muddy runners, another grubby single mattress, rotted, mouldy. Rosie can't begin to imagine what the shed looks like these days and the idea that it houses her precious belongings fills her with shame. All she wants is to take part of her mother's memory out of this fleapit dump. She knocks at the front door, but no one answers, and her knocks turn into a hammering. With every blow, she feels a rage build up inside of her until her knuckles begin to bleed.

She tries the shed next. Finds it padlocked, and there Rosie unleashes the fury that's wound up inside of her since hearing his voice. She's at that splintered timber door with two fists, screaming with a rage she can't contain. Because Rosie is powerless. Every day. All day. No money. No job. No means of identifying herself. No way of climbing out of a rut. All she has is the house her father built, and now Martha's got real estate agents walking in and out, telling them lies. And it always ends with that unfathomable despair that has chased Rosie for years. That she will never see her mother and father again. Toto's birth was a godsend and a curse. It brought back the memory of everything she lost.

Later that day she picks up Toto and meets Yolanda and Tess and the babies. She doesn't know what she has with these women, but they're at Livvi's Place every week and no one's bailed yet. She figures the two see each other more times than every Tuesday, but she couldn't be bothered begging for more. While the babies sit in the sandpit, she fills them in about the nursing home job but doesn't tell them the truth, that she can't identify herself.

'It's really diverse,' she says. 'I saw this Asian woman in the garden and they do a welcome to country at breakfast.'

'Superficial bullshit,' Yolanda says. 'That doesn't make a place diverse, Rosie. Honestly, you come across so racist sometimes.'

'I'm not racist.'

Tess asks about the uni application and Rosie regrets ever telling them about it.

'I'm not going through with it,' she says. 'It's in the too-hard basket for the time being.'

'I thought the guy you're dating from the student centre was helping you,' Tess says.

'I don't want to be that girl who needs help with everything,' Rosie says. 'Not a great way to start a relationship.'

Yolanda has a teacher's look of disapproval in her eyes. 'You are that girl. It's not going to change. So get yourself a profession or you're going to spend the rest of your life making do.'

'Easy,' Tess says to Yolanda.

'You need to support Toto,' Yolanda says.

'Who says I'm not?' Rosie demands.

'On a couple of shifts at a nursing home?'

'You're not my teacher, Yolanda. So get lost with the lectures.'

'Guys,' Tess says, pointing to the babies.

Yolanda's eyes are fixed on Rosie's hands. 'What happened?'

'Nothing.'

'Is that Lachlan guy treating you like shit?'

'No.'

'You're upset about something more than Yolanda nagging you,' Tess says.

'I'm not nagging her.'

'You're nagging me.'

Rosie can feel Tess watching her and gives in. Doesn't know where to start. Begins with the fact that she hasn't enough points to ID herself for a job.

'What about your licence?' Tess asks.

'It needs renewing. The cheapest option is fifty-six dollars for a year and I won't have that until next Thursday when my pension comes through, and my ex-boyfriend has two suitcases of my stuff including my passport and birth certificate . . . and my photos.'

'What do you mean he's got your stuff?'

Rosie explains, her face smarting from the humiliation of having to reveal that she ever went out with a Luke-type.

'Not the baby daddy?'

Rosie shakes her head. 'And I'm not asking him because he'll give me the money and there's just not that much dignity left in the tank.'

'Have you got enough for rent?' Tess asks, removing a coffee cup her daughter Aurora found in the sand.

'I don't pay rent,' Rosie says.

'Well, there's a positive,' Yolanda says. 'Because –'

Rosie's had enough. She grabs her stuff and picks up Toto. 'Let me guess, Yolanda. You pay a shitload of rent or a mortgage, so I'm a whinger?'

'All I meant, Rosie, is thank God there's a positive in your life.'

'I can lend –'

'Don't,' Rosie says, cutting off Tess. 'I'll see you whenever.'

And Rosie figures she won't turn up again. Too much humiliation.

*

165

At home, Eugenia's working with Martha on the garden. They both notice Rosie and she watches them exchange a look. Feels betrayed. Like she did that time her father married Martha eleven months after her mum died. Even more, because Eugenia's not one to be charmed, yet here she is every day digging up the garden with the enemy.

Martha approaches. 'Can we talk?' she asks. Rosie can see her eyeing the way Toto's stomping on the flowerbed.

'What about? The fact that you're selling my house?'

Martha walks over to Toto and takes his hand.

'Don't touch him.'

'He's eating dirt, Rosie.'

Rosie grabs Toto from her.

'And if you bring another agent through the house, I'll trash it.'

Martha looks pissed off. Rosie likes the fact that she can still push her buttons.

'What are the options, Rosie?'

'You move out. That's a great option.'

'This is my house as much as yours. And there's a mortgage, remember.'

Rosie walks inside with Toto, but Martha follows her.

'Eugenia wants you to have a breast check, Rosie.'

Rosie feels her pulse going haywire. Even Toto reacts to it, his mouth beginning to quiver. She storms up the stairs wanting to shut the door on everyone.

'Eugenia's asked me to make an appointment for you to see –'

'I don't need you to do anything for me, Martha!'

'It's for peace of mind, Rosie. I know how you feel.'

'You and I have nothing in common, so don't say that again.'

Toto's squirming in her arms because he wants to stay downstairs with the martyr and Eugenia the traitor.

'How about mothers with cancer, Rosie? Don't we have that in common?'

'Shut up.'

'You saw them,' Martha says. 'In the same ward and they had the same cancer and they died the same week. How can that not be something in common?'

Martha has followed her up and Rosie wants to shove her down the stairs.

'I'm not bonding with you over dead mothers, Martha.'

'You father would have wanted you to do this.'

'Since when do you care what my father wanted for me?' Rosie shouts at her.

'Go for the check-up and put your mind at ease. Loredana –'

'Stop talking about my mother.'

'Rosie, she'd want you taking care of yourself. Toto's going to –'

'*Shut up. Shut up. Shut up.*' And Toto's crying and hitting Rosie and she wants to smash something and Eugenia's coming up the stairs now and she's grabbing Toto from Rosie and pushing him into Martha's arms and then Eugenia's taking Rosie's face between her hands because Rosie can't stop shouting and crying, because she's forgetting what her mum looked like and no one has a photo except Luke the arsehole who won't let her get to her stuff and then she's yelling because they won't give Toto back to her. Just yelling, 'I hate you!' And then Jimmy's there. Rosie doesn't remember him arriving, but suddenly he's at the top of the stairs. He's SES Jesus from the flood, looking calm as he leans over and takes Toto from Martha, his eyes on Rosie the entire time.

'I've borrowed a car,' he says to her. 'Do you want to go for a drive?'

She hasn't sat in the front seat of a car for a long time. Her best memories come from being in her mother's car. She misses the talks and the dialect. Always the dialect. Her dad's as well. At home they rarely spoke English. It made Rosie an outsider from the beginning. No preschool, so kindy was a shock. Seb and Loredana hadn't warned her that the rest of the world spoke a different language. It was a tough lesson to learn when she was five. But there were tougher ones to come.

She looks over at Jimmy. He hasn't shut up the whole time and she can't understand how that's a comfort, but it reminds her of SES Jesus again. Because up until now, here in Sydney, something has silenced him. Maybe two years of loneliness. He's talking about the paramedics and how he's got to the next phase of an application, and how it was Kev who put the idea in his head after the flood, and then he brings up the Monaro. She remembers that he told her back then that the guy who sold it to him had promised it would lead Jimmy to his family.

'You haven't spoken about your father?' she says. 'How did that work out?'

'It wasn't so bad,' he says. 'He's a sweet guy but his idea of bonding was punching a couple of cones or getting pissed, and it's pretty much all we did.'

'On a good behaviour bond?'

'On a good behaviour bond,' he says with a laugh. 'So my choices were: don't break the law, or hang out with my father who I had just met.'

She feels for him. Because she knew how important it was for him not to stuff up back then. But she also knew he was on that odyssey to find his family.

'I headed further north,' he says. 'Up to the Burdekin, and learnt how to drive a harvester, and from there I met a couple of guys who had jobs in the mines.'

He glances at her. 'But I'd like to see him again,' he says. 'My dad.'

'Does it feel like home?' she asks. 'Here?'

He thinks and then nods. 'You?'

She doesn't know how to answer, but tries.

'It feels like a very unwelcoming home sometimes. But I don't want to live anywhere else. It's like . . .'

'Go on,' he says, when she doesn't finish. But what she wants to say sounds crazy.

'Go on.'

'Apart from when I was a baby I never lived anywhere else with my parents. So I'm scared that if I leave, they won't know where to find me if they come back.'

They drive to Balmain and catch a ferry. On board, Jimmy holds Toto tight because Toto seems as though he wants to leap into the beauty of it all. When they get off at Circular Quay, the stench from Toto's nappy is gag-worthy.

'I didn't bring anything with me,' she says.

'Plenty of people with prams,' he says, looking around.

He approaches a couple with a baby Toto's age and starts chatting with them, pointing back to her and Toto. And then he returns with a nappy and some wipes.

'Too easy.'

Although it's cold and the sun's going down, they sit on the concourse and look out at the bridge with Toto wrapped up in Jimmy's hoodie.

'Where was he born?' he asks, pressing a kiss to Toto's padded head.

'Newcastle.'

'How come there?'

If Lachlan were to ask Rosie the same question she'd lie. She'd tell him that she liked the people of the city and that it was great being close to the beach. But she doesn't have to impress Jimmy. He's not a potential boyfriend and he'd pick the lie anyway.

'I'd run out of money by the time I arrived there so I got temp work at a nursing home,' she says. 'Then I found out I was pregnant and they let me board. It didn't make sense to go anywhere else.'

'Did you like it?'

'The job? Not really. The nursing home was sort of a miserable place. After Toto was born I had to move out and I ended up staying in the granny flat of someone related to one of the old people I took care of. So at least something good came out of working there.'

He holds out a hand to her. 'Let's walk.'

They stroll around the concourse as if they're tourists. Once or twice she catches him looking at her and she can't be bothered pretending that he isn't. Toto wants out of the pram and Jimmy removes him and places him on his shoulders. And Rosie is mesmerised by the sound of her son's joy.

*

While she's lying in bed next to Eugenia that night, Lachlan rings. Wants to know if she'd like to come to a music festival at Moore Park. Rosie says yes as though she hasn't a single responsibility in the world. Having Eugenia here is a godsend, but it's meant that she's living in two worlds. One with Toto in it and one without. She knows she has to make Toto part of what she has with Lachlan, but Rosie likes pretending that she can have it all. When she switches off the light, her nonna turns to face her.

'*Sei anamorata*,' Eugenia says, abruptly. She thinks Rosie's in love.

Eugenia may be intuitive, but she's a bit premature on this one. Regardless, the topic of Lachlan is better than cancer. Or Martha. So she tells Eugenia about how they met when Lachlan helped her with her uni application. And that when she's with his friends, it feels good to be part of a crowd. And how she envies them for just being able to pick up and head down the coast or go to a music festival in Byron on the spur of the moment. And how he lives at home and is the type to laugh at a text his mum sends him. Rosie can't help thinking that maybe Eugenia is right in what she's sensing. She may not be in love with him now, but she could see herself being one day.

She feels Eugenia's stare in the dark.

'*L'altro.*'

She means the other one.

The phone beeps at six a.m. and her hand searches for it in the dark.

> *Can your nanna look after the baby*
> *this morning?*

Yolanda.

Rosie sends one back.

When?

Now.

She's confused. Wonders if something's wrong with the baby and Yolanda's got no one else to turn to. It feels good to be relied on.

Okay. Where?

*I'll pick you up in ten
minutes.*

Tess is with Yolanda when they pull up in the hatchback.

'Is everything okay?' Rosie asks at Yolanda's window.

'That arsehole with your stuff would have to be home at this time of the morning,' Yolanda says. 'Where does he live?'

Rosie's stunned. She's not here to help them, but the other way around. 'Maroubra.'

'Get in.'

'Take the City West Link,' Tess says.

It's a good guess. If Luke's going to be home at any time, it will be seven o'clock on a Sunday morning, sleeping off a hangover. He had no concept of having a good night without getting written off. When he opens the door and recognises Rosie, he slams it shut. Yolanda places a nice manicured finger on the doorbell and doesn't let up. They can hear someone shouting, 'What the fuck!' from inside and Rosie figures they've woken up the housemates. Luke opens the door again.

'Get your finger off the doorbell,' he tells Yolanda.

'What, this one?' she asks, holding up her middle finger. He tries to have a stare-off with Yolanda, but he must remind her of every irritating dickhead she's taught, because she's unfazed.

'Where's the key to the shed?' Rosie asks.

'I don't know.'

'Where is it?'

'Are you deaf or stupid, Rosie?'

'Watch your tone,' Tess says.

'Or what?'

Tess puts her finger on the doorbell and there's more yelling from inside.

'I don't have the key!'

'Then it's a good thing we've got boltcutters in the car,' Tess says, removing her finger and walking away. Rosie doesn't know whether she's bluffing, but Tess is heading for the car and Yolanda and Rosie follow.

'I'm presuming you don't have boltcutters,' she says to Tess.

'Of course I've got boltcutters. You said the shed was padlocked.'

Breaking a padlock isn't as simple as it looks in the movies, but the three of them take turns until finally the lock cracks and Rosie pushes the door forward. Inside there's a rank smell and she hears Tess make a gagging sound. She searches for the light and there's a sound behind them. Luke's at the shed door with one of his house-mates. Rosie doesn't recognise him, but her ex-boyfriend's not the type to hold on to friendships for too long so it could be a relatively new arrangement. She feels intimidated and doesn't want to look at the others, in case they feel the same.

'Which are yours?' Tess asks. Rosie points to a couple of grey suitcases with brown trim, a small part of her parents' past. It was the luggage they used when they left Sicily twenty-three years ago, obviously not purchased new because they look like relics. Yolanda and Tess help her drag them out from under a couple of broken heaters and the rusty carcass of a bike.

And that's how simple it is in the end. Taking on Luke with the rejects of a mothers' group. Eighty points. An extra twenty for the Nissan Micra with a car seat. There's a bit of manoeuvring but they manage to squeeze in the luggage with Rosie in the back. Yolanda starts the ignition, but doesn't drive off just yet.

'That first time at mothers' group, I told my husband that you were a Lebanese girl with attitude,' Yolanda says, catching her eye in the mirror.

'I thought she was Greek,' Tess says. 'You all look the same to me.'

Rosie starts laughing and doesn't stop until she's crying, clutching onto the side of the suitcase that still has a luggage tag from Palermo airport, written in her mother's handwriting.

Tess turns around.

'Let's rob a bank next time.'

That afternoon she's dancing to Diplo at the Parklife festival. And in the middle of the crowd, when Lachlan says, 'I don't know whether I feel like a beer just yet,' she looks up at his earnest face and realises the truth. That she can't be with someone who hesitates. Who might be able to get top marks for wages, enterprise and land capital, but can't really think on his feet. And she doesn't blame him. Because he's decent and lovely and funny, and it makes her sad, because by going out with him she got a glimpse of what she was missing out on. Except Rosie can't afford those glimpses. She needs to steer clear of them because they'll force her into mistakes, and having Toto means she can't make as many as Lachlan. Too much collateral damage. In another life she could wait for Lachlan to grow up and be responsible for something other than setting the table at six p.m. or passing an exam. But Rosie needs a functional guy and when she applies the hundred points of ID to Lachlan, he only gets as far as forty.

L'altro. The other one.

SES Jesus had the advantage of meeting Rosie during a natural disaster and carrying Miss Fricker in his arms through floodwaters, wearing his budgie smugglers.

Lachlan never stood a chance, poor bastard.

She hands in her paperwork and gets her shifts at the nursing home. It's a beautiful place with water views and people who seem happy. Both those there and those who visit them. Martha's boyfriend, or whatever he is, walks his dad around the grounds.

'Hi, Rosie,' he says. 'Thanks for the recommendation.'

And Rosie's overwhelmed by the thought that she can influence someone about something so profound in their lives.

'I've got to head off soon, Dad,' he says, introducing them, and then, 'Rosie will take care of you.'

John Healy's worried. He tells Rosie that he has to pick his kids up from school. 'I don't like the look of this weather,' he says.

Rosie eyes Martha's boyfriend and takes his father's arm.

'You know what I reckon, John,' she says, heading back to his room. 'Your kids are going to be fine.'

Chapter Eleven

Martha owes it to Lloyd Cole. Not that she and Ewan planned to be at his concert together. She's there with Sophie and he's with Alana and in the crowded foyer of the Enmore their eyes meet, and that boyish smile is charming the pants off her.

'So you're dating your sister's partner, are you?' she asks, buying him a beer at the bar while Alana and Sophie disappear into the crowd, because there's always someone they know at these things. He's wearing one of those newsboy caps and pulls off the look a thousand times better than she would have imagined. Despite the sacking and the marriage break-up and his father's deterioration, Ewan Healy is a man very comfortable in his skin. It's the first time he reminds her of Seb.

'Hiding the receding hairline is my forte,' he says after she removes his hat and ruffles what's left of his hair.

She winks at him. 'Not your only one.'

He leans closer to her. 'Really. I'm blushing.'

'You actually are,' she laughs.

Alana returns and takes a sip of Ewan's beer.

'Why don't you two just come out and put us out of our misery?' she says.

They don't respond. It's not that Martha wants to keep it a secret. It's that she doesn't quite know what she's keeping a secret. Apart from the night of Charlie P's funeral, they haven't managed to get anything off the ground. Alana is watching them carefully. Martha can imagine the update she's preparing for Julia.

After the concert, Sophie and Alana go home to their families, leaving her with him. She doesn't know whether it's intentional, but she doesn't question it. There's something endearing about her hand being held as they cross Enmore Road, where they end up having Thai and laughing about how many times they would have bumped shoulders at gigs over the years without realising. Lucinda Williams at the State Theatre, The Church at the Opera House earlier that year. They worked out that back in 1986 they were at the same Midnight Oil gig at Selina's and John Cougar Mellencamp in 1988 at the Entertainment Centre.

Ewan's a bit of a Rain Man when remembering dates and venues.

'What's your best gig ever?' he asks. He grabs two napkins, hands one over to her. 'If we write the same thing, I get lucky tonight,' he says. She fishes in her bag for a pen.

'Pity. I was thinking you were going to get lucky anyway,' she says, 'but now it's up to probability.'

She scribbles hers down and hands it over.

*

There's a strangeness in never once ending up in the back seat of his car in high school, but here she is thirty-odd years later doing the deed in a Hilux for the second time, courtesy of Charlie P's funeral and Martha's dead husband's mother-in-law, and Leonard Cohen's 2008 Sydney concert. She manages to get on top, but needs the grab handle above the window, and when Ewan sits up, they're jammed against the door, going at it so fast and hard that she's worried it's going to spring open and they'll end up sprawled naked on some obscure Enmore street.

When it's over, they don't move, lying there, sort of entwined in a less than erotic fashion. She traces his face, feels the bristle and then he's kissing her slowly and there's this terrible guilt at the thought that if she had ended up with Seb for the rest of her life, she would have missed out on this. And that if she had found this earlier, she'd have missed out on the comfort that only Seb could have given her at the worst time of her life.

'My nan needed the Jesus handle to get out of the car,' Ewan says to her. 'That's what she called it. So it's the first time I've ever thought of her during sex.'

'If I thought of Oma Beate during sex I'd be turned off for life,' Martha says.

He chuckles and makes himself comfortable. For a moment the back seat is illuminated by a car turning into the street. 'So what are you going to do with your life beyond this break?' he asks.

'I'm trying not to think about it,' she says. It's been almost three months since she walked out on the job, and Martha knows she has to get used to the idea of returning. 'I can't go back to that department. Paedophiles and rapes and domestic violence and sexual assault. There aren't many good-news days. It chips away at your soul, you know.'

'So what are your options?'

'Oh, you know. An offer from the UK and New Zealand. Not to mention the Queenslanders wanting me.'

He nips at her chin.

'You're making fun of me.'

She thinks of one or two of the jobs that have come up. The attorney-general's department. Infrastructure.

Martha's waiting for a sign. A Gennaro sign. Seb was big on them. Like those seeds they planted in the early days of their grief when the house was just his. One tree for Loredana. One for Lotte. For months there was little growth, even though the soil was drained. The day after Seb kissed her for the first time, it flowered. 'It's a sign from them,' he said to Martha. She had put it down to twenty milli-metres of rain the week before, but she remembers crying because she had wanted some sort of message from her mother. Seb's rule about signs was that they weren't as important as what people did with them.

She lifts her chin from where it's resting on Ewan's chest.

'I have to sell.'

'That could be a good thing, Martha.'

'Really?' she asks and she can hear the bitterness in her voice. 'For who? I'm going to get half of what it's worth, take away what's owing on it and then have to get a loan on a single public servant's salary to buy anything half decent in this area.'

'You can get a townhouse. We can be neighbours.'

The idea of living next door to a lover has Martha contemplating the possibilities.

*

She sees him the next night at training. Looks for a private glance while he takes them through their fitness regime. Sometimes she finds it, other times Ewan's caught up in whatever's going on in his life. He sends the team off on a couple of laps while he takes a phone call.

'Truly the world's shittiest coach,' Elizabeth says. Her daughter is with her again, sitting by the sidelines and, as usual, not getting involved. Although Louise King is in gym gear, the most exercise she does is pick up her phone to check for messages. Elizabeth brings her to everything these days. Training. The games. Drinks. After high school, Louise scored a scholarship at Sydney Uni's St John's College and is now majoring in medicine. She's a humourless girl who doesn't say much, but Elizabeth's days of helicopter parenting certainly aren't over.

Later, Martha updates them on Eugenia's purpose for being in Australia.

'She flies out here so her granddaughter will go for a mammogram?' Julia says with disbelief.

'Well, cancer has wiped out most of the women in her family.'

'I'm convinced they'll find something every time I'm up for mine,' Sophie says.

'We know that, Dr Google. We get the emails,' Alana says.

'White wine contributes to cancer risk,' not-so-quiet Louise says, eyeing Martha and the others when they order another bottle of wine.

As they go to leave, Elizabeth lets Ewan know that she can't play that Saturday.

'I'll be there, but I'm getting my hair done that morning for DJ's Fashion Week.'

'So what?' he says. 'The game's in the afternoon.'

'Did you not hear me, Ewan? I'm getting a cut and blow-dry.'

'Saturday's game is crucial,' he tells them. 'If you lose this one, it'll be three in a row and it's hard to come back from that, especially when we're one person down.'

'Louise can play,' Alana suggests.

'Not a good idea,' Elizabeth answers for her daughter.

'Why isn't it a good idea?' Ewan wants to know, frustrated.

Elizabeth ignores him and walks away with Louise in tow. Ewan broods as they get into the car.

'Can you believe it?' he asks, outraged, directing the question at Martha.

'Can't believe it,' she lies, because there's no way she'd play netball if she were getting her hair done the morning of the game.

A block away from Dalhousie, Martha can see Rosie walking the dog, illuminated by the streetlight. For a couple of weeks, Rosie seemed to be out every second night and Martha figured a guy was on the scene. But apart from nightly walks with Bruno while Eugenia looks after the baby, she hasn't heard Rosie come in late for at least a week.

'Isn't that the girl who serves Dad tea at the nursing home?' Julia wants to know.

Ewan suddenly pulls over, rolls down the window and calls out, 'Rosie!'

'What are you doing?' Martha asks.

Rosie's shocked at first, scared. Then she seems to notice who it is and drags the dog to the car. When Bruno sees Martha, he slobbers all over the passenger side. Rosie glances into the car. Acknowledges Julia with an arrogant toss of her head.

'Can you play netball?' Ewan asks.

Martha's surprised by the question. Rosie doesn't seem to miss a beat, her eyes meeting Martha's with a sense of menace.

'Only if I get to be centre.'

To pay Rosie back, Martha plays *briscola* with Eugenia all night. Because cards and board games are one of the few things you can do with someone who doesn't understand a word you're saying. Last week, when Jimmy was in town, he joined in. Sometimes he'd show Toto the cards and Martha would see the ghost of a smile on Eugenia's usually hard face. The older woman plays with no mercy. Martha can imagine that she's done much in her life with the same mindset. Although it doesn't endear her to people, it earns her a grudging respect from the more formidable locals. Eugenia's most surprising relationship is with the very pious Signora De Lorenzo, who's never had a moment's time for Martha until Eugenia. Signora would have been critical of Seb getting married so soon after his wife's death. Martha, on the other hand, has always been slightly fascinated by the woman's routine. Cleans the church on Monday. Volunteers at the Ella Centre on Tuesday. Boards the Wests League Club bus on Wednesday for *tombola*. Looks after Jennifer and Steve's boys from number 132 on their date night every fortnight. Gets her hair done at Teresa's on Saturday morning in what Sophie and Martha would call the Lotte hair set. And then family over for lunch on Sunday. Martha's gathered too much evidence about the loneliness of the ageing population from her job over the years. She has to respect a woman who's created herself a community from what seems the mundane. Eugenia's recognised this and has used her time here well. Martha knows it's not about getting to know Signora De Lorenzo for the company. It's for the same reason Eugenia's come after Martha. To set up a support system for her grand-daughter and great-grandson once she's gone. Which means that Martha now gets to venture into the house that causes members of the Haberfield historical society's hearts to palpitate every time they walk past. Double storey. Blonde brick. Pillars. Concrete. But once inside, Martha doesn't give a shit about the tiles and wall-paper. The *crostoli* and *sfogliatelle* that have been denied to her all these years are now presented on plates with gold trim that remind her of Lotte's Bavarian tea set. Martha is so charmed, it causes her to tear up.

The same can be said about the women in the delis and IGA and pasticcerias. They've all become Eugenia's translators. The customer in line at Zanetti's tells Martha that Eugenia wants her to keep the pressure on Rosie to get a mammogram. Accompanied by the sign of the cross and a kiss of the fingers. In Lamonica's, Eugenia is trying to explain to Martha that she would like *scarpe*? To escape? Scampi?

'Skype,' the Italian girl behind the counter says, reminding Martha of a young Claudia Cardinale, because Martha's now watching 1960s romantic comedies as part of her pay TV obses-sion. 'La Signora Eugenia wants you to Skype her when she returns to Italy.'

At the pasticceria the owner listens intently to what Eugenia's saying. Sighs.

'*Che?*' Martha asks, hoping she's not channelling Manuel from *Fawlty Towers*.

'Eugenia says not to sell *la casa*.'

Martha should be shattered that the suburb knows her business. Secretly, she's now grateful for the couple of free cannoli she gets every time she pops in. And the fact that she's no longer referred to as *La Tedesca*, the German, amongst the older Italians, who forgave Seb for remarrying soon after Loredana's death, but not Martha.

The main problem is that Martha has no idea how to convince Rosie, especially after last week's meltdown at the mention of Loredana's death. Perhaps she'll go down the brutal path. The one along the lines of, 'If you don't go for a check-up with your history, you could be dead by the time your son's fourteen and Jimmy will marry some girl who'll be the world's worst stepmother.' Maybe a bit less brutal than that.

Tonight, when they've finished playing cards, Eugenia points to the coming Friday on the calendar. Scribbles in the flight number. Her way of telling them she's returning home. Martha wants to drag Eugenia down to Signora De Lorenzo's and ask her to beg Eugenia to stay. But Jimmy tells Martha that Eugenia can't stay. He found out through Rosie that Eugenia works at the local *tabaccheria* and needs to hold onto the job or she won't be able to pay the rent. Eugenia drinks a couple of short blacks as though they're whisky shots, and eyes Martha with that look she's become used to. One that Martha goes searching for because it's all empathy, but zero schmaltz.

'*Coraggio, Marta.*'

Because if anyone's privy to Martha's state of mind, it seems to be Eugenia. And maybe Jimmy as well. During these quiet tea-and-coffee-drinking, card-playing marathons at the breakfast bar while Toto hammers into the walls. Perhaps they've all walked that thin line of despair.

On Friday morning, when Eugenia leaves, Rosie bawls, trying to embrace her, but her grandmother isn't the type. The older woman just keeps on walking until she gets into the cab. It doesn't mean Eugenia feels less. Martha thinks it means that she feels more, but is worried about the dam that'll burst if she ever lets the emotion get the better of her.

At netball the next day, Martha embraces Scarlett and is introduced to Julia and Alana's children, Marley and Samuel, a wary pair, not particularly interested in another adult. But they're tight with Scarlett, the way six- and eight-year-olds can be. And impressed with Rosie's pair of wheels more than the baby inside.

'Can you push a pram?' Rosie asks all three.

They nod, slightly intimidated. She points out the perimeters.

'I want to see you at all times.'

'I'm going first,' Marley says.

'He does,' Rosie says, pointing to the painfully shy Samuel.

The trio take off with Toto and the pram.

'Lot of people,' Martha says, watching the kids and the pram. She's used to trawling newspapers for the worst stories about human nature and what can happen to kids.

'I'm watching them,' Elizabeth says, securing her daughter's hair back as though she's a twelve-year-old and not a medical student who'll be explaining stage-three cancer to a patient in a couple of years.

'Good to see you're contributing, Elizabeth,' Ewan tells her.

'Fuck off, Ewan.'

They lose, but the score is getting better than in previous weeks. Rosie gets into two shoving bouts with her opponent, but she's fast and competitive and proves to be great at multi-tasking, yelling out, 'Give him his dummy', to the kids, while intercepting a ball. She refuses to throw it to Martha, who's in the clear more than once, and it costs them a couple of opportunities.

They go to Papa's instead of the pub.

'We could have won that,' Julia says, coming back with gelatos for the kids.

'But you didn't,' Ewan says. 'So don't be happy with *could haves*.' He points to Rosie. 'And if you want to be part of this team, throw the ball to anyone who's in the clear.'

Everyone seems to agree with Ewan for once. Martha can't help feeling warmed by the support she's getting from a couple of past foes.

'Anyone?' Rosie asks. 'You mean your girlfriend.'

All of a sudden, their support for Martha is replaced by interest in whatever Rosie has to say. She eyes Martha. Enjoys what she's just stirred up.

'They had it off at a funeral.'

Martha hears a combination of gasps and laughs and snorts. Wouldn't mind slapping Rosie senseless.

'Please God, not Sister Mo's?' Sophie says. 'She cursed us enough in our lives.'

'Charlie P's funeral in the Hunter,' Julia says knowingly, looking over at Alana. 'You owe me twenty bucks, babe.'

'Big deal,' Elizabeth says. 'Who hasn't had it off with Ewan?'

'Gross,' her daughter mutters.

'I know, lovely. Mummy had low self-esteem in her teens.'

Sophie goes to speak. Martha knows that she'll refute the idea that she was one of those who slept with Ewan. Sophie's miraculously reinvented herself into the not-so-wild Sophie of her youth, but Elizabeth puts up a disdainful hand.

'Caves Beach. 1980. Our version of schoolies. The caravan. Don't deny it, Sophie.'

Martha wasn't invited to the 1980 bonding session. That would have been Julia's doing at the time. Not that Martha's parents would have let her go.

'I didn't sleep with Ewan,' Alana says. 'But I did pash him when I was thirteen. It's how I worked out I was a lesbian.'

Ewan takes any ridicule in his stride and Martha can't help laughing with the others. In her thirties, she lived with a man who didn't take well to anyone taking the piss. Almost to the verge of violence.

'It's true,' Alana says. 'I had the biggest crush on him and I thought that if Ewan Healy can't turn me on –'

'His sister can?' Martha asks.

'Well, we didn't work that out until our twenty-firsts.'

'When you've all finished laughing at my expense, can we talk about my game plan for next week?' Ewan says.

Martha's forgotten about Rosie, but she's watching them all with Toto on her lap making a mess with gelato.

Later that night, lying with Ewan in the back of the Hilux, Martha brings up his sister.

'Can you believe Alana and Julia made a bet about us?' she says.

'They bet on everything. The winnings go into the same account.'

She tries to get comfortable. 'Why do you think your sister left me out of everything in high school?'

'Does it matter? It was over thirty years ago.'

'I feel as if it still lingers.'

'She's stressed about Dad,' he says. 'She overstresses about the kids mostly. The courts are dragging this on and it's getting to both of them, but Julia has more time in the day to dwell on it. So I don't think she cares about whatever both of you clashed about back then.'

She leans her chin on his chest.

'Did she like the wives?'

He laughs. 'You make me sound like a Mormon.'

'How does someone decent end up with two broken marriages?'

He thinks for a moment.

'Shooting blanks killed the first marriage. Not having kids consumed her. It consumed us. She said it wouldn't, but it did, and when we worked out it was me and not her . . .' He shrugs. 'She's got four kids now and never seemed to look back. I don't know what killed the second marriage. Maybe the wrong decision in the first place.' He's contemplative. 'My biggest mistake was being introduced by someone in the League world, and thinking we had something in common.'

'Are you trying to tell me that the love of footy isn't enough to sustain a relationship?'

He laughs. 'What? You never met someone you thought you had everything in common with?'

'Yes, for the first twenty years of my dating life. And the moment I met someone I had nothing in common with, except for a dying loved one, he ended up being the one.'

'So I'm up against "the one"?' he asks, softly. Their eyes meet and she presses a kiss against his lips.

'The strangest thing I'm ever going to say to you is that I wish you got a chance to meet him.'

'Well, I can't say the same about my ex,' he says. 'And to answer your question, no. My sister and Alana didn't like the wives. They tolerated them. My father was heartbroken by the end of the first marriage. He loved Jeannie. Wasn't as fussed by the second.'

He links his fingers with hers. 'So are we going to move our sex life to your home anytime soon now that scary Eugenia's gone?' he asks.

'Her aura still lingers. Give me a couple more days.'

Martha feels the intensity of his stare.

'Is it his aura that still lingers?'

'Well, Seb did rebuild the house so he's part of every inch of the place,' she says.

It's not what he wants to hear, but she can't find the exact words to reassure him.

*

In her kitchen she makes herself a cup of tea. The house already feels a touch lonelier, and Martha wonders how Eugenia and the activity she brought down the stairs became part of her normal.

She hears a sound and looks up to see Rosie. Martha's at a loss about how to make things right before they sell this house and never see each other again. Because Rosie is a link to Martha's short and profound life with Seb. She feels a great sense of failure that there'll be nothing to take away except for money that may purchase her bricks and mortar, little else. Deep down, she wants to find a better way of telling Rosie that Loredana wasn't forgotten. There had been times, even after they were married, that Martha would come home early from work and hear Seb crying as he sanded the walls.

'When's that appointment?' Rosie asks.

Martha's confused for a moment. Wishes she was better prepared for this conversation. She fumbles for her phone and looks at the calendar.

'I made it for the fifteenth at two p.m.'

She's about to go into an explanation about why she didn't cancel it, but Rosie's already turned and walked away.

Martha imagines this is what progress looks like.

Chapter Twelve

He arrives at Central, same time as always. Figures he'll take a chance and just head out to Rosie's. Except today she's on platform twenty-three with Toto on her hip. At first Jimmy thinks it's one big coincidence and that Rosie's taking the train to the airport, but she's peering over everyone's heads and he knows they're waiting for him. Jimmy whacks everyone he passes with his duffel bag just to get to them.

'What are you doing here?' he asks, taking Toto from her, and his voice sounds croaky because Toto's chortling into his neck and at that exact moment Jimmy's never loved anyone so much in his life.

'Obviously waiting for you,' she says.

He wants to hug her too, but instead he hitches Toto up in one arm and his duffel in the other and they head out together.

'Do you want to get a bite to eat?' he asks. 'My shout.'

'Why not?'

*

They end up in a beer garden on Glebe Point Road where Jimmy goes off to find Toto a highchair. It's pretty crowded for a Monday night because of Trivia.

'You want a beer or something?' he asks. 'A Coopers?' Because it's what she drank the night he met her. Rosie nods and when he returns with the menu, she studies it and then puts it down.

'I'll have the wedges.'

'Naw. I'll do the ordering.' Jimmy doesn't want to come across as chauvinistic, but he thinks she's only picking the wedges because they're the cheapest on the menu.

When her steak and his pasta arrive she makes up a little plate for Toto and they take turns eating from each other's plates as if they've done it all their lives. Trivia's about to start and they're interrupted a couple of times by some of the diehards asking for the spare chairs at their table.

'Have you heard more from the paramedics?' she asks.

'Yeah, but it's taking them forever to get to the next step.'

Rosie gives Toto a taste of beetroot and he seems to like it.

'What about your plans?' he asks.

'I don't have an ATAR, but I can sit for a special tertiary admission test.' She shrugs. 'It's pretty competitive, but I'm tossing up between a Bachelor of Nursing and Bachelor of Midwifery.'

'You're smart,' he says. 'You'll get in.'

'I don't feel very smart at the moment.'

He thinks of the phone texts she was getting from some guy the last time he was in Sydney, and how dressed up she was for her date. Wonders if it's that guy who doesn't make her feel smart at the moment. Jimmy's never been one to beat around the bush, so he asks, 'Is it serious? The guy you're dating. Not to be nosy or anything, so if you don't want to talk about it, I'm totally fine. Although if you want to ask any questions about me, go ahead.'

'Have you told your girlfriend about Toto?'

He ignores half of what she says because Jimmy's already told Rosie that he doesn't have a girlfriend.

'All of my friends know Toto's my number one priority.'

Rosie studies him. Raises her eyebrows in a challenge, as if he's not telling the truth. She puts down her knife and fork.

'Your number one priority, is he?'

'He's my number one, two, three, four, five, and I could count to a hundred and he'd still be on the list,' Jimmy says.

A smile appears before she picks up her knife and fork again. 'His name is Lachlan,' she says, 'and he's really funny and smart and sweet, but a bit immature and useless.'

It's a strange description for Jimmy to process, but it brings him hope.

'No one seems to know how to do anything useful,' she says. 'Well, maybe you do.'

'Good to know that I'm the least useless person you know.'

'No, you're the most useful person I know.'

'Is there a big difference?'

'Big difference.'

Their eyes meet.

'Do you want to come back to the house?' she asks.

And because the only way Jimmy and Rosie know how to connect is by having sex, he spends his first night under the same roof as his son, and they need to be quiet because Toto is in the cot and Martha's downstairs and Rosie's shushing Jimmy the entire time because he's talking a hundred miles an hour. He can't stop. Because home's just had a whole new dimension added to it. Her and Toto and this house and a kitchen that smells of comfort food and a glimpse . . . a glimpse of how it can be, and she's straddling him and he's about to tell her that maybe in that top-one-hundred priority list Rosie's there, but she's just saying, 'Shut up, shut up,' and it's muttered into his neck as they shudder together.

And then life gets simple and complicated and back again. He learns to compartmentalise. Lies to Mackee, Tara and Frankie. Tells them he got into Sydney a day late. Lies to them again and says he has to look after Toto so he'll probably spend the night on Rosie's couch. On the nights he stays at Mackee and Tara's, he tells Rosie that he'll be working on the paramedics' application and it's all on Tara's computer. There's a voice in his head demanding to know why he's not telling the truth, and Jimmy figures it's because he's never had to balance people before. He's frightened that those he cares for won't like each other.

In his daytime world, life is more simple. Jimmy goes to swimming lessons with Rosie and Toto and she introduces him to friends with babies who are Toto's age. He likes that Rosie has these women looking out for her when he's away. One of them, Yolanda, comes from Moree, where Jimmy spent a couple of months back in 2008, so they end up knowing a few of the same people. On Wednesday night, he watches Rosie and Martha train for netball with a bunch of women who drink a lot of wine afterwards.

Has a conversation with the guy Martha's flirting with and it lasts five minutes. It's not that he doesn't like Ewan. It's that they have absolutely nothing in common. He gets an exchange of texts from Will on Thursday and he sends him a photo of Toto. *Too good-looking to be yours* is the response, and then a, *How's Frankie?* Jimmy goes for the truth and texts, *Missing you. Feeling underrated*, and despite it all Will's response makes him chuckle. *I didn't know you felt that way about me, Hailler.*

On Saturday, Mackee convinces him to bring Toto along to a birthday party at his aunt Georgie's house. The guy Georgie's married to has a son, Callum, from a previous relationship, who's turning ten, a wrestling fanatic and devotee of his step-cousins Tom and Anabel Mackee. They've set up a wrestling ring in the backyard and Anabel's wearing Viking horns while Mackee's got a pair of tights on, his jocks on the outside. They're both a comedy act waiting to be discovered, and when they put on a show, the roar of laughter from the kids is matched by the adults. Jimmy has never seen Tara crack up so much, her arm around Mackee's mum. He can't help thinking how some families break and can be put back together again. Others, like Jimmy's, cave. Four years ago the Mackees were a mess. Scattered across two states. Grief-stricken, angry at the world and at each other. What he's worked out about other people's families is that the lifeline can come from any direction. He figures that the key to it is a good foundation to begin with. The Haillers were doomed from the start. They didn't even have a grip on reality. Their lives were fuelled by alcohol and drugs and unemployment and failed relationships and bad luck and stupid decisions and a lack of faith in each other. His grand-pop lied about everything. One day he'd get a job. One day he'd stop gambling and drinking and smoking and flushing the pension down the toilet. Jimmy spent his childhood being sent into pubs or the TAB or down to the greyhound races. 'Tell him there's no fuck-ing food in the house,' Jimmy's mum would say. She, at least, was truthful about 'one day'. One day she was going to leave. One day she'd get out of this shithole of a family.

It was his nan who had made some sort of difference when she was alive. A martyr to the parish, volunteering to organise flowers for weddings, typing up the minutes, cleaning up the sacristy. The reward was that it got her grandson into St Sebastian's on a community scholarship. It's where Jimmy spent four years known as the school crazy guy until Frankie and the girls came along in Year Eleven, dragging Mackee in with them. Standing in Georgie's backyard, holding his son and watching the Mackee lunacy, Jimmy wants to believe he can be like all of them. A lifeline to himself, so he can be one for Toto and Rosie.

Mackee joins him with a plate of assorted God-awful kids' party food. He holds a devilled egg up to Toto. 'No? Are you sure?'

'He's more than sure,' Jimmy says with laugh, putting Toto down because he's beginning to squirm.

Mackee introduces Jimmy to a whole lot of people whose names he won't remember, but they seem to know about him. Either because Jimmy had helped out the Finch-Mackees in Walgett, or because they're somehow connected to Martha, of all people.

'Abe's sister is friends with her,' a woman called Lucia tells him, pointing to her partner who he figures is Abe. 'Alana? They're in the same netball team.'

'The school principal?' Jimmy says, pleased he remembers being introduced to Alana earlier that day at the game.

'Anabel reckons she spotted you there this morning,' Mackee says.

'Just babysitting Toto while his mum plays,' Jimmy says. 'Vicious, vicious game.'

'I'll join you next time.'

Toto stumbles and falls and Mackee's father, Dom, picks him up.

'I was younger than you when we had Tommy,' Dom tells Jimmy. 'I miss them at this age.'

'Any advice?' Jimmy asks, because someone like Dom Mackee had seen the dark side, but managed to get his family back.

'Yes,' Dom says. 'Don't be scared to ask for help.'

That night he goes out with Rosie. Ewan is at the house and Jimmy attempts small talk in the kitchen.

'It's sort of our first date so I wanted to put thought into it,' he explains, after telling Ewan that they're going to the drag races up at Eastern Creek.

'Your first date?'

At the netball, Martha had introduced Jimmy as Toto's father so the first date thing doesn't seem to make sense to Ewan.

Rosie has organised for the Italian woman across the road to look after Toto. He figures from the body language that Signora and Rosie have attitude between them, but the woman seems to love Toto, so it's an easy handover.

'She's a bitch,' Rosie says as they walk up to the bus stop.

'Then why are you leaving him with her?'

'Because she'll never let anything happen to him.'

At the speedway, they eat hot dogs and chips and Rosie talks about adrenaline and noise, and how sometimes it's just Toto's crying, or the feeling that there's no one around that gets to her. She looks sad when she says that, and he senses it's about missing people, so he asks about her father and Rosie tells Jimmy that he used to fix racing cars and most of their Friday nights were spent at the speedway.

'I'm sorting through my photos with Teresa next door, so once I'm finished, I'll introduce you to my family,' she says.

When they go to pick up Toto, Signora sends them away because he's sleeping, so Rosie lets Jimmy stay again. Later, she's lying on him and he feels like he's under inspection.

'I don't even know how to describe you,' she says, grabbing at his face, pinching at his cheek, checking out his hairline. 'What colour are your eyes?'

'Murky grey. And my hair is murky brown and my skin's pasty white.'

She places her head on his chest and stays there and Jimmy knows he loves her. Is frightened to say it because he's scared the words will come out lame. Knows there's a cruel side to Rosie who'll react badly because she doesn't know how to trust anymore.

'We don't even have a photo of us dating to show Toto one day,' she says. 'Everyone else does. Just a little glimpse of us together so we can say, "This is who we were before you came along."'

'Is that important?' he asks.

'My favourite photos of my mum and dad are those from before I was born. Because they were so into each other and I can see this love in her eyes that says, I trust this guy to fucking bits.'

*

After dinner at Frankie's the next night, Mia and Bob Spinelli take Toto for a walk while Jimmy works on the next phase of the paramedics application with Frankie.

'The good behaviour bond won't go down well,' he says. He's sitting on her bed studying her walls as if seeing them for the first time. Loads and loads of photos. She must be the only person left alive who still gets them printed. He thinks of Rosie working with her next-door neighbour to get the family photos organised. Jimmy has none. A few on his phone of Toto. One or two of these guys when they were in high school.

Frankie is reading the criteria and shakes her head. 'I disagree about the good behaviour bond. They'll want good character references and they'll want to know how you feel about the charges, but there's nothing here that says they'll discriminate.'

'Can you copy some of those photos of us at school?' he says.

She looks to where he's pointing and there's a soft smile on her face. 'I remember in Year Eleven when it was just the six of us,' she says, wistfully. 'We were sort of losers who found each other. I miss that a bit. I love every one of my friends now, but I miss us. I feel as if Siobhan is never going to live in Australia again and I wish Justine was here, and I even miss the double Ts. They just know so many other people and I don't get to see them as much as I want to.'

'They say the same thing about you and Will.'

It's Will who dominates Frankie's photos. Jimmy thinks of what Rosie said earlier and knows there's enough evidence on these walls to say that Frankie trusts this guy to fucking bits.

'How do you get eight years together to work?' he asks.

She thinks for a moment.

'We let each other keep our own friends,' she says. 'We respect each other's families. We have the same values. We want the same things. We're best friends. We don't get turned on by fights or drama.'

'You need to be over there, mate,' he says, because he knows how much Frankie misses Will. 'You know that. You promised him.'

'Do you want to know a secret?' she asks. 'I could live with my parents for the rest of my life.'

'That's not a big secret, Frankie,' he says. 'I could live with your parents for the rest of my life. I haven't even questioned where they've taken Toto.'

She holds up a red plastic folder from one of the trays on her desk. 'ANU has an exchange program with the University of Milan so I'm thinking of working on my PhD over there,' she says.

Jimmy spins the globe on her desk. Studies the proximity and points.

'You can have a dirty weekend in Liechtenstein whenever you want. It looks halfway between Milan and Stuttgart.'

She takes a ragged breath and Jimmy thinks she's going to cry.

'I'm not angry because Will stopped asking me to marry him, you know. As if he has to. I'm angry because he stopped asking what I want to do with my life.'

When he leaves, Mia helps rug up Toto for the bus ride home, and because he asked Dom Mackee for advice he asks her the same. She hugs them both.

'Guilt is a burden, so forgive yourself for the mistakes.'

*

Jimmy and Rosie sit together on the bus to Central with Toto on his lap. He can sense her looking at him and when his eyes meet hers, Jimmy feels tenderness beyond anything. He's never used that word in his head to describe the longing for anyone in his life. Not even with Frankie, because maybe tenderness belongs to lovers or kids, not necessarily your own. He can see a resigned sadness in Rosie's expression and he figures they both want whatever this is between them, but it's not as easy with Toto in the picture. Yet unfathomable without him there.

At Central he kisses her, hugs Toto and walks away. But she follows him up to the gates.

'Can you tell whoever you're sleeping with that it's over?' she asks. 'Even if it doesn't seem anything special.'

'Why?' he says with false bravado. Because he wants to hear the truth about how she feels.

'You're sort of like an ID thing,' she says. 'Twenty points for usefulness, twenty points for being good in bed, twenty points for being decent, and you get triple bonus points because Toto's your top-one-hundred priority.'

He moves closer to her. Kisses her again. Can't stop, despite Toto trying to pull his hair.

'Can you shave off points from usefulness and decency and give me extra for being good in bed?'

She laughs, but there's a shrewd challenge in her eyes. 'It would have to come out of your Toto triple-bonus points.'

'Thanks, but no thanks,' he says, not missing a beat. 'I think I'll hang on to those bonus points.'

Chapter Thirteen

Rosie spends every afternoon next door at Teresa's, going through the photos she took back from Luke's garage while Bianca babysits Toto and the dogs out back. Teresa and Signora De Lorenzo are the only two who know where to place most of them chronologically in an album. When Rosie looks at the images scattered across the table, she can't help thinking that the life of the Gennaros is reduced to a size eight Hush Puppies shoebox.

Teresa slides a photo towards her.

'It's a beautiful one, regardless of where it was taken, Rosanna,' she says quietly.

Rosie glances at it, pushes it away and concentrates on one where she's sitting on the bonnet of her mum's car when she was about eight years old. She shows it to Teresa.

'Sometimes she'd turn up at school and I'd have to interpret for her,' Rosie says. 'She'd make me tell my teacher that I had to leave early because we had an appointment, but it was bullshit really. She just wanted to go for a drive.'

'She was a cool one, your mother. Most of us would have gone crazy living in that house the way it was for years, but Loredana never seemed fazed. That shrug of hers said it all.'

'Did people think my dad was a loser for taking so long?'

'No. Some said he should have sold it when he was getting the offers, because he could have made a profit.'

'My father would never have sold.'

Rosie knows that there were years the house stayed untouched because they didn't have a cent.

'And then when Loredana got sick, he just didn't have the heart to work on it.'

The coffee's ready and Teresa gets up to turn off the stove.

'The council and the historical society would be on his back, because they said it looked like a hoarder's house with all the material out front.'

'Yeah, well, look at it now. It's amazing.'

'That house has been built by many hands, *bella*.'

Rosie doesn't want to bring Martha into this discussion.

'For my mum and me and Nonna Eugenia.'

Teresa doesn't respond.

'It's what he used to say all the time, isn't it?' Rosie demands, because she wants the vindication from someone who heard those words.

Teresa stares at a photo of the house, its front lawn packed with rubbish and building material. A skip forever out front.

'*È una casa per la mia famiglia,*' Seb would say. 'A house for my family.'

*

She takes Toto to swimming lessons with Tess and Yolanda, who suggest the three of them join a basketball team.

'The comp doesn't start for a couple of months, so we've got time to get fit.'

'I haven't played for years,' Tess says. 'If it's during the day and they have a creche, I'm in.'

Rosie likes the idea of being in a team with them. Although she knows they're not going to bail on her, deep down she'd like to hang out with them more.

'I know someone who can get us fit,' she tells them, although she doesn't mention Ewan Healy's name because they might not rate a guy who got sacked from being a coach. 'If you guys are free Wednesday nights he trains a netball team down at Nield Park.'

Out of all the visitors at the nursing home, she sees the Healys most. Rosie shouldn't have favourites, but John Healy goes from long periods of silence to bursts of conversation and reminds her of Jimmy.

'It was a knock on for sure,' he tells her while she's serving him lunch. 'And that idiot ref Frank Crombie needs a bloody pair of glasses because anyone can see.'

Rosie thinks it's a sad sort of peculiar that someone can't remember the people he loves, but can recall every single detail of a game that took place almost forty years ago. When she returns with afternoon tea, Julia Healy is there with her daughter Marley who looked after Toto at the netball that one time. Julia takes a longneck bottle of beer out of her backpack and opens it, pouring a glass for her dad.

'That's not his tee-shirt,' she says to Rosie. 'Can you tell the nurses to stop dressing him in other people's clothes?'

'You should tell them.'

On the mantelpiece there's an old black-and-white wedding photo and Rosie suspects it's John and his wife because he looks exactly like Ewan.

'Where's your mum?' Rosie asks Julia, who is now sorting her father's clothes and chucking on the ground anything that doesn't belong to him.

'She died when Ewan and I were babies.'

'Are you twins?'

'No, but we were born in the same year.'

Marley is sitting outside on the verandah playing chess with John. Julia catches Rosie looking at them.

'He was Pop John from the moment our kids came to live with us,' she says. 'It's as if their hearts had met and the moment they came face to face, Marley and Samuel belonged to him.'

Julia Healy is about to cry, which is strange because she seems the type who makes other people cry. Rosie looks at Marley and John Healy instead, sad that Toto won't ever have that relationship with her father, or Jimmy's crap parents.

'How did he look after you?' Rosie asks. 'Two babies in the old days?'

'I don't appreciate the "old days" comment,' Julia says, and she's not joking either. 'They wanted to put us into St Joseph's Home at Croydon, but the Charbels moved in next door. Leila, Alana's mum, took over. We were sort of raised with all of them.'

'Were you always in love with Alana?'

Julia eyes her. 'You're chatty today.'

'Just asking.'

'Alana was Ewan's best friend. They were inseparable because they loved sport. I was the third wheel when we were at school.'

One of the registered nurses pokes her head in, and then keeps on walking because Julia is the Healy most of the staff try to avoid. Julia goes after her anyway. A moment later, Marley comes back inside wanting to know where her mum is.

'Hassling the nurses,' Rosie says, grabbing the fresh sheets from a cupboard. 'Come and help me.'

'Who's looking after your baby?' Marley asks, starting on the pillowcases.

'The lady across the road from where I live.'

'Just say she hurts him.'

'She won't hurt him.'

'How do you know that?' Marley demands to know.

'Because I trust her.'

Ewan arrives just as his sister and niece are leaving. He flicks Marley on the brow with a finger, and she laughs, doing it back to him. Julia orders her brother to tell the registered nurses that she wants John's medication reduced. 'They're turning him into a zombie, Ewan.'

'Give this place a chance, Jules.'

When the others are gone Rosie asks him about training.

'How many?' he asks.

'Three of us.'

'Because I'm not interested in adding another couple of chatty Cathys to the mix.'

'What's a chatty Cathy?'

'I'm just saying.'

He tests the heat of the mug and puts it into his dad's hands.

'And you'll have to find someone to look after Toto because I don't want kids and babies at training.'

'It's not *Toetoe*,' she says, mimicking the way he says it.

'Don't tell someone named Ewan how to pronounce names,' he says. 'I've spent a lifetime correcting people.'

Rosie understands Ewan's irritation, because at training on Wednesday night Martha and the women are annoying and talk too much. Later, they go down to the pub and Rosie sits with Yolanda and Tess at the end of the table. Louise sits with them. She's Elizabeth's daughter and twice Rosie has seen her turn up and not get involved.

'They're always this loud,' Louise tells them.

'I'm embarrassed to be around them,' Rosie says.

Tess leans close to her. 'Does the coach and your stepmother have a thing going on?'

Rosie glances over to where Ewan is laughing at something Martha's said.

'He's apparently slept with most of them,' Louise tells them. She delivers everything in the same tone. Rosie hasn't worked her out yet.

'Why don't you like Martha?' Yolanda asks. 'I think she's cool.'

'She stole my house,' Rosie tells them. 'You don't know how it feels to –'

Yolanda puts up a hand to stop her. 'Don't go there.'

Rosie counts to ten because she doesn't want to go around sounding insensitive or racist.

'What else don't you like about her?' Tess asks.

'Isn't that enough?'

'My stepmother's a cow,' Yolanda says. 'Don't get me started.'

'So now we're going to have a competition about whose step-mother is the worst?' Rosie asks.

'I'd win, Rosie.'

Louise is looking from one to the other.

'I haven't worked out whether you're friends or not,' Louise says.

'We're friends with different versions of evil stepmothers,' Yolanda says.

Later, when they're leaving, Rosie tells them she won't be at Learn to Swim.

'I'm going for a check-up.' The others are eyeing her. 'A mammogram.'

'Why?' Tess asks.

'Just to work out if I have that breast cancer gene that runs in my family.'

'The BRCA gene,' Louise tells them. 'Everyone has it, but some have a mutant one.'

'Does that mean you have cancer?' Yolanda asks.

Rosie shakes her head, but looks at Louise who seems to have all the answers.

'If it's the mutant gene she has a higher chance of getting it,' Louise says, bluntly.

That stops conversation for a moment.

'I'll come with you?' Yolanda says.

Rosie shakes her head. 'Martha's taking me.'

'That's pretty evil of her.'

*

Parramatta Road is a car park the next morning as they drive to the Strathfield Breast Clinic. Four lanes of traffic and they're stuck in the one that's about to turn onto the M4, when that's the last thing they want to do.

'This city is a joke,' Martha mutters, beeping her horn and trying to get into the left lane for the third time.

'Are you a mutant?' Rosie asks, doing her bit and sticking her hand out the window to stop the car coming up beside them. Martha squeezes into the lane and gives the obligatory wave of thanks.

'Yes, I am,' she says.

'Does it frighten you?'

Martha doesn't answer for a moment.

'I have a mammogram twice a year and a scan once a year. I get very nervous around that time, but I tell myself that, even if they find something, they'll catch it in time because I'm checked regularly.'

'What do you think you'll do if they . . . find something?'

'I know exactly what I'd do,' Martha says. 'Without a doubt.'

'Is that why you haven't committed to Ewan?'

Martha turns to her, stunned. A car beeps behind them because she's driving too slow. Martha gives them the finger, without looking away from Rosie. 'Why would you say that?'

'What's stopping you from going out properly? It's not as if you're both too young to date. Have you told him?'

'There's nothing to tell.'

'It's pretty obvious to me that you don't want to commit to him because you're worried –'

'That's none of your business, Rosie!'

It ends any conversation until they turn off Parramatta Road.

'There's a chance you might not have the mutant gene,' Martha says, as if the subject of Ewan never came up. 'It skipped Eugenia.'

'My nonna's got nine lives, regardless of how fucked they all are.'

Rosie misses Eugenia. She misses the buzz of nights in the kitchen, and belonging to someone. Without Eugenia around, she has to try harder to connect.

'Your father never had a bad word to say about her,' Martha says. 'Despite him being furious when you went to Palermo to live with her.'

Rosie can't bear to think of that time. Not only because of the betrayal of her father marrying Martha, but because she wants that year back. She wants every one of those days, every hour and minute, so she can build up more memories with her father. Because the photos in the shoebox aren't enough to tell the story of their lives.

'When I turned up on her doorstep that time, Eugenia slapped me so hard across the face that she split my lip.'

Rosie doesn't know why she admits that to Martha, who takes her eyes off the road for a moment.

'She wanted you out of there?'

Rosie nods. 'I remember walking past one of the bars in San Filippo Neri and this man made a gesture like he was going to cut my throat. I thought my father had got up to no good when he was younger, but I think it was Eugenia. There were heaps of rumours about her.'

'Such as?'

Rosie can't forget the sickness in her stomach when she first heard the worst of the stories. Doesn't know whether she wants to tell Martha, and then can't find a reason why not.

'That Eugenia was raped by more than one man and that's how my mum came about.'

'Christ! Who told you that?'

'Just these dickheads I used to hang out with over there. They heard it from their fathers and uncles. That Eugenia deserved it.'

She glances over at Martha. 'I smashed one of them in the face for saying that, you know. He cried worse than Toto ever has.'

'Good for you.'

'When my parents met, Eugenia gave my father a wad of money and told him to take her daughter away. He didn't know where she got it from, and my mother told him not to ask.'

'You reckon that's what he used to buy the house?'

Rosie nods. She doesn't want to say the obvious. That if it wasn't for Eugenia, Martha wouldn't have a home.

'Then if she knows these lowlifes, what's kept her safe?' Martha asked.

Rosie shrugs. 'She says that when you get old, men stop looking at you, but they also stop wanting to kill you.'

'I have a feeling that men haven't stopped looking at Eugenia.'

The mammogram is the weirdest thing Rosie's ever had done to her boobs. Like some sort of crazy sandwich press, except it's cold and it pinches. After that, she sees the breast specialist, who asks her to remove her tee-shirt again. Her kindness makes Rosie feel safe. She thinks of Jimmy. Another one of the kind ones. Such an underrated word. Rosie wishes she had gone searching for that quality in people when she was younger.

'Do you know who your mum's breast doctor was, lovely?'

Rosie shakes her head. 'Martha might know,' she says.

The doctor asks her a whole heap of questions while she's feeling Rosie's boobs and then gets her to sit up.

'All good.'

And then she tells Rosie that nothing's come up in the mammogram, but it's best for her to have the test to see if she's got the BRCA mutant gene.

'My friend says it's expensive.' Last night, Louise had said it was.

'You don't have to worry about paying for it, lovely. It's offered to people under fifty with a family history.'

'What if it comes back positive?' Rosie asks.

'Having the mutant gene doesn't mean you have cancer.'

'But it'll mean I've got a higher chance of getting it.'

'How about you don't worry about any of that now? First work out if you want to have the test, and we'll take it from there.'

After that, Martha drives Rosie down to Westfield and announces that she's going to buy her a dress.

'Why?'

'Because I didn't get to buy you an eighteenth or twenty-first birthday dress.'

'What's such a big deal about an eighteenth and a twenty-first?'

'In my day it was a big deal. On your eighteenth, you had your first drink. On your twenty-first, you wrote yourself off. Coming-of-age stuff.'

'I did that when I was fifteen.'

They end up in David Jones. 'Go on, choose something fancy,' Martha says. 'You can wear it next time you're go-karting with Jimmy.'

Sometimes Rosie wants to laugh at what Martha says, but doesn't want to give her the satisfaction. She doesn't want to ever let Martha know that there are things around the house that bring Rosie comfort. Like the porcelain figurine in the kitchen of the little boy in the apple tree. Or the cuckoo clock in the front room that always makes Toto chuckle. She finds a couple of things she likes and heads to the dressing rooms.

'Too short?' she asks. It's lace with a tight bodice and skinny straps.

'You're not going to have that body forever, Rosie, so flaunt it as much as you can for as many years as you can.'

Rosie does the rounds the next day with the teacart and finds Ewan in his father's room setting up a big flat-screen TV. There are more photos in the room, as though Ewan and Julia are coming to terms with the fact that John's not going home again. Alana's mother turns up. She's been around once or twice and calls Rosie, '*habibi*'.

'Let's go for a walk, John,' Leila says, an accent in her voice because she was born in Lebanon. Rosie remembers Julia saying that Leila had helped raise John's children so it must feel like double family if their daughters are partners.

'Your father must have never got over your mum,' she says to Ewan, looking at the old wedding photo.

'I don't know, because he never spoke about it.'

'My father forgot about my mother. Eleven months after she died.'

Ewan looks up from scanning the TV. 'It doesn't work that way, Rosie. I don't think people forget a person they loved just because someone else comes along.'

'No offence, but you're twice divorced. You're not exactly a pin-up boy for everlasting love.'

He chuckles. 'True. But I think I'm in love with a woman who still loves the man she was married to.'

Rosie wonders if Ewan's told Martha any of this.

'Martha hasn't forgotten your father,' he says. 'And I can't imagine him forgetting your mum. I'm sure Martha had to cope with her ghost in the same way I have to deal with Seb's.'

There's a grimace.

'And he's a bloody big ghost. As big as that house.'

Rosie knows that there's more than her father holding Martha back.

'Well, the house is going to be out of your way soon,' Rosie says.

'Like I've said to Martha, that might not be a bad thing.'

When Toto and Jimmy are both sleeping that night, Rosie hears Martha in the kitchen and she ventures down with a photo. There are times at night when Rosie would like to sit in the kitchen like she used to when Eugenia was here, but it's an unspoken rule that it's Martha's territory after eight p.m. Martha's studying her computer screen, maybe checking out jobs because Rosie heard her mention it to Ewan.

'I thought you might want this,' Rosie says, sliding over the photograph. She couldn't bear to look at it the other day at Teresa's. But when she finally did in the confines of her room she had to agree that it's pretty beautiful. Martha stares at it, her mouth trembling, so Rosie walks away, because she doesn't want to think of Martha being that human.

*

In the morning, when she goes to leave the house to drop off Toto at Signora's, she sees the photo on the sideboard, next to the porcelain figurines. Rosie and Martha's mums, in the cancer ward at the RPA, with their heads bare, laughter in their eyes. Taken by her father, no doubt, or maybe that lovely woman who used to cheer everyone up at chemo. Rosie can imagine that some of those patients are gone. Others, she hopes, have been seven years cancer-free. Her father used to say that cancer isn't racist, or ageist, and it's not homophobic. It lets anyone in. An equal opportunity club. She studies the photo because Rosie's obsession with wanting to connect with her mum has grown ever since she had Toto. She sees her father in Toto all the time, especially his eyes and the colour of his skin. She gets a sense of Sebastiano Gennaro, in the house, in the neighbourhood. Everywhere. But she can't find enough to bring Loredana back. Rosie had thought the photos would work magic. But once again, her mother only comes in fragments. And Rosie owes Toto more than pieces of their lives.

Chapter Fourteen

Martha wakes to Lotte telling her not to respond to text messages. Which is ridiculous really, because Martha's mother wouldn't have known what a text message was back then. Lotte still had one of those telephones that required the force of a finger. But the voice that wakes her is clear and emphatic. So when the message comes from the real estate agent advising that a response is needed urgently if Dalhousie Street is going to make the spring market, Martha ignores it.

That day, the netball team win their first game by one point. In her humble opinion it's a clear example of brilliant teamwork, although most of the opposing players are in their thirties. She finds them the least competitive demographic because they haven't hit the desperation of wanting to be fit in their forties, or fabulous in their fifties. They're more like the 'fuck off, we're in our thirties' lot.

'Why don't we go to the pub and celebrate?' Martha suggests, avoiding the three text messages on her phone.

'You go to the pub and celebrate when you lose,' Rosie says. 'What's the difference?'

'You don't have to come.'

They're at Briars in Concord because they have the kids with them and Sophie's the expert on kid-friendly beer gardens in the inner west. Ewan's writing out next week's game plan on a napkin, as if any of them give a shit.

'Let's just live in the moment, Ewan,' Martha says, taking the napkin and neatly folding it.

She tells them about Lotte's instruction this morning.

'You do know it's your subconscious desire instructing you,' Julia says.

'What a thing to say,' Sophie says. 'Of course, it's her mother.'

'Really, Sophie,' Elizabeth challenges. 'I'm going to put this all down to ethnic superstition.'

'That's a generalisation,' Julia says. 'Alana's not into ethnic super-stition and she's a Leb.'

Alana nods in agreement. When Julia goes to break up an argument between the kids just as Elizabeth's phone rings, Alana leans in close to Martha. 'Of course it's your mother.'

It's only Elizabeth's tone in her phone conversation that stops Martha from wanting more analysis.

'Where are you?' Elizabeth asks, and then there's a whole lot of, 'It's all right. You're fine. Just turn off the ignition,' which renders everyone at the table silent. When Alana clicks her fingers for her attention, Elizabeth mouths, '*Louise*', and they wait to see what it all means. Elizabeth doesn't look distressed, but resigned. Sad, really. She questions how and what *Lou-Lou*'s feeling and Martha hears Rosie clicking with frustration beside her.

'Let me try,' Rosie says, giving Toto to Scarlett and holding her hand out for the phone. For once, Elizabeth does as she's told.

'Panic attacks,' she tells them, grabbing her bag. 'She's pulled over on the City West Link.'

'I'll go,' Ewan says. 'You're over the limit anyway, Elizabeth.'

Elizabeth waves away his offer, but the others convince her to stay. Rosie's still on the phone, walking away as if she's some counselling expert.

Elizabeth gives Ewan a couple of details and he heads off. She's still watching Rosie, who doesn't seem fazed by the conversation she's having.

'When did they bond?' Elizabeth asks.

'The southern end of the table bitch about us all the time, especially when the basketballers join us,' Sophie says.

Elizabeth rubs her eyes. Martha doesn't know whether it's from exhaustion or whether she's hiding tears, because her expression never changes.

'How long has Louise had these attacks?' Alana asks.

'Beginning of the year. A lot of anxiety to start with. It came out of the blue and it's just crippled her.'

'Oh, Elizabeth.'

'I spent a fortnight delivering her to the exam hall and sitting in the car park at Sydney uni last month. She doesn't want to lose her scholarship, but I've had to move her back home.'

'Why didn't you tell us, you goose?' Sophie says.

'And what can you do about it?'

'Nothing, but we could hear you out.'

Elizabeth waves them off. 'It's all I talk about. To psychologists, naturopaths, GPs. Sometimes I just want to talk shit and forget about it.'

About twenty minutes later, Rosie returns with the phone. 'Ewan's there. He said your other daughter's arrived and he's following them home.'

Rosie takes Toto from Scarlett and sits down to her cold French fries.

'What did you say to her?' Elizabeth asks.

Rosie shrugs. 'I just told her about the netball game and how you guys went berserk when you won. By a point.'

'Oh, come on, Rosie,' Alana says. 'We were fantastic.'

Rosie ignores everyone agreeing with Alana and concentrates on Elizabeth.

'When these attacks happen, Louise doesn't want to talk about how she's feeling,' Rosie says. 'She wants the stress in her head to pass, and the only way that happens is if she keeps preoccupied.'

Elizabeth is nodding, taking it all in.

'So next time just talk about banal stuff,' Rosie continues. 'Like your lives.'

'When did you turn into Obi-Wan Kenobi?' Martha asks.

'It's Yoda to you, Martha.'

Elizabeth stands up, grabbing her purse. There's protest from all around.

'Stay, Elizabeth!'

'Ewan's got it under control!'

'Chill,' Elizabeth says. 'I'm just getting Yoda some hot chips.'

When she returns they discuss it more.

'I think Lou-Lou regrets not taking a gap year from being the best at everything,' Elizabeth says.

'She's too young to have regrets,' Julia says. 'Tell her to buy a backpack and head overseas.'

'I regret not doing that,' Alana says. 'Back in the eighties, all my teaching friends ended up in London.'

And that gets them talking about regrets, which Rosie says is her cue for telling them she'd rather take the bus home than listen to them a minute longer.

'Off you go, then,' Martha says.

The others watch Rosie walk away with Toto.

'I'm sorry, but I just can't help liking her,' Julia says, laughing. 'She's great with Dad.'

And was such a shit to her own, Martha wants to say. But she doesn't, because she has to take some of the blame.

'What's your regret, babe?' Alana asks Julia.

'Keeping you waiting until I had the guts to come out.'

'How long?' Sophie asks.

'Long enough to go out with a guy and get engaged.'

'We love him,' Alana says. 'He's been our financial adviser for years.'

'Your turn, Martha.'

Martha's regrets are too many, but she concentrates on the one that wakes her every morning.

'I regret not taking my mother to Oberammergau,' she says. 'My father refused to go back all their lives, and then, after he died,

I was too busy working. Next minute she had cancer and was dead within a year.'

Sophie looks like she's going to cry because she loved Lotte and was inconsolable when she died.

'Oh and I regret losing my virginity to the guy behind the bar at Jacksons on George,' Martha adds.

'I begged you not to order that fourth Kahlúa and coke,' Sophie tells her, opening up a bag of crisps for the kids and sending them to the next table. 'I regret spending four years married to a dick,' she whispers when Scarlett's out of earshot.

'Big dick,' Martha agrees, because she couldn't stand Sophie's first husband.

'He had a big dick or he was a big dick?' Elizabeth asks.

'Definitely the latter,' Sophie says. 'But I was determined not to marry a Greek guy. So I regret not listening to my cousin Ariadne who kept on telling me about her accountant. I didn't get to meet George for another fifteen years.'

'And has St George, hero of the Peloponnesus, got a big dick?'

'Shush, Elizabeth!'

Elizabeth pours herself another glass of wine. 'Well, I'm sure you all know what mine is,' she says, and Martha figures they'll finally discover the truth about the disappearing husband.

'Obviously that perm I got for the Year Twelve formal.'

'That's probably why Ewan dumped you,' Alana says, just as he walks back in, oblivious to what they've been discussing.

'What about you?' Alana asks him. 'Do you regret doing the Men of League calendar and showing off that hairy chest?'

'I regret agreeing to coach you lunatics.'

*

224

Martha keeps herself busy that week. Sophie's helping George out at the office because his receptionist is off sick, so Martha picks up Scarlett every afternoon and takes her back to the house until Sophie comes to collect her. Elizabeth's off to a buyers' conference in Brisbane on Wednesday, so she takes her to the airport.

'What time does your plane get in?' Martha asks, when she pulls up in front of the terminal.

'Don't be ridiculous, Martha. You're not picking me up during peak hour.'

'Course I am. The taxi line will take ages.'

She decides to do a St John's Ambulance course with Julia, who needs to be up-to-date because of the adoption application. Later, they go down to Papa's for a coffee.

'Every time I do one of these courses I sort of wish someone will have a heart attack near me so I can put them in the recovery position.'

Julia laughs. 'You're an idiot.'

Their cannoli arrive along with a little box of Italian pastries for Julia's father.

'How much longer is this adoption going to take?' Martha asks.

'We stopped playing with numbers about five years ago,' Julia says. 'But we're no longer in the Children's Court, so that's a relief. Hopefully we'll get a date for the Supreme Court and we'll be a tiny step closer.'

She's drained. Martha doesn't know anyone coming out of the Children's Court who isn't.

She soon finds herself under Julia's scrutiny.

'But let's talk about you.'

'Nothing to talk about. I'll be back at work by October.'

'And the house? Because no disrespect to your mother, but you can't be taking real estate advice from the dead, Martha.'

'Not true. I've been watching this *Medium* show on the Entertainment Channel and it's exactly what she does.'

Julia is still studying her.

'I like seeing my brother happy.'

Martha doesn't want to speak about Ewan. Because last week when she drove Rosie to the breast clinic, it reminded her that, back in February, she had almost worked out exactly what she was going to do about the family's history with breast cancer. And then Charlie's funeral happened and she met Ewan.

'When he came back from Charlie P's funeral there was something different about him,' Julia says. 'The sacking had turned him into a hermit and all of a sudden he came back to life.'

She smiles and it softens her. Martha has only seen the side of Julia stressed by her children's legal status and her father's Alzheimer's.

'Back then, Alana and I found him going through my old photo albums. He pointed to one of us back in Year Twelve and asked, "Is that Martha Newman?" I've driven Alana crazy ever since.'

'So a bit of a coincidence that Sister Mo wanted me at her funeral?' Martha says.

'Sister Mo didn't give a rat's arse about any of us except Elizabeth.'

'Not even Sophie?'

'Sophie was "that Greek Orthodox girl",' Julia says, mimicking Sister Mo's Irish brogue. 'I was the motherless one.'

'Who was I?'

Julia grimaces. 'She didn't remember you. Martha who?'

'I knew it. What a cow.'

Julia shrugs. 'I just want my brother to be happy, so Sister Mo's funeral seemed a good opportunity to get in contact with you.'

'If I had been forced to do a liturgical dance because of a lie, I'd have to kill someone.'

They finish their coffee and sweets and Martha walks Julia to the car.

'What did we fight about at school?' Martha asks. 'I can't remember, but it had to have started in First Form because there was never a time you weren't mean to me. And I feel as if I hadn't forgiven you all these years, when I should have, because it all seems so petty now.'

Julia laughs with disbelief. Goes to speak, but changes her mind.

'No, say it,' Martha says.

Julia hesitates.

'You were the first person to call me a dyke, Martha,' she finally says. 'We were thirteen and you must have suspected. Maybe at the same time I was figuring it out.'

Martha feels as if something hard has been slammed into her chest.

'And I have forgiven how you made me feel. But I've never forgotten. Because I'm reminded every once in a while.'

'So you've thought I was homophobic all these years,' Martha asks.

'God, no. I just thought you were a bitch.' Julia shrugs. 'But back then . . . that word made me frightened of everything I felt.'

Martha wants to remember saying it, so she can take it back, but Julia's already moved on to another conversation.

*

She goes to get a haircut, but her regular hairdresser isn't there. Martha gets advice she doesn't need from the guy who's tugging at her hair with a grimace.

'I don't get my hair cut often, so just a tidy up,' she says.

'Mm, it's not really age appropriate, is it?' he asks.

'I'm more into the European model of longer hair at any age.'

'It's all rather schoolgirl.'

Martha wants to point out that what Michelle Pfeiffer and Julianne Moore and Monica Bellucci have in common is a non-sexist and ageist hairdresser. And that she's sick of adding to the list: what people her age can't wear anymore, or do anymore, or be anymore. But she doesn't. Except she gets a sense that he's going to do whatever he wants with her hair, so she puts up a hand to stop him, stands up, takes off her cape and walks out.

Teresa ends up trimming it, and the capable hands kneading her scalp make Martha cry. She can't bear the idea of not living next to Teresa and Marco and their family, or Jennifer and Steve and the boys. She's lived in enough houses where neighbours seemed absent. Hostile. Cold. Polite. She'll miss those conversations while she's dragging out the recycling bin. The ostentatious Christmas lights that bring people out of their houses for a stroll up and down the streets. Of Teresa waving off Jennifer's apology for the noise made by her kids at night because, according to Teresa, when your sons get their P plates in this area, who sleeps anyway. But spring has come and there was no warning from Lotte this morning. Just another text message from the agent.

And this time Martha responds.

Chapter Fifteen

Jimmy's worlds collide in the bakery section at Coles in Leichhardt while Toto's enjoying a ride in the trolley and Rosie's analysing use-by dates.

Frankie's there. Studying the ingredients of the pull-apart cheese and bacon bread, and for a moment he contemplates walking past, but she sees him. Smiles with surprise at first, delight when she sees Toto. And then Rosie. Jimmy's supposed to introduce them. He knows that, but he doesn't. He's sure it's as simple as, 'Frankie, this is Rosie.'

But he doesn't say a word.

'I'm Francesca,' she says.

'Rosie.'

He figures it's Italian instinct that has them kissing each other on both cheeks. Coldly. Politely.

Frankie takes Toto's hand next. *'Ciao-ciao, tesoro.'*

And then she glances up at Jimmy.

'I'll see you around.'

He got it wrong. Cold and polite wasn't meant for Rosie. It was meant for him.

The dog-food aisle proves to be worse than the bakery section. Rosie puts in the same ingredient analysis for Bruno as she does for them.

'Are you embarrassed about being with me?' she finally asks.

'No,' he says. '*No.*' He's angry that she even thinks it.

'You didn't even introduce us. She had to do it.'

'I didn't know what to do.'

'Why?'

'Because she's my best mate and I don't keep –'

'Secrets. So being with me is a secret?'

He wants to say that being with her and Toto means every-thing to him and that he knows that, because he spends a week away from them and the loneliness eats away at him as if he's been away a year.

But he doesn't say a word.

At netball, Rosie wants him to keep an eye on Toto while she's playing. They're surrounded by girls and women, thousands of them. Even Toto is fascinated, leaning forward in his pram, peering out at the world with a crease of confusion in his brow, as if he's already worked out that the opposite sex is strange and colourful and animated and loud.

'When's your game?' he asks Rosie as they walk between a couple of courts.

'2.30.'

'Then why are we here so early?'

'Because Scarlett and Marley are playing!'

He's worked out that they're the children of a couple of the women, but doesn't need to be told in a tone that says, *dickhead, how did you not know that?*

And nothing intimidates Jimmy as much as Martha and those mothers watching the Under 8s Dolphin team. Rosie's one of them. 'GET IN THE CIRCLE, MARLEY!' This Rosie is an alien that Jimmy and Toto haven't met before. 'SHOOT! SHOOT, SCARLETT!' Maybe that's Martha voice, because Jimmy can't differentiate between them anymore. They belong to the animal kingdom of netball mothers and associates. Tears in most of their eyes when Marley gets a shot in, but Jimmy understands. Because the look on the kid's face, when she looks over at both her mums, is priceless.

Mackee approaches with Anabel and a girl named Fern, who's about six feet tall with a lot of braids and different team colours. They've just started going out together. Fern smiles when Anabel tells Jimmy that. In a way that maybe Rosie would smile if Jimmy told everyone that they were sort of going out together. Or sleeping together. After having a baby together. Fern has to ref a game, so Anabel sticks around with Jimmy and Mackee, and then Alana joins them because her brother is one of Aunt Georgie's best friends.

Jimmy likes being a netball bystander. When he's forced to watch a League game with Will or Mackee, they talk about the players and the ref and the odds and their footy tipping. But here, Jimmy's fascination for other people's lives is rewarded. Today he gets the inside story of the Anabel and Fern dilemma. Fern's parents are in denial about her going out with a girl, whereas the Mackees are accepting. The problem, however, lies with the Mackees. Anabel's fear of being told by her school that she can't take Fern to her Year Twelve formal is surpassed by the fear that her parents will protest and make it a big deal.

'But it is a big deal,' Jimmy says.

'But not theirs. Ours,' Anabel says.

Alana sees herself as an expert on the topic because she's a school principal and a lesbian. Her belief is that there'll be no directive from the principal of Anabel's school about who to take to a school formal. And in the space of an Under 8s netball game, Jimmy has a discussion about being teenage and lesbian, listens to Alana interrogate Tom about his teaching credentials, learns more about the family history of the Charbels and the Finch-Mackees and accepts that he will never understand team sport.

'I'm going to grab a couple of sausage rolls for the kids,' Alana says. She tells Mackee to come along with her.

'Which one's Toto's mum?' Anabel asks Jimmy.

Jimmy points.

'Yeah, that figures.'

'Why?'

'It just does. I like her hair. Where did you meet?'

'In a flood. You?'

'Here,' Anabel says. 'We played each other's team on the first game of the season and during a toss up, our eyes sort of met.'

'That's pretty romantic.'

'Yeah, so's meeting the mother of your child during a catastrophic event.'

The final whistle blows and Anabel's on her feet. 'See you next week.'

And Jimmy hopes he does.

Mackee returns with a sausage in a bread roll, looking relaxed and pleased with himself.

'I think I just got offered a job,' he says.

Jimmy decides to go see Frankie down at the Union during one of her breaks.

'It's like you didn't want us to meet,' she says, putting a beer on a coaster in front of him and sitting down. 'As if I wouldn't be interested in meeting Toto's mother.'

Jimmy wants to channel Anabel Mackee and tell everyone that he's going out with Rosie.

'I've been staying there at night.'

'What does that mean?'

'We're sleeping together.'

'Is that a good idea?' she asks, and he feels irritated by her expression, but feels vindicated because this is the exact reason he didn't introduce her to Rosie.

'In what way wouldn't it be a good idea?' he asks.

'She's Toto's mother, so when you break up it'll have big consequences, Jimmy.'

'Why would you instantly think we'll break up?'

'I've never got a sense you were interested in a relationship, so just make sure you don't feel forced into this one.'

'She's not forcing me into anything!'

'I didn't say she was,' Frankie says. 'It's you who might be doing the forcing on yourself.'

They're interrupted by one of the bar staff who wants Frankie to sign off on something. Jimmy waits until the guy's out of earshot.

'I don't understand what you're getting at, Frankie.' His tone is a lot more hostile than he intends.

'Are you interested in her because she's Toto's mum or is it something deeper?' Frankie asks. 'Because you need to make sure you're not getting the two confused.'

'Why are you getting aggro, Frankie?'

He can see the hurt in her expression, but he can't stop feeling pissed off at her.

'I'm not getting aggro,' she says. 'You are!'

'No, mate. You are!'

There's ice in her stare. 'Maybe I'll be shitty if you walk away from Toto.'

'I would never walk away from him.'

'You haven't been given a reason to walk away. Yet. A broken relationship would be a reason.'

'*You don't know that.*'

'Yeah, I do,' she says. 'Because it's what you do, Jimmy. After your pop died we didn't see you for a year. A *year*. And then you came back and nicked off again.'

'You're the one who told me to go looking for my mum, Frankie!'

'Yes, and when that didn't work out, you kept on going, and another two years went by and we didn't see you! But this isn't about us, Jimmy. It's about Toto. Because if things don't work out again, you can't go looking for yourself.'

'Thank you for reducing my life to a cliché.' He sculls his beer and stands up.

'I bet Mackee didn't get a lecture when he decided to bail out on us all those years ago!'

'You weren't here,' she says. 'So you have no idea how hard it was for Tom, and Tom has no idea how hard it was for you. You guys are so slack and we do all the work. Siobhan lives on the other side of the fucking world and she checks in, and so does Justine. But you guys fall to pieces and don't give us another thought. Well, you can't do that when you've got a kid. That's a game changer. That's all I'm saying.'

She's crying now and he feels like shit, but he's angry at the same time.

'My mother's depression screwed me up for such a long time, Jimmy. And it was out of her control. But I'll never forget it. That little boy needs you, no matter what.'

Jimmy has to get out of there, so he walks out without saying goodbye.

He's got laundry to collect from Mackee and Tara's, so he heads over to Petersham. Tara's home, and if she's been given a Frankie update she doesn't let on.

Jimmy asks her for a bag to put his clean clothes in. She hands him a canvas one and he heads outside to the laundry.

'Need help?' she says, following him out.

'I don't appreciate someone telling me how to live my life,' he says to her, because he's bursting to say something.

'Fair enough.'

'Or having an opinion on who I am and what I should be doing and what my responsibility is. And that's what Frankie did today, and she was out of line!'

'I know how you feel,' she says. 'I have the Mackees and they're like that with Tom. So you have to make a choice. Accept it and be subject to it for the rest of your life, or walk away. Because you can't have the watered-down version of family, Jimmy. Not with Tom and Frankie.'

Chapter Sixteen

She overhears Martha telling the netball women that her mother Lotte's voice wakes her up each morning. Everyone seems to have dead-mother stories, except for Rosie.

What she's sure about is that she's not going to wait for any gangster cancer to win. Decides to go for the blood test, to work out if she's got the BRCA mutant gene. If this thing's coming after her, Rosie's going to get to it first. And because she doesn't want to ask Martha again, or do it alone, she calls Yolanda.

'It's a blood test,' Rosie tells her in the waiting room.

'Do you want me to go in with you?'

'No, just sit out here with me and then we can go for a coffee and muffin after.'

'Too easy.'

Yolanda flicks through a magazine. Shows Rosie a picture of some reality star in a bikini.

'Fake boobs,' she says, but then realises what she's said. 'Sorry I mentioned the boobs.'

'Why? Mine aren't going anywhere.'

And then they're laughing. Yolanda takes Rosie's hand and gives it a squeeze and goes in with her, after all.

When she gets home, Jimmy's waiting on the doorstep and they go across the road to pick up Toto from Signora and then head back to the house.

Upstairs, she runs a bath for Toto and figures she should tell Jimmy about the BRCA mutant thing, because she doesn't want to be like Martha. Jimmy listens intently, nodding, and then she sees his eyes water.

'Don't be a fucking crybaby, Jimmy.'

'I'm not,' he mutters. He picks up Toto from where he's playing in his pen.

'I'll bathe him,' he says.

She lies on the bed and listens to their chattering. Toto's found the perfect companion because Jimmy can chat for hours once he loses his inhibitions.

'Where do you want to go?' Jimmy asks, when Toto's dressed in his trackies.

'Anywhere.'

What she almost says is 'anywhere with you and Toto', but she doesn't want to come across needy, especially since he didn't introduce her to his best friend. They put a hoodie on Toto because the weather's still unpredictable and head towards the bus stop. Jimmy takes her hand, like he always does when they cross the road.

'You're hurting me,' she says, because he's squeezing so hard. He lets go, but she takes his hand again, and he presses his lips to it. They head into Chinatown for dinner and a stroll because Rosie likes the colour and the crowd and then, on the tram trip home, while Toto sleeps in his arms, they just pash the whole time.

Back in the kitchen later that night, she grounds the beans for coffee, and Jimmy tells her that he's got an interview with the paramedics.

'Why didn't you say?' she asks, setting the *caffettiera* on the stove. Toto has refused to settle down and he's banging at the laundry cupboard where he knows his toys are.

Jimmy doesn't respond and she looks over at him, wanting to see his expression.

'You're going for that interview, Jimmy,' she says.

'Maybe.'

'No maybes.'

'The mines pay better than any other job I'll get with no qualifications, Rosie.'

'You don't want to work for the mines. You want to be a paramedic.'

'I just want to look after you and Toto.'

His phone rings. He looks surprised because it's after ten.

'Yes, this is him,' he says, picking up Toto, who is clinging to his legs. Jimmy takes him out to the backyard. Rosie's curious about who's on the phone, but isn't sure how much of it's her business. Wonders if it's about his mother, or his father. The coffee percolates and she pours him a cup and gets him one of Signora's almond biscuits. By the time he's back inside, his cheeks are flushed with excitement.

'That was the cops in Rockhampton,' he says. 'They found the fricken Monaro.'

'No way.'

'Yeah. They picked up a guy just outside town for speeding, and ran the plates.'

There's the sound of the front door opening. Rosie knows Martha won't go straight to her room because Jimmy's here.

'We're celebrating,' Jimmy calls out. Toto gives her a '*Marta*' shout just in case they all forget his growing obsession with her. Bruno joins in the adoration, jumping all over her as if Rosie hasn't shown him affection for years.

Martha joins them in the kitchen. Puts down her handbag and takes off her jacket and shoes. 'You've got into the paramedics?' she asks.

'No. They found my Monaro.'

Martha looks taken aback. 'You lost a Monaro?'

'Stolen.'

Rosie thinks it's funny that Martha has the same reaction as she did.

'It's how I met Rosie.'

'When Jimmy met Rosie with a Monaro thrown in,' Martha says. 'Seb would have loved that.' She points to the *caffettiera* for permission, but doesn't even wait for Rosie's response.

'My mum would have loved it,' Rosie corrects.

'True.'

Jimmy's hyper and Rosie likes seeing him this way. He can't sit still. Grabs his phone and begins to text.

'Toto will love it,' he says, crouching to hug him. 'We're going to have to get a car seat. A proper one.' He's up, hugging Rosie next and his arms are trembling. Jimmy had never gone into how much the car meant to him.

'I've spent the past six months totally avoiding Catherine Street,' he says. ''Cause I didn't want to bump into the guy who sold it to me. He would have been cut knowing it was stolen.'

The microwave makes a *ding* sound at the same time the *ding* goes off in Rosie's head. And Martha's. Their eyes meet.

'Who sold it to you, Jimmy?' Martha says.

'A guy with an accent,' Rosie answers for him and she hurries to Martha's room where she knows there's a photo of her dad. Back in the kitchen, she shows it to Jimmy. This time it's her hand shaking.

Jimmy studies it and Rosie can hardly breathe, because it's all there in his expression.

'You met Seb,' Martha says.

And the three of them can't find the words.

'*Dadda.*'

But Toto does.

Jimmy crouches down again, holds him close and Rosie can see that he's overcome.

'My dad kept the car at work after my mum died,' Rosie says. 'Wouldn't sell it for years. I thought he was keeping it for me . . . because it belonged to her.'

'Why would he go and sell it then?' Jimmy asks.

And her eyes meet Martha's again. Rosie can't recall the exact words she spoke that day, but she remembers her rage. After that, she moved out with Luke the deadbeat and hardly saw her father for the rest of that year. Rest of his life. She blamed Martha for that.

'We had spent too much on legal fees,' Martha finally says. 'Challenging the council to let us build upstairs. The irony was that we won but didn't have enough money to finish it.'

She points up the stairs.

'That's what the Monaro paid for.'

Rosie and Toto's attic.

She lies awake for most of the night. Tomorrow, Jimmy's going to fly back to work and in a week's time he'll hitch a ride to Rockhampton with one of his workmates and pick up the car. And it's at about three in the morning that Rosie knows she needs to travel back to Sydney with him and Toto in her mother's car. Sort of a pilgrimage. She shakes him awake.

'Can you lend me money for a ticket to Rockhampton?' she asks.

He turns to her and they're so close, she feels his breath on her face.

'Are you and me together?' he asks.

'Yes.'

'Then there's no talk about me lending you money again.'

Chapter Seventeen

Martha sits out on the verandah. She hasn't had a moment's sleep and can't bear to deal with the breakfast trio in the kitchen. And what right does she have to take over a kitchen when she can't even cook? But she wants Seb's photo because it's still sitting on the butcher's trolley. Because she doesn't trust memory anymore. For years it's painted a different picture of the past. Rosie's aggression and rage. Julia's antagonism. And Ewan. Now it's Martha who can't remember the song they supposedly danced to when they were in Year Ten. Maybe there wasn't a song in the first place. Maybe Martha's one of those delusional people who invents hoops for those around her to jump through.

And then Ewan's there, parking out front, and Martha's in destructive mode. Knows she has to put a stop to these quirky sessions because what they're aiming for won't stand the test of time.

'I don't think this is going to work,' she says while they stand out on her verandah.

He's been talking about a couple of job offers, but she hasn't taken in a word.

'I probably should have told you this the first time we saw each other, except it's not exactly an opening line at a funeral. But my mother and grandmother and aunts died of breast cancer and I've been tested, and I'm one of the mutants and, just before I met you, I worked out that I didn't want to live with the fear every six months that they'd find a lump, so I made a decision about what I was going to do.'

And Martha just keeps on talking and says words she's never spoken out loud before. Double mastectomy and hysterectomy and reconstruction.

Ewan is shaken, confused.

'But you're not sick?'

'No.'

He looks relieved.

'So we'll deal with whatever you decide to do,' he says.

'No. I'll deal with it.'

He looks wounded. Add vulnerability to Ewan Healy's many traits.

'I don't want us to start something and then it be over,' she says.

'We have started something, Martha. Why would it be over?'

And then she sees his anger, because the penny's dropped.

'You're presuming I won't want to be around if you go ahead with it,' he says.

Martha wants to deny it because she didn't think he'd articulate it so quickly.

'I've never even seen them,' he says. 'I actually told Alana that I thought maybe you were hiding something because every time we have sex, it's in the car and most of your clothes stay on.'

'You've spoken about not seeing my boobs with Alana?'

'I talk about everything with Alana. Even Bavaria.'

'I just don't want the disappointment.'

Now she sees fury. 'Oh fuck you, Martha. What right do you have to predict how much of a weak prick I'm going to be?'

And then he walks away.

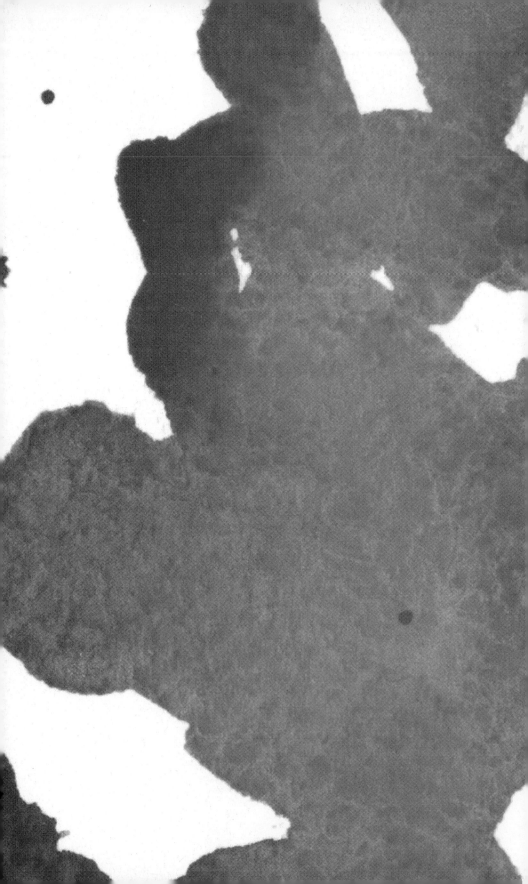

PART THREE

Going home

Chapter Eighteen

Rosie looks tired when she walks off the plane and Jimmy can't imagine sitting for a whole flight with Toto on her lap, including a stopover in Brisbane, being fun. Some guy beside her offers to carry her bag, and she lets him, adjusting Toto in her arms. When she reaches Jimmy, he takes her face in his hands and they kiss, with Toto squirming between them, but Jimmy doesn't want to stop, because these days, a week away seems like forever.

They pick up the Monaro at the cops on Bolsover Street, and when she sees it, Rosie cries in a way Jimmy hasn't seen before. It hurts to watch, but he doesn't look away because he knows she's going to make tough decisions in her life and he doesn't want to be the guy who looks away every time something breaks her heart. The car breaks her heart. Because it's the most concrete reminder of her mother. The house isn't, because the rooms have been torn apart, walls have been knocked down and so much has changed. But the car has stayed the same.

Toto whimpers in his arms as though he knows.

'Mummy's just sad,' Jimmy whispers to him.

Rosie wants to drive and they're on the Bruce Highway heading to Brisbane. Toto's sleeping in the back and for a while there's silence, but it doesn't make Jimmy feel lonely and he senses the same for her. Later, he puts on a CD that Mackee burnt for him and, while they're listening to a song by some band he's never heard of, about belonging to you and belonging to me, Jimmy senses that nostalgia is planted. He knows they'll look back on this moment and remember it with great clarity, and when they see the A3 turn-off she glances at him, and they must see the same thing in each other's eyes. Because she turns left instead of going straight and Jimmy knows they won't be getting to Brisbane for a while. He remembers the first time he made this journey, driving the car through strange-sounding towns like Dululu. Wowan. Goovigen. Baralaba. Before he met her. Before the rest of his life happened. And it brings back memories of desperate loneliness, and the suffocation Jimmy had felt knowing he couldn't return home for another two years because of the good behaviour bond. But today, as they pass the town sign, he can't help feeling that it's a home-coming of some sort. Last time he was here, Jimmy got to stay long enough to be part of a community's healing. He can't say that the people here were the most resilient he had met, because he grew up in Waterloo and his housing commission neighbours were a pretty hardy bunch, but in this town they had taken care of each other when they needed to, and Jimmy had travelled through communities where that didn't happen. Where there was plenty of blame and division. The sameness of the place is a comfort to him. The wide streets with no pavements, the Queenslander houses, the gold XXXX sign on the top of the pub, the water tower dominating the skyline to the east. This was the place where Jimmy met Rosie and he hopes it hasn't changed.

Rosie wants to go to the hospital first, but Min's not there.

'Drinks in town,' the nurse tells them. Jimmy and Rosie don't recognise her and they'd ended up knowing most of the medical staff back then in some capacity, so she must be new. Jimmy thinks of drinks in town the night before the floods. How Kev got up there to warn everyone about the flood. Jimmy had been bone-tired from sandbagging and was about to head up to his room when he first saw Rosie. Thought she was so fucking gorgeous in a sad way. Spent about an hour watching her without doing anything about it, because he never thought he stood a chance. Except a voice in his head challenged that.

Outside the hospital, he takes Toto from her. 'Let's walk,' he says, because there's something special about a town on the Dawson at sunset when the breeze is close to perfect and the sky is sort of another world.

The only change in the pub is the carpet, but the stench of beer soaked into its foundations smells the same. Kev's making a speech again. Because Mick the butcher, who Jimmy worked along-side during the floods, is also an amateur photographer and is having an exhibition of some sort. Min is sitting at a table with a couple of the other women, drinking a beer and eating scones that are doing the rounds. She glances up and it takes a moment to register, but then as they make their way towards her surprise turns into joy and she shakes her head in wonder, her arms held out for Toto, who holds out his own, as if he's known her in some other life.

'Have we got ourselves a flood baby here?' Min asks him. Toto's loving the attention after being cooped up in the car, and Min embraces the three of them as if they mean something to her and Jimmy knows he'll spend a lifetime collecting people who make them feel that way.

'I dream of you,' she says to Rosie, almost in disbelief. 'Ask Kev. I'll wake up and say, "I dreamt of that Rosie again."'

They sit and talk for a while, surrounded by Mick's photos. Of flood. Of drought. Of getting on with life.

'People down south think you get over it as soon as the floodwater goes down, but it took us so long,' Min says.

'But at least we didn't get it as bad as those poor bastards in the Lockyer Valley this year,' Kev says. 'I was hoping you weren't down that way.'

'No,' Jimmy says. 'Just up north when Yasi came through.'

'How long are you staying?' Min asks.

Jimmy looks at Rosie and they both shrug.

'I'm off for ten days, so we're going to take our time getting back to Sydney,' he says.

'Miss Fricker?' Rosie asks. 'Is she still alive?'

'That one will outlive us all, doll.'

Jimmy tracks down Mick, who's playing pool, and buys him a beer to toast his work.

'Got a bit blue after, eh,' Mick tells him while they're sitting at the bar, drinking. 'Not just because of the deaths, but . . .' he shrugs.

'It sorta gives you purpose when you're workin' and helpin' out. And then everyone gets on with their lives, and it's as if you don't know who you are anymore.'

Rosie approaches with Toto and Jimmy reintroduces them. 'Do you remember Mick? He drove the truck when we came to get you from Miss Fricker's place?'

Mick's eyes light up. 'Thought I knew your face.'

'You saw me for five minutes and you remember my face?' Rosie asks. 'I'm flattered.'

Mick stumbles to his feet. 'Come with me,' he says, with an urgency they don't understand. But they follow him to the back wall where his photos are on display. He searches and then points up high, grabs a chair to stand on and removes a photo, handing it down to Rosie. And Jimmy sees her eyes well up.

'You're lovely,' she says to Mick. 'Thank you.'

And she holds out the photo. It's of Jimmy in his jocks, carrying Joy Fricker through floodwaters. And Rosie's right behind them, staring up at Jimmy. The look in her eyes promises the world.

'This is us before you were born, Toto,' he says, showing their son.

Later, after Min's taken Rosie and Toto to Miss Fricker's, Jimmy sits out back on the verandah with Kev and Mick.

'Your name came up last week when the paramedics rang me for a reference,' Kev says.

'I'm not going to take it,' Jimmy says. 'I can't support them on a three-year traineeship.'

'Where are you living?' Kev asks.

Where is Jimmy living? On a couch, or in her bed, or in a mining camp. He knows he has to get a place for the three of them, especially if Dalhousie Street gets sold at auction in early November.

'In Sydney,' he says.

'Bloody expensive in Sydney, eh?' Mick says. 'Move up here, Jim. It's closer to the mines and you can rent for next to nothin'.'

'Don't listen to him,' Kev says. 'You'll end up losing your kids to the big towns.'

In the room above the pub, Toto's sleeping beside Rosie. Jimmy watches him a while. Wonders how this golden-skinned gorgeous being could have come from him. He strips and gets into bed, gathering them both closer. She turns and faces him. 'You smell like a brewery.'

'Had to keep up with them,' he says with a laugh. 'Honestly, I'd end up a drunk if I lived up here.'

She traces her finger over his mouth.

'It took me a couple of months to work out Toto wasn't Luke's,' she says. 'He was so miserable, always sick. And then his smile just appeared one day and I can't begin to explain what I felt when I recognised it. Even if I never saw you again, at least I could tell Toto good things about his dad.'

Jimmy doesn't know how to be a good dad. He just wants to be a decent human being.

The light from the street lamp outside illuminates the bedside table and he sees the photo Mick took.

'You want to get married?' he whispers into her ear.

It takes her by surprise, but only for a moment. 'Yeah, I do.' And then she seems to think about it more.

'Let's get married here.' She looks down at Toto and brushes sweaty curls away from his eye. 'Where we made something good for once in our lives.'

Talk of a wedding gets around by the next afternoon. One of the farmers who owns a property outside town turns up at the pub and offers his paddock for a barbecue because Jimmy once helped rescue a couple of his prized cattle. Mick volunteers to take the photos and pledges the sausages, and Maeve from the newsagency wants to make the cake.

'So does that mean Maeve's invited,' Jimmy asks Rosie, 'because I thought maybe it'd be just us and Mick and Kev and Min?'

'And Miss Fricker.'

The members of the CWA bring them a hamper of local goodies and Rosie invites them as well. And by the time the guestlist hits thirty, Jimmy knows that sooner or later he has to tell Frankie. After their last conversation he doesn't know whether she'll understand, but he knows she'll never forgive him if she finds out from someone else, so he rings her.

'I'm up north,' he says. 'They found the Monaro.' Of course she'd know that because he had texted Will.

'We're getting married here,' he says, waiting for the reaction.

'What are you talking about?'

'It's where things began with Toto,' he says. 'And this car being up this way, and a thousand other things. It means a lot to Rosie.'

'When is it? I'll be there.'

'Frankie, you're not going to fly to Rockhampton and drive a hundred k's west.'

'Why not? Don't be ridiculous. Of course I am! Aren't I invited?'

'As if I wouldn't invite you to my wedding.'

'Then why are we having this conversation? When is it?'

'Saturday.'

'Are you kidding me?'

'We're going to have to get the paperwork done in Sydney,' he says. 'Who knew you had to apply to get married, but the Catholic priest comes once a month and I have to get back to work in about a week, so it's this Saturday.'

'How the hell are you going to organise a wedding in five days?'

'There's not much to organise really. We're having a sausage sizzle in a paddock.'

'Give me a list of things to do.'

He speaks to Martha next because, despite everything that's gone on between her and Rosie, Jimmy thinks she should know.

There's silence at the other end of the line.

'Martha, I know it's a lot to ask, but if you'd like to come along . . .'

'Is that what she wants?'

'I know she'd want you to be there.'

'Did she tell you that?'

'She doesn't have to.'

In the end Jimmy can't convince Martha that Rosie would want her there, but she agrees to pack a few things for Frankie to pick up, including Loredana's wedding dress.

*

Four days later, he drives to Quilpie airport to pick up Frankie, who's come with an entourage. Not only are Mackee and Tara there, but Justine as well, grinning from ear to ear, with that same infectious energy she had back in school. She links her arm with his as they follow the others.

'I wouldn't miss this for the world,' she says.

'What? Me getting married?'

'No, you being happy, Jimmy.'

'We've been practising one song,' Frankie tells him. 'So if you've already got a wedding band, tell them we want ten minutes on stage.'

'Sausage sizzle in a paddock. Radio on. That's our entertainment.'

'Where's the luggage conveyer belt?' Justine asks.

Quilpie airport is a one-room affair. Check-in, arrivals and departures all in the same place. Jimmy points to the ute that's just driven up, packed with luggage.

'This isn't fucking Melbourne, Justine,' Tara says.

Justine laughs, obviously in on the joke, while Mackee and Frankie head towards the luggage ute and start collecting what's theirs.

'By the way, I forgot to ask if it's okay that I bring a plus one,' Frankie calls out, dragging a suitcase off the trailer.

'Me too,' Justine says. Tara hugs Jimmy's arm. All three girls are giddy and Jimmy's confused.

'Who are their plus ones?' he calls out to Mackee, because he's not going to get anything from the girls.

Mackee points. 'Them.'

Jimmy looks to see Will and Siobhan standing near the exit.

'You're getting married!' Siobhan says, leaping onto him.

Will looks heavily jetlagged and wants to know where the Monaro is. 'Can't believe you lost it for two years, Hailler.'

'Stolen,' Jimmy corrects. 'You look like crap, mate.'

'Will and I have been travelling for thirty-six hours,' Siobhan says. '*Thirty-six.*'

'We met these two at Brisvegas airport,' Tara explained. 'They haven't even gone home to see their families.'

Jimmy embraces the two. 'You came all the way here for me?'

'As if he did,' Siobhan says. 'He came all the way to make sure everything's okay with Frankie.'

'I told you that in confidence, Siobhan,' Will says, irritated.

'You told me that because we've been stuck together for *thirty-six* hours, Will.' She's got an audience in a local family who are fascinated by the arrival of very loud dramatic foreigners.

'He thinks he stuffed up by taking the Stuttgart job, not reading the signs and wallowing in self-pity instead of coming back and making things right.'

Siobhan looks at Will.

'Did I leave anything out? I've got a good memory for reluctant male crying.'

Will mutters something under his breath and walks away to help Frankie who's now on the ute's tray helping to off-load the luggage.

Siobhan points to her cheeks, mouths the word, 'Tears.'

They arrive at the pub and Will goes off to organise a couple more rooms down at the motel. Mackee and Tara are still to arrive because they had to hitch a ride with a local. The girls, meanwhile, have taken over the main bar with their luggage.

'What does one wear to a country wedding?' Siobhan says, holding up two outfits.

'Sausage sizzle,' Jimmy reminds them.

There's the sound of footsteps on the stairs, and Siobhan looks up. 'Oh my God, I'm going to cry,' she says. 'That's him, isn't it?' Rosie is coming down the stairs with Toto on her hip, staring at the invasion of frills and tulle on the ground. Jimmy figures it's her mother's wedding dress spilling out of Frankie's luggage. Siobhan is advancing on Rosie and Toto with arms open. 'I just want to eat him.'

Jimmy removes Toto out of the impending fray and introduces Rosie. She doesn't say much, but crouches down beside the wedding dress. When she holds it up, there's a gasp amongst the others, and then silence.

'I'm presuming we've got a circa late 80s, early 90s gown here,' Frankie says.

'It's pretty awful,' Rosie says.

Frankie and Jimmy politely agree.

'Let's hit the shops,' Siobhan says.

'Shop,' Rosie says.

'That's what I'm saying,' Siobhan shouts. 'Let's go shopping!'

'There's one shop in town,' Jimmy tries to explain.

Frankie is searching for something amongst the tulle of the dress. 'Before I forget.' She finds a pocket and unzips it. 'Your stepmum –'

'Just Martha,' Rosie says.

'Martha said to tell you that when she sent the dress for dry-cleaning, she found these in the pocket.'

Frankie holds out two rings. Plain gold. Rosie stares at them.

'Are they your mum and dad's?' Jimmy asks.

Rosie nods, takes them from Frankie, clenches them in her fist.

'I can fix the dress,' Frankie says. 'Pull it in a bit, cut it at the knee, get rid of the puffed sleeves.'

Rosie doesn't respond. Jimmy tried to explain to them on the drive from Quilpie how Rosie was feeling at the moment. Raw, because her parents aren't around for her wedding. Hopes they understand her mood.

Will walks in holding a couple of keys and Frankie does the introductions.

'Rosie's dad sold Jimmy the Monaro,' Frankie tells him.

'No way.'

Jimmy nods. He can see it's too much for Will's pragmatic mind.

'Go sleep off the jet lag, babe,' Frankie says to him. 'It'll make better sense when you're awake.'

Will goes to leave, but turns back to Rosie.

'I was with Jimmy when he bought it, you know,' he says.

They seem to be magical words for Rosie. 'You met my dad.'

Will nods. 'When we walked into the workshop, he didn't know who was interested in the car, but I got a sense that if it were me, he wouldn't have sold it.'

Will has a think about it.

'Your dad just took a liking to this one,' he says, pointing in Jimmy's direction. 'And then Jimmy tells him that he needs a car because he's looking for family, and that was it.'

Will looks at them both. 'Pretty big coincidence,' he says.

Later that night, while Rosie and Toto are staying at Min's, Jimmy and the others end up in a meadow, lying on the grass, staring up at the stars.

'Best night sky I've ever seen,' Justine says.

'I've seen the northern lights in Norway,' Siobhan says.

Frankie sits up from where she's lying beside Will, who is still half asleep.

'We don't want to steal anyone's thunder, so don't even say congratulations until we land in Sydney,' Frankie says, 'but we did this on the plane.' She holds up a hand that has a ring on it.

'Can't we –' Tara begins.

'Nope,' Frankie interrupts. 'And stop crying, Justine.'

'Are you at least having an engagement party?' Jimmy asks.

Will opens an eye. 'We're going to find the closest paddock in Campbelltown and have a sausage sizzle.' He gives up on sleeping and sits up next to her. 'Once we get married, Frankie's dad's going to renovate the double garage in my parents' backyard,' he says. 'Turn it into a granny flat.'

'That's practical,' Tara says.

'Yes, because people who get engaged in seat 10b and 10c on a Rex flight to Quilpie are pragmatic about such things,' Siobhan says.

'Very challenging,' Frankie says. 'I'm going to have to wash my hair in seven minutes because of the water tank.'

Mackee is looking unimpressed by the news.

'Justine in Melbourne. Siobhan in London. Frankie in fucking Oatley,' he laments.

'Tom, it's a twenty-minute drive from your house, and it's on the train line,' Frankie points out.

'Guys, we're going to be thirty years old before we know it,' Siobhan says.

'In five years' time, mate.'

'I'm already counting it down. Jimmy's got a baby and these guys are talking granny flats. And do I need to confess that I now holiday with my father? *My father.* My parents get a divorce from their toxic marriage and I start enjoying the company of the middle-aged.'

She shakes her head with disbelief. 'Our fun days are gone.'

'As opposed to being in Year Twelve and watching Jimmy's nudie runs down Maroubra beach,' Tara says.

'And Siobhan flashing,' Mackee says. 'Remember we'd be like, "Not again, Siobhan. Put 'em away. We're begging you."'

'You're a dick, Tom,' she says, but they're all laughing. And it's what they do all night, talk and drink and laugh, because Jimmy figures it's the last time they'll be together again for a while.

'So now for the wedding presents,' Justine says.

'No presents,' Jimmy says. 'We don't have room in the car anyway.'

'These won't take up room,' Justine says. 'You've got three days to get to Byron because we've booked you in to a five-star resort there.'

'And my parents bought you a suit for Saturday,' Frankie says.

'And my parents are covering the drinks bill,' Mackee says.

'Too much,' Jimmy says. 'You being here is enough.'

And they toast to them being together.

'Speech, Jimmy,' Tara says. 'Because I bet you won't do one at the sausage sizzle.'

Jimmy's never made a speech in his life.

'Go on,' Frankie says.

He doesn't know where to start, except for the truth.

'After I found my mum, it sort of fucked me up a bit,' he says. 'And I'm driving for days and days on the Bruce Highway and it's just me and my head and the trees, and for a moment I tell myself to drive straight into one. And I know you guys want to be enough to have stopped me, but at the time I didn't have space in my head to think of anyone. And then in a split second I get an image of the guy who sold me the car, and I knew I couldn't wreck something he seemed to love so much. And that was it. The moment was gone. And a week later I met Rosie.'

None of them speak, and Jimmy doesn't know what to say. He catches Mackee's eye.

'Best man?'

'Shit, yeah.'

Jimmy's wedding day is literally the best day of his life. He hasn't had many of those, so he's able to differentiate. After the barbecue is lit, he holds Rosie's hand and they watch it all in silence. And like always, Jimmy is amazed by the kindness of strangers. By the coincidences in life. By how much his friends love his son. By Miss Fricker's sullen tenderness towards Rosie, matched by her total hostility for Jimmy and Toto.

Min joins them, holding a muddy Toto.

'How about Kev and I take this one home with us tonight?' she says. 'We've got a cot set up for my daughter's little one in the rumpus room.'

Jimmy likes a world where Min and Kev are in charge. It feels safe.

'Any advice, Min?' he asks.

She thinks a moment. 'Easy. The kids always come first.'

Frankie, Mackee and Justine put together their version of Toto's 'Rosanna', a sort of ballad for the bridal waltz, and although there's not really a dance floor on that paddock Jimmy takes Rosie in his arms.

'You look great in that dress,' he says.

'You look great in that suit.'

'It's the best thing I've ever worn,' he says. 'You?'

She thinks about it. Holds up a hand with her mother's wedding ring.

'This is the best thing I've ever worn.'

Tara and Mackee fly out the next day to visit his Nan Agnes in Brisbane. Jimmy drives them back to Quilpie. Doesn't know how to thank them for letting him stay in their home, but he knows he'll find a way.

'Can I ask you something personal?' he says, just as they're about to board.

'Depends on how personal?' Tara asks, suspicious.

'When you do that whispery thing to each other in the morning before you go your separate ways, what do you say?'

They exchange a look and laugh.

'Should I pick up a couple of chops for dinner, petal?' Mackee asks her.

'A thousand times yes,' Tara says.

'Was I a dick last night, poppet?'

'A thousand times yes.'

'Can you make sure our health insurance premiums are up to date, honey bunny?'

'A thousand times yes.'

The boarding gate opens and people start filing past them. 'Nothing deep,' Tara says, giving Jimmy a hug. 'Just a personal joke from before we were going out.'

Jimmy thinks it's profound enough.

'See you in fucking Sydney,' she says.

Chapter Nineteen

At 5.47 p.m. when the sun is meant to set, Martha waits patiently for the solar lights to switch on.

They're placed along the path that leads to the vegetable patch, exactly where Seb meant them to be. She lies back on the banana chair and waits. And waits some more. But they don't come on.

'Fuck you, Seb. *Fuck. You.*'

She hears the back door open behind her and Rosie is standing there, home from the Monaro retrieval and from the wedding. Martha would love to point out that girls who look twelve years old shouldn't be getting married, but she already knows the response to that one. 'What would you know, Martha?'

*

When she gives up on the solar lights, she heads back inside to where Rosie's warming up Toto's milk bottle.

'Thanks for finding the rings,' Rosie says.

Martha doesn't respond. Her job application is spread out all over the butcher's trolley so she shuffles it together, placing it into a plastic sleeve.

'Am I presuming a congratulations isn't on the cards?' Rosie says, arms folded. Slap-worthy expression on her face.

'Congratulations, Rosie. I'm so happy for you.'

'Really, Martha?'

'Yes, really. How about we have some people over to celebrate the nuptials?'

Rosie looks surprised and then suspicious. 'The what?'

Martha starts taking her own suggestion seriously. She grabs the notepad off the fridge and starts writing names.

'Everyone who knows you will want to toast the bride.'

'I don't know that many people.'

'What about the neighbours, and those girls from your mothers' group?'

'It's not a mothers' group.'

'Whatever it's called these days.'

Rosie's suspicion hasn't eased. The microwave pings while Martha's scribbling down names and ignoring the scrutiny.

Marco, Teresa, Signora De Lorenzo and *mothers' group x 2*. Their names will come to Martha soon. Those capable young women who sit in judgement of Martha and the others.

Rosie walks over to examine the list.

'What about Ewan and Julia?'

Martha finds herself in an arms-folded Rosie pose. 'You hardly know them.'

'I belong to the netball team, Martha. Ewan trains us, plus I take care of their father, so we chat sometimes.'

'You and Julia chat?'

'What of it?'

'I'm not inviting Ewan and Julia.'

'Why not? He's your boyfriend, isn't he?'

'If I do, Alana will come along and then Sophie and Elizabeth will get offended.'

'Invite them all, then. It's not as if you're throwing this party for me!'

'I'm throwing it for all three of you!'

'Bullshit. This is your way of having a house-unwarming. It'd be nice if you just admitted it.'

'Well, it would have been nice to attend your wedding, Rosie. But it looks like no one's getting what they want these days.'

'As if you needed to be asked!'

'Of course, I needed to be asked!'

'Jimmy asked you.'

'No offence to the lovely Jimmy, but I would have preferred that it came from you.'

'I didn't think it'd be such a big deal, Martha!'

Lotte is telling Martha to bite her tongue, because it's loaded with something she'll regret saying. She scribbles down Ewan's and Julia's names. Shows Rosie.

'Happy now?'

The doorbell rings and it's Ash from the real estate agency, who beat four others because of less bullshitting and a touch of warmth.

Martha takes her out to the backyard, wondering if the solar lights are going to make an appearance. When they don't, she turns on the floodlights instead.

'It looks amazing, Martha.'

Rosie is watching them from the kitchen the whole time, and once they're back inside Martha puts on the kettle.

'Rosie, this is Ash. We're going over the contract if you'd like to join us.'

Rosie doesn't respond and Martha leads the agent to the front living room where they sit down on the three-seater. Martha skims through the advertising plan, shaking her head. 'I'm not interested in redecorating.'

'You've got a better chance of attracting buyers,' Ash tells her.

'What part of this house, this street and this suburb won't attract buyers?'

'If you play your cards right, Martha, you can get over the one-million-dollar mark. It's pretty amazing for a place that used to be a dump.'

'So obviously Seb looked past the decorating last time it was on the market.'

Martha can tell that Ash is choosing her words wisely. 'All I'm saying, Martha, is that we want to attract a certain type of buyer.'

'Someone not like my father.'

Ash looks over to where Rosie is leaning against the door.

'No, not like your father at all,' she says. 'You don't need someone with vision and a dream to buy this house. Just someone with money.'

*

The party list goes from six people to twenty-five. Feeding a large number of people is not something Martha's ever quite accomplished in her life, but she refuses to let on to Rosie that she's out of her depth. She goes next door to Teresa, who's happy to take over.

'I'll get Signora to help and we can make a tray of lasagne and *cotoletti*.'

'So where do we start?' Martha asks.

'Go buy what's needed and leave it to us.'

'I can help with the cooking.'

'No, you can't, *bella*,' Teresa says, diplomatically.

'How about German potato salad?'

Teresa seems to pretend that Martha hasn't spoken. 'And I'll make the tiramisu, and I know that Signora will make the *crostoli*.'

Who's Martha to deprive the newlyweds of Signora De Lorenzo's *crostoli*?

Marco comes home and Teresa tells him to check out Martha's solar lights.

'Have you had them out in the sun long enough?' he asks as they head over to the house.

'Four days.'

'Maybe you should return them.'

'I don't know where Seb bought them from.'

Marco looks taken aback.

'Seb bought them? When?'

'Five years ago.'

Marco laughs. 'Martha, I'll buy you new ones.'

She nods to fob him off, because there's no way she's buying new lights. If Seb's don't work, she's finished with solar energy in her life.

*

269

She decides to make it a mid-afternoon affair, and for the first time since Martha's lived in this house she has guests over for a party. Rosie wears the dress Martha bought her and Jimmy is looking smart in a skinny black suit. Both are effortlessly gorgeous, and Toto's resemblance to Seb throws Martha every time he bursts into her space. Which is often. The guests all come at the same time, which makes things less awkward when Ewan arrives. She misses the banter and the chemistry between them. Misses getting the texts. Misses their intimacy. Martha spends the afternoon floating around, refilling glasses and listening to snippets of conversations. Either Yolanda's or Tess's partner is having a conversation with Marco about water conservation because he's a country boy and he reckons that water distribution is all they talk about where he's from. Jimmy's outside being grilled by Sophie and Elizabeth.

'. . . no, I'm putting that off for now,' he says. 'Sticking to the mines.'

'Where are you looking?'

'Anywhere. We're budgeting for a two-bedroom.'

'Tempe's great,' Sophie tells them. 'And you can still get a bargain in Dulwich Hill.'

'We'll work it out,' Jimmy says. 'Rosie doesn't want to lose any of her shifts, so it's best if we stay in the area.'

'You won't find anything in the area, darls,' Elizabeth says.

It seems to be the question on everyone's lips, because Rosie's having the same intense conversation with the girls.

'He's away every second week, plus they only fly him to the closest capital city, which is Brisbane, and from there he has to pay his own way to Sydney and back again.'

'But he's still making more than if he was on a traineeship, Rosie, so the mines are a better option,' practical Louise says.

'Mark and I are struggling on a single wage at the moment,' Yolanda says. 'Who knows whether we'll stick it out until the end of the year.'

'You said you were struggling back home, Yolanda,' Rosie says. Martha can sense she doesn't want these girls leaving town. 'At least he's got a job here.'

'But we had family around us. The aunties, the cousins.'

'Babysitters,' Tess says.

Teresa has excelled with the food, and there's praise all round for the menu.

'I'm not the best of cooks, as my friends will tell you,' Martha says as she pours Yolanda and Tess a glass of wine.

'My father said it's because she's German,' Rosie says.

'What is?' Martha asks, politely.

'The fact that you can't cook, Martha.'

'If that was said about the Italians, there'd be cries of racism.'

'No one would say that about the Italians,' Rosie says. 'When was the last time you heard someone say, "What's your favourite German restaurant?"'

'Una's,' Alana volunteers, overhearing on her way to supervise the kids upstairs.

'How about we throw around the names of two world leaders, Rosie? Angela Merkel and Silvio Berlusconi. Wonder who I'd prefer leading my country.'

Rosie won't give Martha the satisfaction of laughing, but Martha knows she wants to. She can see Seb's quirk dancing on Rosie's lips.

'German riesling, anyone?' Martha asks, holding up the bottle.

Later, Signora De Lorenzo approaches with Toto who's feverish and miserable and Rosie is about to take him upstairs, but Signora won't hear of it. There's a mini exchange or argument between them, but who can tell? Signora always looks like she's telling someone off, when all the while it could merely be a discussion about the weather.

'Walk them to Signora's,' Rosie tells Jimmy, kissing Toto's cheek.

And throughout it all Martha's aware of Ewan, who sticks close to Julia and Alana and the kids. What she'd really like to do is walk over and ask if it's true that he's taken a job at a sporting clinic in the south-west. But he doesn't look at her, and she doesn't blame him because she wishes she could have revealed how she was feeling without causing so much hurt and damage.

Outside it's getting dark and Martha goes to check the solar lights, but there's nothing.

Except Sophie and Elizabeth sharing a cigarette.

'You two are a disgrace,' Martha says.

'Can I just put something out there, Martha?' Sophie asks.

'If you bring up Ewan, I'm going to find George and tell him you're smoking.'

'She was the one who dobbed on us in second form when we smoked at your slumber party,' Elizabeth tells Sophie. 'You always had blinders on when it came to St Martha.'

'It's about Rosie,' Sophie says.

Martha shakes her head. She doesn't want to speak about Rosie.

'Has it ever occurred to you that she didn't come back for the house?' Sophie asks. 'That she knew they'd be safe with you?'

'You've made her cry, Sophie,' Elizabeth says.

'I just can't get my solar lights to work,' Martha sobs.

When she walks back inside, she's overwhelmed by the feeling that pretty much everyone she loves most in the world is enjoying themselves in the home that Seb built. That both of them did. All of them. Eugenia's money. Loredana in the early days before she got sick. Rosie as a kid. She watches Scarlett and Marley and Samuel playing with Lotte's old radio. Martha hopes they don't break the figurines next to it, but doesn't want to go over and be a party pooper. The kids get Ewan to help and he shows them how a tuner works, because that generation has no concept of anything but a scanner. Suddenly music blasts clearly through the speakers. Lionel Richie crooning 'Three Times a Lady'. Ewan looks up, stunned at first, and then he catches Martha's eye. Knows exactly where to find her. And she can't help smiling. Laughing, really. And while the others are oblivious because there's too much going on, they smile at each other across the room, and Martha's fifteen years old again, in that school hall, dancing with him to this soppy song and thinking that this is the beginning of something big.

It's late by the time everyone's gone home. Rosie and Jimmy come back from picking up Toto at Signora De Lorenzo's, and Jimmy heads upstairs with him, while Rosie prepares his bottle.

'Thanks, Martha,' Jimmy says from halfway up.

Martha forces a smile, doesn't respond.

Most of the plates have been put in the dishwasher, but she picks up a stray glass or two and hovers around the sink, listening to the sounds she's become used to as part of Rosie's nightly rituals for Toto.

'There's probably a better way of saying this, Rosie, so you're going to have to forgive me for my bluntness, but I don't think you two are going to make it.'

Rosie reaction is instant. A deer caught in headlights. The week's contentment gone.

'What planet do you kids live on that makes you think it's possible? Even with the money you'll get from us selling this place, you are still going to end up with mortgage repayments, or Sydney rent prices, or just trying to keep your heads above water. And then every second week you're on your own dealing with Toto, trying to get to work, trying to get him into day care, spending more money and then having to pay at least six hundred dollars a month flying Jimmy back and forward to Brisbane. It's like the universe is setting you both up for failure before you've even started.'

Rosie's bawling. That silent cry that makes her look so vulnerable. Because she's gone through this in her own head. Martha can tell. Jimmy can live on hope alone, but Rosie's never been one to romanticise a situation.

'You kids deserve better than that.'

Upstairs, Toto starts wailing.

'I don't think we should sell the house, Rosie.'

She says it. Maybe she's been wanting to say it forever but was frightened to. But, deep down, Martha knows that she owes Rosie a life in this house. Owes it to herself.

'That way, you can go to uni and Jimmy can take the paramedics traineeship, and staying here will mean there's always someone around to look after Toto, whether it's one of us, or Teresa or Signora or the netballers or Jimmy's friends.'

Jimmy comes down the stairs with a blubbering Toto.

'Rosie?' he says.

'Just deal with him, Jimmy,' Rosie says.

He hesitates, sees her tears. Toto's crying becomes deafening. Up until now, Jimmy hasn't had to cope with a crying wife and a sick child.

So Rosie follows him up the stairs.

Martha finishes up in the kitchen and switches on her laptop. Finds a plethora of Sophie emails from last week. Same as always. Chain letters about love, the sisterhood, friendship, ageing. She's about to delete them all but doesn't. Sends an email instead.

From: justmartha@me.com
Subject: You are one of the loves of my life
Dear Sophie,
Before you go into a panic, I'm not suicidal or contemplating a big sea change, but you are one of the loves of my life and I wanted you to know.
Love,
Martha

She realises too late that she's sent it to Alana, Julia and Elizabeth as well. So she just keeps on writing.

From: justmartha@me.com

Subject: I'm sorry for calling you a dyke in first form

Dear Julia,

I'm sorry for calling you a dyke in first form. It was probably my only retaliation against you beating me in the maths prize, although I blame Sister Mo for that.

Love,

Martha

And it's as if she can't stop herself.

From: justmartha@me.com

Subject: Sorry for dobbing on you for smoking at Sophie's birthday party

Dear Elizabeth,

What a little whistleblower in the making I was back then. All this time —

Halfway through it, she hears the sound of an email arriving.

From: queenelizabeth3@gmail.com

Dear Martha,

I'm responding before anyone decides to drag this into the wee hours of the morning and none of us gets any sleep. So three things:

1.   We love you.

2.   We think that Ewan, the loser who dumped me at our school formal, is the best you're going to get at your age so stop fucking around.

3.   Get a bloody job. You've got too much time on your hands.

Love,

Elizabeth

Chapter Twenty

After she puts Toto to bed and talks to Jimmy about the life she wants, Rosie comes down the stairs. The stairs that Jimmy's Monaro money made. The Monaro her mother drove. The one her dad promised would lead Jimmy to his family. The one that led him to her, and her to Toto.

From the kitchen she can see Martha sitting in the dark outside on one of the banana chairs.

'Do you want a cup of tea, Martha?' she asks from the French doors.

'I'd love one,' Martha says.

Moments later, Rosie hands the tea to Martha and sits down on the banana chair beside her.

And the solar lights come on.

Acknowledgements

To Amy Thomas, who has now edited five of my novels. I love sharing these characters and stories with you.

Thank you to Nikki Christer, Laura Harris and Ben Ball.

To Adelina Marchetta, Marisa Donovan, Daniela Marchetta, Anthony Catanzariti, Brenda Souter, Janet Hill, Maxim Younger, Toby Younger, Chloe Michele, Jutta Goetze and Melissa Montuori, all who either read the manuscript or agreed to be interviewed, or knew something about the subject material that I didn't.

To Jill Grinberg and Jennifer Naughton and everyone on their teams.

Thank you to Phil Crowley and Matthew Lamb from the *Review of Australian Fiction*, and Christie Neiman, editor of the *Just Between Us* anthology, who gave me a chance to write *When Rosie Met Jim* and *The Centre*. Both short stories began the journey for this novel.

And finally, to my family and friends, and my neighbours, and to the school and netball families, because this is a novel about communities, and B and I love belonging to yours.

Room to Read®

ABOUT MELINA MARCHETTA AND ROOM TO READ

Melina Marchetta is a committed writer ambassador for Room to Read, an innovative global non-profit which seeks to transform the lives of millions of children in ten countries in Asia and Africa through its holistic Literacy and Girls' Education programs.

Founded in 2000 on the belief that World Change Starts with Educated Children®, Room to Read's innovative model focuses on deep, systemic transformation within schools in low-income countries during two time periods which are most critical in a child's schooling: early primary school for literacy acquisition and secondary school for girls' education. We work in collaboration with local communities, partner organizations and governments to develop literacy skills and a habit of reading among primary school children, and to ensure girls can complete secondary school with the skills necessary to negotiate key life decisions.

Room to Read has benefited more than 10 million children across 18,000 communities in Asia and Africa and aims to reach 15 million children by 2020. Room to Read is changing children's lives in Bangladesh, Cambodia, India, Laos, Nepal, South Africa, Sri Lanka, Tanzania, Vietnam and Zambia.

As Melina says, 'Two of my great passions are education and reading. The third is community. I've always belonged to one. Room to Read builds communities not just with bricks, but with words. When I first heard about Room to Read, all I heard were the words "building schools and filling libraries with books" and I was there. I have never heard anyone from Room to Read speak about what they can't do. It's always been about the great possibilities and hope.'

For more information, www.roomtoread.org.